THE KISSING EXPERIMENT

He kissed her very carefully until she kind of melted against him, and then all bets were off. Her hand stole around his neck and her nails dug into his skin in a way that made him shudder with need. She kissed him back, and he wrapped one arm around her waist to keep her exactly where he wanted her.

She ripped her mouth away from his. "I thought we weren't doing this."

"We're not. That was just a little experiment." Noah made no effort to hold on to her.

"About how infections spread between people?" Jen asked.

He shrugged. "Maybe."

She made a huffing noise, retreated to the far end of the kitchen, and busied herself cleaning the stove and emptying the rest of the pork into a bowl. He leaned against the countertop and watched her as he waited for his unruly body to calm down. If kissing her had been an experiment, then he'd fallen even harder for her than before. She tasted like heaven, and he wanted more. . . .

D0964421

Books by Kate Pearce

The House of Pleasure Series
SIMPLY SEXUAL
SIMPLY SINFUL
SIMPLY SHAMELESS
SIMPLY WICKED
SIMPLY INSATIABLE
SIMPLY FORBIDDEN
SIMPLY CARNAL
SIMPLY VORACIOUS
SIMPLY SCANDALOUS
SIMPLY PLEASURE
(e-novella)
SIMPLY IRRESISTIBLE
(e-novella)

The Sinners Club Series
THE SINNERS CLUB
TEMPTING A SINNER
MASTERING A SINNER
THE FIRST SINNERS
(e-novella)

Single Titles
RAW DESIRE

The Millers of Morgan Valley
THE SECOND CHANCE
RANCHER
THE RANCHER'S
REDEMPTION
THE REBELLIOUS
RANCHER
THE RANCHER MEETS
HIS MATCH
SWEET TALKING RANCHER
ROMANCING THE RANCHER

Three Cowboys
THREE COWBOYS
AND A BABY

Anthologies
SOME LIKE IT ROUGH
LORDS OF PASSION
HAPPY IS THE BRIDE
A SEASON TO CELEBRATE
MARRYING MY COWBOY
CHRISTMAS KISSES WITH
MY COWBOY
LONE WOLF

The Morgan Brothers Ranch
THE RELUCTANT COWBOY
THE MAVERICK COWBOY
THE LAST GOOD COWBOY
THE BAD BOY COWBOY
THE BILLIONAIRE
BULL RIDER
THE RANCHER

Published by Kensington Publishing Corp.

Three Cowboys and a Baby

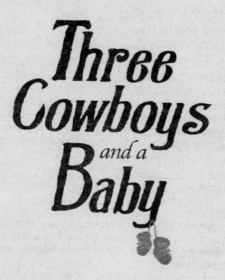

KATE PEARCE

ZEBRA BOOKS
KENSINGTON PUBLISHING CORP.
www.kensingtonbooks.com

ZEBRA BOOKS are published by

Kensington Publishing Corp.
119 West 40th Street
New York, NY 10018

Copyright © 2023 by Catherine Duggan

This book is a work of fiction. Names, characters, businesses, organizations, places, events, and incidents either are the product of the author's imagination or are used fictitiously. Any resemblance to actual persons, living or dead, events, or locales is entirely coincidental.

All rights reserved. No part of this book may be reproduced in any form or by any means without the prior written consent of the Publisher, excepting brief quotes used in reviews.

To the extent that the image or images on the cover of this book depict a person or persons, such person or persons are merely models, and are not intended to portray any character or characters featured in the book.

If you purchased this book without a cover, you should be aware that this book is stolen property. It was reported as "unsold and destroyed" to the Publisher and neither the Author nor the Publisher has received any payment for this "stripped book."

All Kensington titles, imprints, and distributed lines are available at special quantity discounts for bulk purchases for sales promotion, premiums, fund-raising, and educational or institutional use.

Special book excerpts or customized printings can also be created to fit specific needs. For details, write or phone the office of the Kensington Sales Manager: Kensington Publishing Corp., 119 West 40th Street, New York, NY 10018. Attn. Sales Department. Phone: 1-800-221-2647.

ZEBRA BOOKS and the Z logo Reg. U.S. Pat. & TM Off.

First Printing: January 2023
ISBN-13: 978-1-4201-5494-8
ISBN-13: 978-1-4201-5495-5 (eBook)

10 9 8 7 6 5 4 3 2 1

Printed in the United States of America

Acknowledgments

A big thank you to Jerri Drennen and Sian Kaley for critiquing the book for me. A very special thank you to Tamara Worlton for introducing me to LCDR Chaia McAdams DNP CNM IBCLC, who served on one of the USNS ships and let me ask her all sorts of stupid questions. Thank you both for your service. Any mistakes are on me.

Chapter One

Noah Harding walked toward the unknown car that had just pulled up in front of the barn and waited for whoever was inside to reveal themselves. Even though he'd left the military three years previously, his fingers curled around the grip of an imaginary weapon as he automatically tried to work out how many people were in the vehicle. He was surprised anyone was out in the appalling weather, especially in a car that wasn't four-wheel drive. But tourists did occasionally get lost in the vast redwood forests. He was more than happy to set them on the right road if it meant he was left in peace.

He tensed as the driver door opened and a guy with long, fair hair in some kind of bun on top of his head got out and grinned at him.

"Arkie. Long time no see, big guy. How's tricks?"

It took a second for Noah's memory to click into place. "Riley. Dave Riley."

"Yup. Top gate wasn't locked so I just drove right in!" Dave looked around, his blue-eyed gaze encompassing the two barns and the old ranch house. He looked like the kind of guy who surfed and lived on the coast rather than a retired Marine. "Nice place." He sniffed loudly. "Pine and cedar. Smells like my grandma's closet."

Noah still hadn't moved closer. "Who's in the car with you?"

"Just my little buddy." Dave grinned again. "Are you going to invite me in or is this how you treat your old comrades in arms these days?" As he was talking, Dave walked around to the passenger side and opened the second door. He half disappeared inside the vehicle and then emerged, shaking his head.

"Still asleep. Maybe I should leave him be."

Noah glanced up at the leaden sky as a gust of freezing air coming straight off the mountain peaks swirled around the buildings and buffeted his face.

"It's going to get cold real soon. You'd better come in."

He didn't wait to see if Dave was taking his advice and turned toward the side door of the ranch house. There were three steps up to the covered porch and a screen door that led into what had once been the kitchen but was now a decent-sized mudroom. Even though he'd only been outside for a few minutes, the heat of the house enfolded him like a warm blanket.

There was no sign of Luke or Max, who were still out working. The only reason Noah was home was because he'd been waiting on the farrier. What would Dave have done if no one had been around? Knowing the guy, he'd probably have gone in, made himself comfortable, and waited for someone to come and find him.

After taking off his boots and sheepskin-lined jacket, Noah walked through into the new kitchen and set some coffee on to brew. He had no idea what had brought Dave to the middle of nowhere, but he guessed he would soon find out. He didn't know the guy well; he had more of a connection to Luke, who put up with everyone with a calm good humor Noah sometimes envied. But his boss had told them a million stories about Dave and his propensity to get into trouble, so Noah was expecting the worst.

"Thank God it's so warm in here." Dave arrived and dumped a large, bulky backpack and a series of bags on the kitchen table. "I thought I was about to freeze my nuts off on the drive up to this place. Whatever possessed you to come out here?"

Noah shrugged. "It's Luke's family home. The Nilsens have been here since the gold rush."

"I see you're as chatty as ever, Noah," Dave said. "To be honest, I was expecting to see Luke. I didn't realize you were staying here, too."

"I live here. Luke didn't mention you were visiting when I saw him this morning." Noah poured two mugs of coffee.

"Weird." Dave frowned. "Maybe the internet sucks up here as well as the weather."

"Nothing wrong with the cold."

"Can't argue with that. Ever since Afghanistan, I hate the heat." Dave shuddered and held out his hand for the mug of coffee. "When are you expecting Luke back?"

Noah glanced at the kitchen clock that sat on the high mantelpiece. "Any time now. We've been moving the cattle closer to the house because we're expecting a snowstorm to come through."

"Glad I made it then," Dave said. "What's for dinner?"

Noah gave Dave a sidelong glance as he went to check the list on the refrigerator, which divvied up the household chores between the three of them. Since Luke's Mom, Sally, had left for Texas to help her daughter Brina with her two young kids, the freezer and microwave were getting a work-out. Luckily for them, Sally had left explicit instructions on how to cook everything.

Slow cooked beef in freezer. Heat in electric pressure cooker for forty-five minutes.

He could manage that okay. He got the cooker out; plugged it in; dumped the bag of prepared beef, veg, and stock into the pot; and set the timer.

"Should be ready in about an hour."

"Awesome!" Dave said. "Okay if I use the bathroom?"

"Sure." Noah pointed the way and then went to check the cooker was doing its thing before pulling out his cell phone. Time to give his friends a heads-up about what awaited them when they finally got home. Dave was right about reception being spotty up in the middle of the Plumas National Forest, and the inclement weather made it worse. Noah's cell beeped immediately as Luke replied.

WTH. 5 minutes away.

Noah refilled his coffee mug and contemplated setting the table before realizing he'd need to get Dave to move his stuff off it first. It didn't sound like Luke had been expecting Dave either, which wasn't exactly a surprise. From everything he'd heard about the guy, thinking ahead hadn't exactly been his strength. He was an excellent shot, though, and had once saved Luke's life, which meant he had to be tolerated.

Noah was just about to check how much beer was in the fridge when a small cooing sound came from behind him. He tensed as he slowly turned to stare at the table where something was waving at him. He blinked hard and advanced toward the starfish-shaped little hand. What he'd thought was Dave's kit bag was actually some kind of carrier.

"Dada."

Big blue eyes stared into his as he blinked like a fool.

"Da?"

"*Hell,* no," Noah said rather more forcefully than the baby probably appreciated because its lip started to tremble.

"Hey! You met junior!"

Noah jumped as Dave came up behind him and reached around to unbuckle the kid, who smelled really bad.

Dave made a face. "Man, you stink little dude. I'll need to change you right now." He handed the baby to Noah. "Hold on to him while I find the stuff, okay?"

Even as Noah went to protest, the kitchen door opened, and Luke and Max came in and stopped dead.

"Something you want to tell us, big guy?" Luke asked. "He doesn't look much like you, and I never saw Dave standing in for the stork."

Dave laughed. "This is my kid, Sky. He's almost a year old, aren't you buddy?"

"Someone had a kid with *you*?" Max asked. He was always happy to be the plain speaker of the group. "Like, for real?"

"Yeah. Amazing, isn't it?" Dave grinned. "But it's kind of why I'm here." He took the baby out of a relieved Noah's arms. "Let me change his diaper, and then I'll come back and tell you all about it."

"It's like this." Dave sat at the table with Sky on his lap and a beer in his hand. "I'm off on an assignment in Africa—like a consulting thing—and I've brought the kid here for Jen."

Luke pretended to look around. "No Jen here, although I think I went to school with about a dozen of them."

"Her aunt lives in Quincy. You must know her."

"What's her name?"

"Betty, Brenda, something beginning with B?" Dave grimaced. "Jen did tell me, but I kind of forgot to bring the intel with me."

"What's Jen's last name?"

"Rossi." Dave looked expectantly at Luke. "Does that ring any bells?"

"Nope."

"It might not be the same as her aunt's. I think I would've remembered that. When I realized I'd forgotten the name and Jen wasn't replying to my texts, I decided to make my way up here and get some help."

"Quincy is small, but unless you go door-to-door you're not going to find this woman if all you know is that she's Jen Rossi's aunt," Luke pointed out.

"Yeah. I wish Jen had been more specific. I mean it's her kid, too. And we did agree to share custody, and she's been gone for way more than the four months we agreed."

"Where exactly has she gone?" Noah inquired as he gently removed Dave's fork from Sky's waving hand. Trust Dave to blame his girlfriend when he'd been the one to turn up without the information he needed.

"How the hell should I know? We're not exactly friends or anything."

"You have a kid," Noah pointed out. "You should at least be on the same page about that."

He had no idea why he was bothering to lecture Dave when he knew firsthand that thousands of parents only thought about themselves rather than the impact they had on their kids.

"I guess." Dave gave the baby a stick of carrot from his plate. The beef stew had been excellent. "I could try again in the morning and see if I can find this aunt of hers. Jen's supposed to be there tomorrow."

"But she hasn't contacted you?"

Dave shrugged. "She says it's hard for her to do that when she's traveling."

Noah's opinion of the absent Jen went down another few notches. But anyone who took up with an airhead like Dave was probably just like him.

Luke pushed back his chair. "I'll call my mom and ask if she knows which Jennifer we're talking about and who her aunt might be."

"Thanks, buddy." Dave picked up the baby and groaned. "Damn. I need to change him again. It never stops."

Luke waited until Dave closed the door behind him and then turned to Max and Noah.

"I don't like this."

"I agree. It's just all too vague for my liking. You'd think having a kid would've settled him down," Noah said as Max nodded. "Something's off. I think we should escort him to town tomorrow, make sure he finds the right women, and let him get on with it."

"And what if we can't find her?" Luke asked. "I'll check with my mom, but it's not guaranteed she'll know who the hell I'm supposed to be looking for."

"If your mom doesn't know, no one will," Noah agreed. "But let's just remember this isn't our problem. It's all on Dave and the kid's mother for not getting their shit together."

"I was about to say I can't believe he'd mess up something so important, but we are talking about Dave here," Luke mused. "He's the biggest screw-up I've ever met."

"Who agrees to hand over their kid in the middle of nowhere?" Noah asked. "What is this? A hostage situation?"

"Maybe," Max said. "Not all relationships end well."

"Is this Jen planning on living with her aunt for a while?" Luke asked.

"None of our business," Noah said firmly. "We just escort Dave down to town, help him find her, wave, and walk away."

"You're right." Luke nodded as Dave came back into the kitchen with a sleepy-looking Sky on his hip.

"You'd better stay the night," Luke said to Dave. "There's a crib in the spare room my sister uses for her kids when she visits, which should be fine for Sky."

"Thanks," Dave said. "He's getting tired now. It's been a long day for both of us."

"What do you plan to do if you can't find Jen or her aunt?" Noah asked.

"Well, I can't take the kid to Africa. I think that's against the custody agreement." Dave looked around the table. "But don't worry. I'm sure we'll find Jen. It's not like this is a big town or anything. She'll probably call in the next hour or so."

"I admire your optimism." Luke stood up. "I'll check in with my mom right now."

"Thanks, dude," Dave said cheerfully.

By the time Luke came back, they'd cleared the table and moved on to coffee. Sky was now fast asleep in his father's arms.

"Mom says there are at least twenty Jennifers who have a connection with the town, and she doesn't remember any Rossis. She's given me all the possible addresses, so I guess you'll at least have somewhere to start."

"Yeah, because even if Jen hasn't made it yet, I can dump—I mean leave—Sky with her aunt."

"Does the aunt know Jen's coming?" Noah asked.

"How would I know? That part is on her."

Dave and his ex seemed remarkably unconcerned about the fate of their own kid, which was starting to grate on Noah.

"Does Jen usually turn up on time?"

"Not really. But it's never been an issue before." Dave glanced down at his sleeping son. "This is the first time I've been offered a real job in a long while, and I don't want to screw it up. I'm just praying she keeps her word and comes through for me."

"Aren't we all," Noah said with a glance at Max and Luke. "I'll show you where you can sleep, and let's hope we can reunite you with your family tomorrow."

* * *

Noah held the door open as he, Luke, Dave, and Sky filed into the small coffee shop in town. They'd left Max behind to manage the ranch. It was almost midday, but there was no sign of the sun breaking through the ominous snow-filled clouds. He found a table near the back where it was warmest and took the drink orders.

When he returned to the table, Sky was struggling to get off Dave's lap.

"He wants to stand all the time," Dave groused. "It's like, really annoying."

"You wait until he starts walking and you have to chase after him," Noah said as he put the tray in the center of the table and sat down. They'd each taken part of the list to speed up the process. "I guess none of you found the right Jen either?"

"Nope." Dave sighed. "And no one seems to know who her aunt is. I've got to get on that plane soon or I'll lose my job."

"We've only covered half the names my mom gave me," Luke said and looked out the window. "But we have to get back to the ranch."

Noah cleared his throat. "Lucy at the B and B across the street has space to put you up while you continue your search, Dave."

"Sure." Dave was looking at Sky, who was standing on his knees and bouncing up and down. "I'll come up to your place, get my stuff and my car, and we'll move out."

"It should be easier for you to operate down here," Luke said tactfully. "You're closer to the highway and the concentration of houses."

"You've been great. Thanks." Dave set Sky on the floor and waited for him to get his balance before reaching for his coffee. "I guess if the worst comes to worst, I can take him to my mom."

"Good idea." Noah drank his coffee and wondered why Dave hadn't done that in the first place.

"She's not happy with me right now, but I know she'd do anything for Sky."

"Problem solved, then." Luke checked his cell. "I hate to rush you, but we need to get back before the snow starts coming down and the roads become impassable."

Noah gathered up the drinks. "I'll get these to go."

Dave was uncharacteristically silent on the way back to the ranch, but that might have been because Sky had nodded off and he didn't want to wake him. It wasn't long before the first wisps of snow appeared on the windscreen, melting as they made contact with the warm glass.

"This is going to be a bad one," Luke commented as he slowed down to take another blind corner. "Glad we got all the cattle close to home."

"You have to wonder why your family built their place out in the middle of nowhere, Luke," Dave said from the back seat.

"I guess they just weren't into crowds," Luke replied as he made the final turn and activated the electric gate. "I told Max to stay near the house today."

"Like he'd take any notice," Noah murmured. "He's a free spirit, that one."

Even though it was still afternoon, the lights were already on in the main house, which was situated in the shadow of a large redwood grove. From what Luke had said, the original Nilsens had been loggers and after claiming the land had felled the trees to build and fence their own place.

There were still remnants of the original hand-sawn wood in the barn, and the wide-planked flooring in the house had been there forever. Noah liked the idea that the house and the grove of trees were made from the same materials. You couldn't get more organic or natural than that. If he ever built his own place, he'd likely do the same.

"Come on, kid." Dave unstrapped the car seat and brought Sky inside still sitting in it. "Time for a nap while I call Grandma."

The weather grew steadily worse throughout the afternoon. Luckily the snow was still too skittish to settle, which at least meant they weren't cut off from the town—yet. Dave spent a while using the washer and dryer because Sky went through a lot of clothes. He repacked his stuff into a separate backpack.

Noah put his head around the door where Dave was folding his laundry.

"Did you get hold of your mom?"

"She's super salty with me, but she'll take him if she has to."

"Great."

"Yeah."

Noah left it at that and went back to the kitchen to cook up some steak and baked potatoes for dinner. If Dave was traveling halfway around the world, he'd need to keep his strength up.

Luke peered out into the darkness and turned back to the dinner table, where they'd all just finished eating.

"It's not too bad out there."

Dave finished his beer. "I guess that's my cue to leave."

"It can wait until morning." Luke closed the drapes against the draft. He'd always been the nicest of the three of them. If it had been up to Noah, he'd be helping take Dave's bags out to the car and waving him off. "I wouldn't want your kid catching a chill out there."

"Will the roads be okay for my rental in the morning?" Dave asked.

"Should be, if the snow doesn't settle too deep. If it gets icy, I'll take you down in my mom's old truck, which has four-wheel drive and a set of chains."

"Awesome." Dave looked over his shoulder at the refrigerator. "Maybe I've got time for another beer after all."

When Noah's alarm went off at five, he opened his eyes into a deathly stillness that didn't bode well. He reached out an arm, snagged his jeans, knitted socks, and thermal Henley and put everything on before he even considered getting out of his warm bed. Despite being almost fully dressed, he was still dreading it, but horses wouldn't wait, and the dogs needed feeding, so he'd have to make the effort.

He went to the bathroom and then padded down the stairs into the kitchen, where someone had left the light on over the stove. There was a faint hint of coffee hanging in the air, and the pot was tepid to the touch. Either Max had had one of his sleepless nights or someone had been up early. Noah refilled the jug with water and set it to brew while he nuked some oatmeal in the microwave.

While he waited for the oats to turn to mush, he wandered over to look out of the window, which faced the larger of the two barns. There was about a foot of snow deadening the sound, and ice glinted off the metal roofs of the trucks and the barn. It wasn't as bad as he'd feared, but if it didn't thaw out, Dave might have some problems getting down to town without a four-wheel drive.

The microwave beeped. He added a lake of maple syrup to his bowl, made some fresh coffee, and sat down to eat with one eye on the clock. As soon as he was done, he'd go over to the barn, feed the dogs, and start in on the horses, leaving the cattle to Luke and Max. He'd always liked to be up early, and the other two were more than happy to let him start the day.

By the time he'd made it across to the barn, his bearded face was stinging from the snap of the cold. He fed the outdoor dogs, let them out, and then turned his attention to mucking out the stalls of the half-dozen horses they used to get around the ranch. All-terrain vehicles were great, but there were still places where wheels couldn't go and horses could.

It wasn't until his return journey to the house that he noticed something was missing. He stomped his booted feet hard on the outdoor mat and went in through the mud room, slipping his boots and jacket off before he walked into the kitchen. No one else was up yet, so he went along the hallway and paused outside Dave's room. All was quiet. He was just about to move on when he heard Sky.

"Dada?"

The words were accompanied by a loud banging on the side of the crib that should have woken the dead.

"Da?"

Noah eased the door open, stared at the unmade bed and then at the crib where Sky grinned at him and held out his arms. His first thought was to run like hell, but he couldn't do that to such a hopeful little face. He picked Sky up and walked back through the silent house until he was at Luke's door.

He went in without knocking. "Hey, we might have a problem."

Luke sat up like he'd been shot. "What?"

"Dave's disappeared, and he's left the baby behind."

Chapter Two

Jennifer Rossi rang the bell of Martha's condo for the third time and glanced anxiously up at the second-floor windows. Where the hell was Dave's mom? It was two in the afternoon, which usually meant afternoon soaps, coffee, and a discreet nap in front of the TV.

"She's not there, dear."

Jen lowered her gaze to Mrs. Friedman, who lived in the apartment below.

"She's out shopping?"

"No, she's gone."

Jen tried to gather her scattered thoughts. Two nights without sleeping while traveling on a Greyhound bus weren't helping.

"But she's expecting me."

"I guess she got fed up waiting." Mrs. Friedman shrugged. "Well, that's what she told me, anyway." Her gaze softened. "Would you like to come in? You look like you need a drink."

With one last worried glance upstairs, Jen stepped into the wonderful coolness of Mrs. Friedman's front room. It wasn't the first time she'd been in the apartment because

Mrs. Friedman was Martha's best friend as well as her neighbor.

"When you say she's not here, what exactly do you mean?" Jen accepted the lemonade with thanks and immediately drank half the glass.

"She's gone to her place in Florida."

Jen just blinked at her. "With Sky?"

"I guess."

"Then . . . where exactly is Dave?" Jen croaked. "He's supposed to be with Sky." She glanced wildly up at the ceiling. "She didn't leave him here by himself, did she?"

"Of course not, dear. She's very fond of Sky, but everyone needs a break sometimes, and she has been dealing with the baby all by herself for months."

The usual guilt swamped Jen. "But wasn't Dave here, too?"

Mrs. Friedman made a dismissive noise. "Not that anyone would notice. I think that's why Martha eventually decided she was going to Florida."

"To force Dave to pay attention to his own son?" Jen sank down onto the peach velvet couch and groaned. "Sounds right on brand."

Mrs. Friedman sat beside Jen and patted her knee. "Martha said Dave expected her to become a full-time care giver while he gadded around like he was single again."

"That wasn't how we arranged things at *all*. Martha agreed to help Dave get started and to keep an eye on Sky for me, but I didn't expect her to have to do *everything*." Jen sighed. "I wouldn't have gone if I hadn't believed everything would be okay."

"She's not getting any younger, and she wants her life back."

"I'll kill him," Jen muttered. "He *promised* me he'd take on the majority of Sky's care. To be honest, I didn't really believe him, but Martha reassured me that she'd always be there to keep him on the straight and narrow. . . ." She took a deep, steadying breath and looked at Mrs. Friedman. "Maybe I was expecting too much. So, Dave doesn't have Sky now?"

"I don't really know, dear. He drove Martha and Sky to Florida, and she called the other day to let me know they'd all arrived safely."

"Then I'll have to go to Florida."

Jen mentally reviewed the perilous state of her finances and realized flying or renting a car was out of the question. She'd have to go cross country by bus, which would take some time. She'd only just arrived in San Diego. The last thing she wanted was to start traveling again, but she had no choice.

She found her cell and tried to call Martha, but it went straight through to voicemail. Jen left a message, but as Martha detested using her phone, she didn't expect a call back.

"I'd better get to the bus station." Jen smothered a yawn.

"Not until you've had something to eat and a nap," Mrs. Friedman said firmly. "Martha would never forgive me if I let you go in such a state."

Jen quickly checked the time again. She hadn't realized how late it was. "Are you sure? That would be awesome."

"Absolutely. I'm glad to have some company." Mrs. Friedman beamed at her. "I'll go and set the table. I made lasagna yesterday and was worried I would have to eat it all week. I keep forgetting I don't have a big family to feed anymore."

"I'll definitely help out with that." Jen rose to her feet.

"Why don't you go and freshen up, first?" Mrs. Friedman suggested tactfully. "It'll take at least ten minutes to heat the lasagna and make a salad."

"Do I look that bad?" Jen grimaced and smoothed a hand over the coffee stain on her pants. "Maybe I'll take a quick shower."

"You do that." Her hostess ushered her out into the hallway and pointed at the bathroom. "And take your time."

When Jen saw her reflection in the mirror, she almost shrieked. Her naturally curly brown hair was standing on end, deep purple shadows highlighted her eyes, and her skin was the color of spoiled milk. She didn't look like a professional person, let alone a mother. No wonder everyone on the bus had given her wide berth.

With a sigh, Jen turned on the shower, stripped off her clothes, and stepped under the free-flowing warm water.

"Thank God for American plumbing," she murmured as she borrowed Mrs. Friedman's orchid shower gel and all-in-one shampoo and completed the fastest shower ever. She'd have liked to stay in there for days, but she might fall asleep. The thought of the diminutive Mrs. Friedman trying to drag her naked body out of the shower—or even worse, calling the fire department to help—was a great incentive not to lose consciousness.

"Unless the firefighters were hunks," Jen said aloud. "And one of them—the really tall, hot, one with a degree in microbiology, and a trust fund—fell instantly in love with me." She got out of the shower and wrapped her wayward hair in a towel, adding, "I've been reading too many romance novels on my days off."

She found some clean clothes in her backpack and hurriedly put them on before heading downstairs where the heavenly smell of lasagna now perfumed the air.

"What can I do to help?" Jen asked as she poked her head around the kitchen door.

"Nothing." Mrs. Friedman smiled at her. "Just go on through and sit down."

Jen did as she was told and waited expectantly for her hostess to join her. She almost moaned with greed when the lasagna hit her plate in all its cheesy, meaty, stuffed-pasta goodness.

"Please, eat as much as you'd like." Mrs. Friedman plied her with salad. "You know Martha was expecting you about a month ago."

"Yes." Jen grimaced. "But I couldn't exactly up and leave when I was stuck in the middle of a natural disaster."

"To be fair, I think Martha's frustration was directed more at Dave and his reluctance to parent his own child than at you."

"That's Dave for you."

"I assume the two of you aren't getting back together any time soon, then?"

"We were barely together in the first place. I stupidly thought he was 'the one,' only to find out he was dating two other women and had no intention of settling down with any of us."

Mrs. Friedman tutted and poured Jen some lemonade. "He's a charming rascal, I'll give him that."

Jen yawned around a mouthful of salad. "Sorry. The change of time zones is getting to me."

"Then finish up and go and take a nap in my spare room."

"That's so kind of you," Jen said. "I checked the bus times, and the last one goes at eleven tonight. If I leave here at eight, I should be fine to get on it."

"What time is the next one?"

"Eleven in the morning, why?"

"Because that's the one you're getting on. You can stay the night, and I'll drive you to the bus station tomorrow." Mrs. Friedman held up her hand. "Rushing off when you're tired isn't going to change anything. Sky's perfectly safe with his grandma and father until you get there."

Jen contemplated that and sat back. "As long as Martha's in charge, I'm sure you're right."

If it was just Dave . . . then she'd definitely be in trouble.

"Where the hell is he?" Luke stared at the empty bed as if willing Dave to appear again. "He can't just have gone— *can* he?"

"You tell me." Noah balanced Sky on one hip. "He's your friend."

"He said his mom would take Sky if he couldn't find his girlfriend."

"I know, but he's obviously decided not to stick around and make that happen."

Luke disappeared in the direction of the kitchen at some speed and stared out of the window, Noah following behind him.

"He must have gone out for a walk. His car's still here."

"Sure, his rental's here, but what's missing?"

Luke's gaze traveled around the circular drive. "Mom's truck. The absolute dickhead!"

"That's what made me go check on him. I was coming back from the barn, and I noticed the truck was missing." Noah settled Sky into the high chair. "What the hell do you think he's doing?"

Luke gazed at the baby. "Did he leave a note anywhere?"

"No, he left his kid!" Noah wasn't in the mood to be nice. "Because, as you mentioned earlier, he's an inconsiderate, lying jerk!"

"What's going on?" Max came into the kitchen, rubbing his eyes. "You're scaring the baby with all that shouting."

Aware that he could sometimes be classed as loud, Noah warmed some milk in a sippy cup and handed it over to Sky, who was looking a tad apprehensive. Noah patted him on the head.

"It's okay, little buddy. We're not mad at you, just your dad."

"Da," Sky said as he drank his milk.

"I was just trying to work out if Dave left us a note," Luke explained to Max.

"Like that one stuck behind the clock?" Max pointed. "With your name on it?"

Luke went over to pick up the note, opened it up, and began to read.

"Please share," Max said, sarcasm dripping from every word. "We're all dying to know what Dave's thinking was on this."

Luke looked up. "He says, 'I couldn't change my ticket so had to leave the kid with you overnight. My mom or Jen will pick him up tomorrow afternoon for sure. I've given them your address and cell number so keep an eye out for a call. Thanks for everything, buddy. I owe you one.'"

"Like anyone's going to make it up here in the next twelve hours." Noah looked out the window as the snow started to fall again. "He's run off and left his kid."

"Sure looks like it." Max helped himself to coffee.

"But it's not our job to look after his kid!" Luke said as he furiously texted with his thumbs.

"Really Captain Obvious?"

Luke frowned. "You're not helping, Max." He contemplated Sky, who was banging his empty cup against the tray. "We have a ranch to run."

"Maybe he can help?" Max suggested. "I mean, my dad put me to work the second I could sit on a horse."

"He's too young," Luke said. "He wouldn't be able to keep his balance."

Despite the current emergency, Noah still wanted to smile at Luke's carefully considered opinion.

"He would if we tied him on." Max was obviously intent on winding Luke up. "Or we could use him as bait."

"Max . . . ," Noah said. "You're not helping."

"I'm not trying to." Max met his stare head on. "I just like watching how Luke's mind works and how he tries to find a solution for everything."

"There is no solution right now," Luke said. "We're not going anywhere. If the storm keeps up, no one will be able to get to us, either."

"Dave did say he gave his mom and Jen your number," Noah reminded him.

"Shame he didn't give me theirs." Luke grimaced. "What's the chance they get here today, anyway?"

"Knowing Dave, approximately zero percent?" Max suggested.

Luke stared at his phone. "He doesn't want me to contact them, does he."

"Damn straight." Noah looked back at Sky. "Does the little dude eat oatmeal?"

"Eat would be a strong word. From what I saw yesterday at feeding time, he prefers to wear his food," Max said. "It got in his hair and everything."

Noah set his jaw. "I'll cook him some breakfast and make sure he eats it."

"Good luck." Max winked at him. "I'm going back to bed." He set down his mug and sauntered toward the door.

"Hold up," Luke said. "I need you to help me check the cattle are okay."

Max looked pained. "Why can't Noah do it?"

"Because he's feeding the baby." Luke paused. "You can do that if you prefer."

"No thanks." Max shuddered. "At least I understand cows. I'll go and get dressed."

"Thanks." Luke poured himself some coffee while Noah

fussed around with the microwave to make sure the oats were cooked through but were also cool enough for the baby.

"I'm going to call Mom and tell her what's happened," Luke said. "I think she still has a list of charitable organizations and government agencies that might be able to help us out."

"By shooting Dave?" Noah asked. "I'm all for that."

"No, by taking care of Sky until someone can locate one of his parents." Luke paused to check his cell. "Did Dave say how long he planned to be in Africa?"

"At least three months."

"Did he happen to mention which country he's going to?"

"He said that was restricted information." Noah rolled his eyes.

"Which probably means he's up to no good and not affiliated with any official military sources or suppliers." Luke sighed. "The thing is, if I don't know where he's gone, I can't attempt to track him down."

"Which is probably exactly how he wants it."

Noah took the cooked oatmeal, added a ton of milk, and tested the temperature. Sky was at an age when he wanted to do everything for himself but didn't quite have the skill set, so Noah would have to be firm.

"Good luck." Luke handed Noah the kitchen towel, a wet dishcloth, and a plastic bib. "From what I saw yesterday, you're going to need all of these."

"Thanks. Where are you going?" Noah asked.

"To call Mom and then out to check the cattle. It's a good thing we have all that baby stuff my sister left behind to use for Sky. You can cope for an hour, can't you?" Luke kept walking, his phone jammed to his ear. "Hey, Mom. We have a situation here . . ."

"Looks like I don't have a choice," Noah muttered as he stared at Sky. "Okay little buddy, listen up. It's chow time, and no, you can't feed yourself."

* * *

"I made you some sandwiches and there's some of that lemonade you like in there, too." Mrs. Friedman handed Jen a plastic lunch box with a cartoon princess on the lid that probably belonged to one of her grandkids. "You should be fine until you reach the next stop."

"Thank you." Jen took the box.

They were parked outside the bus station. She'd already bought her ticket online and just had to find the right departure bay. The California sky was turning blue, and the sun was just waiting to burn off the lingering fog creeping in from the bay. She'd slept like the dead in Mrs. Friedman's spare bed and felt about as ready as she could to embark on yet another journey.

"If Martha calls, I'll tell her you're on your way."

"Thanks. I'll keep leaving her messages, but I never know if she picks them up." Jen got out of the car and took her backpack out of the trunk.

When she turned around, Mrs. Friedman was waiting to say goodbye, her expression concerned.

"Now remember to stay safe and don't talk to strangers."

"Will do." Jen accepted the kiss on her cheek. "I'll let you know how things turn out."

"Good girl." Mrs. Friedman patted her arm. "Now off you go. I don't want you to miss your bus."

"Thanks again for everything."

Mrs. Friedman waved and got back in the car. She was already driving away as Jen made sure she had all her possessions and turned toward the entrance of the bus station. It was surprisingly busy, but she guessed that most people who had somewhere to go wanted to get an early start. She certainly did.

She consulted the information board and walked over to the bay where the bus was already waiting. She showed her ticket on her phone, stowed her bag, and boarded. To her secret relief, no one sat beside her, meaning she might get some sleep on the first leg of her journey across country. She was used to cramped quarters, but it was always nice to stretch out a little.

It wasn't going to be easy to get to Miami. She'd be traveling through at least eight states, transferring buses three times, and making around forty-three stops. If she was lucky and all went to plan, she'd arrive at Martha's in just over three days.

Eventually the bus pulled out into the heavy morning traffic, and Jen settled in. She had reports to finalize and notes to turn in, so she wouldn't be at a loss for things to keep her busy. She gazed out at the congested streets and pictured the calmness of the ocean, which always centered her. Mrs. Friedman was right. Martha would never let anything bad happen to Sky. All she had to do was get to Florida, apologize profusely to Dave's mom, and reclaim her son.

After that, things got more complicated, but she'd learned at a young age not to look too far into the future. She tried to picture how big Sky was now. She'd managed the occasional Skype and FaceTime with them both, but the fuzziness of the images hadn't been great. It only occurred to her now that Dave had rarely been around to talk, and that Martha, who had taken most of her calls, probably hadn't wanted to worry her when there was nothing Jen could do to change anything.

She'd just been so glad Martha and Dave had her back. . . . Had Sky stayed blond like his father, or had his hair darkened like hers? The thought of seeing him again was both frightening and exhilarating. She only hoped he'd remember who she was. . . .

Chapter Three

It took Noah twenty minutes to work out how to get the kid into his outdoor snowsuit. The constant wriggling didn't help. It was like trying to stuff a bowl of wet noodles into a small paper cup. As soon as he got one limb in and turned to the next, the first one was out again, which Sky thought was the funniest game ever. After three tries Noah managed to get the zipper up and rose to his feet, the baby stationed on his hip.

It was two hours since breakfast. All he'd done was feed the kid, bathe the kid, change the kid's diaper, dress the kid, and clean up the kitchen. He was already exhausted. The weather hadn't gotten any worse, but it was still gently snowing, and the temperature was well below zero. Neither Max nor Luke had come back to the house. Noah couldn't decide if they'd simply been busy or had cravenly decided to stay away and let him deal with the baby all by himself.

He suspected the latter, which was why he was determined to get out to the barn. Despite the workload, he couldn't complain too much, as the little guy hadn't cried and had regarded Noah with great interest at every turn. But he hadn't signed up to be some baby's nanny, and he wasn't about to let the other two guys shirk their responsibilities either.

"Come on, kiddo." Noah turned Sky's face into his shoulder

to protect him against the cold and went out into the frozen air. "Let's go see what Uncle Luke's up to."

His suspicions were confirmed when he went into the tack room and found Max and Luke comfortably ensconced in two folding chairs, sharing a flask of coffee and a bag of cookies.

"Cowards." Noah dumped Sky on Luke's lap.

"We were just coming in," Max said.

"Sure, you were." Noah leaned up against the countertop and scowled at his two friends. "Any news from Jen or her aunt?"

"Nope." Luke sighed as he offered Sky a sliver of his cookie. "No one's called except my mom."

"And did she have any advice for us?"

"She said that when the weather improves, we could call the sheriff's department or social services and ask them to come and take Sky away."

"What would they do with him?" Max asked suspiciously.

"Probably put him with temporary foster parents." Luke shrugged. "And then try and contact the parents."

"So Dave and Jen would probably have to face consequences of some kind," Noah mused. "Good. And they might lose custody of their kid."

"Maybe that would be for the best," Max spoke up. "I mean, the poor little dude. Having Dave as a dad isn't great, but where the hell is the mom? From what Dave said, it sounds like she spends the majority of her time wandering around the world without a thought for anyone but herself."

"Come on, Max. They're both equally to blame," Luke said. "Dave insisted they had an agreement to share childcare duties."

"Which she broke," Noah reminded him. "And not for the first time, according to Dave."

"Just because your parents couldn't work things out,

Noah, doesn't mean everyone else is the same. We only know one side of the story right now, and we all agreed earlier that Dave isn't the most reliable of guys."

"You think he's been lying to us?" Max asked, his tone withering. "Like, really?"

Luke gave Sky another piece of cookie. "My mom always says that sarcasm is the lowest form of wit."

Max snorted. "You know I love your mom, but she's totally wrong on that one." He sipped his coffee and handed the mug to Noah. "Here you go."

"At some point either Dave's mom or Jen will call me," Luke said. "We'll hand over the baby, and everything will be back to normal again."

"And what if they don't?" Max asked.

Luke frowned. "They're Sky's family. Of course, they'll come and get him."

"Okay, what if they can't?" Noah added. "I mean look at the weather right now. There's no way anyone except emergency services is getting up that road."

"Then we'll take the kid to Dave's mom when we can. It's not difficult, guys."

"Or we hand him over to the proper authorities and let them do all the hard work." Max reclaimed his coffee from Noah.

Noah glanced over at Sky, who was happily gnawing away at the cookie Luke had given him. For a kid who had been basically abandoned by both parents, he seemed remarkably chill, but maybe he was used to being passed around like a parcel.

"If you give me the number, I'll call the county and the hospital," Noah offered. "I used to date a pediatrician there, Mary. She might know someone who can take Sky."

"She's still talking to you?" Max asked.

"Unlike you, I always try and stay friends with my exes," Noah said.

"No point in pretending to be friends with someone you dumped," Max stated. "What's the end game with that? You'll make her think you might get back together some-day."

"She dumped me."

"Then feel free to go ahead." Max winked at him. "If she'll take your call."

Noah stood up. "I guess I'll find out." He took Max's empty mug and headed for the door.

"Hey!" Luke called out to him. "Haven't you forgotten something?"

Noah looked back at Sky. "He's totally comfortable with you right now. How about you show him around the barn while I'm making my calls?"

Luke sighed. "Sure, but don't be too long about it."

"I'll be as considerate of you as you were of me this morning," Noah said as Max groaned. "So take your damn time."

He returned to the house, making sure not to slip on the already icy flagstone path that led from the barn to the side door. When the weather got bad, they rigged up a rope from the barn to the house to stop anyone getting disoriented and wandering off in a blizzard. Noah had originally scoffed at the idea until he'd lived through his first winter from hell and realized the immense power of Mother Nature to screw you over.

He found his cell and checked his texts to see that Luke had sent over the necessary information for the county social services department. He called them first and wasn't surprised to learn that their offices were closed. He had the choice of calling 911 or leaving a message. Fully aware that the county's already tight resources would be stretched to their limits with all the snow, he opted to leave a voicemail.

It took him a while longer to find Mary's number and call her. She didn't pick up either, but he wasn't surprised. She worked shifts at the hospital and often turned her phone off. It was one of the reasons their relationship had never gone anywhere. Just scheduling a day when they were both free had proven challenging, and she wasn't the kind of woman who would blow off her job just to be with some cowboy like him. He admired her for admitting that and being the first to acknowledge things wouldn't work out.

Luke came in the door with the baby. "How did it go?"

"Left a couple of messages." Noah shrugged. "Any news on your end?"

"Nothing from anyone, including Dave, who is probably halfway to Africa right now." Luke glanced down at Sky. "What do you want me to do with the kid?"

"Why are you asking me? You're the one who has a niece and a nephew."

"Whom I barely get to hold when my mom and Brina are around." Luke set the baby on the couch and started to unzip his snow suit. "You had lots of siblings, right?"

"Yeah, which means I'm totally over parenting kids that don't belong to me."

"But at least you know what to do."

"My skill set is fifteen years out of date," Noah said flatly. "I bet you good money that anything I did back in the day is now all wrong."

While Luke's attention was on Noah, Sky took the opportunity to roll off the couch.

"Watch out!" Noah stuck out a hand, but it was way too late. Sky landed on his face and immediately started to wail.

Noah picked Sky up and gave him a cuddle while Luke rushed around muttering about concussion, ice packs, and what the correct dosage was for a baby if you had to give them a painkiller.

"He's fine," Noah said. "He fell on his snowsuit."

Luke had his head in the medicine cabinet. "I wish Mom

was here. She might be semiretired, but I could sure do with some medical advice right now."

"Luke, he's fine," Noah repeated. "Look. He's not even crying."

Luke turned around to stare at Sky and blew out a breath. "Good. I mean he rolled off that couch like a champ. He almost gave me a heart attack."

"Babies do that shit all the time. You have to watch them twenty-four-seven." Noah put Sky in the high chair and offered him a cup of milk.

"Which is why we need to get this little dude home as soon as possible." Luke ruffled Sky's blond curls as he went past him. "I'll call Blair down at the sheriff's department. She might be more helpful than her boss."

"She might be for you," Noah murmured. "Seeing as she's got a crush on you a mile wide."

Luke shrugged. "I can't do anything about that, can I? If it helps get this little dude home quicker, I'm willing to take one for the team."

It was only after Luke exited the kitchen that Noah realized he'd been left with the baby again. He stared at Sky, who smiled back at him, reminding Noah forcibly of Dave. Except none of this was the kid's fault, and if Dave did suddenly indulge in a fit of remorse and come back, Noah was still going to let him have it.

He sighed and checked the time. "I guess I should get you a snack. Do you like apple slices?"

Sky nodded as if he understood every word. Noah took an apple out of the bowl on the countertop and started slicing it. If Sky's mom turned up before Dave, Noah had a few choice words for her as well. . . .

Jen woke up from an uneasy doze somewhere around Atlanta and scrambled to get her stuff together to make the transfer to the final bus that would take her to Miami. After almost three days when she'd had no response from Dave, his mom, or Mrs. Friedman, she felt as if she'd accidentally strayed into an alternate universe. Every mile the bus ate up made her worry more. She'd seen disaster close up, and her imagination as to what might happen to her son knew no limits.

She reminded herself for the millionth time that Martha would never let anything bad happen to Sky, and that even if she'd gotten tired of looking after him full time, she wouldn't abandon him.

Like Jen had done. . . .

She shoved that thought back down. She'd had no choice. Her job didn't allow for quitters, and she'd been obliged to finish out her contract regardless of her inconvenient personal life. She had the opportunity to change that now, and once she had Sky back in her arms, she'd make sure he was there to stay.

The bus pulled into the Atlanta terminal and Jen prepared to disembark. Bus travel didn't bother her, as she was used to close quarters and being trapped with a group of people with all their individual quirks and annoying habits. She'd made her peace with the lady who snored like a tsunami warning, and the dude who sang along off key to all his music two states ago. Forty stops down and less than five to go. She could do this. She had to. And if Dave was with Sky? She'd be giving him a piece of her mind for scaring the crap out of her as well.

She checked her cell as she exited the bus and noticed a text from Mrs. Friedman.

Spoke briefly to Martha. She is expecting you.

Thanks! Jen immediately texted back as she made her way through the busy terminal to her next boarding point. I'll be there tomorrow morning.

The Miami bus was already there, and the doors were open. Even as her body protested the mere idea of being squashed into another small space, Jen mounted the steps and looked for her seat. One more night of discomfort and then the joy of seeing Sky. She couldn't wait. She only hoped that after five months apart, he'd know who she was.

"Jennifer." Martha opened the door of her ground-floor condo. She still wore her bathrobe, and her brown hair was in a messy topknot with a pencil stuck through it. "Come on in."

"Thanks."

Jen eased her backpack off her shoulder and set it carefully beside the door. The last thing she needed was to break any of the two thousand china ornaments that covered every available surface. She followed Martha through into the sun-drenched kitchen, noting the box of toys in the hallway and a stuffed rabbit on the formal couch.

"I'm so sorry—"

Martha had her back to her. "Coffee, dear?"

"That would be awesome." Jen gathered her courage. "You must be mad at me."

"I'm pretty mad at both of you right now." Martha handed her a mug of coffee. "But more so with Dave. He really isn't taking parenting seriously at all."

Jen took a quick gulp of coffee. "The ship was delayed because of the hurricanes and then we got turned around to help out. There wasn't much I could do about any of it."

"I understand that." Martha sighed. "But Dave didn't take it well. You'd think he'd been the one caring for Sky the last few months, the fuss he made."

"He left Sky with you?"

"Pretty much." Martha nodded. "Officially, he was staying

at my place, but I hardly saw him except when he wanted a meal or to do his laundry. I had to nag him to spend any time with Sky at all."

"I'm so sorry."

"That's hardly your fault, is it? We both hoped Dave would step up and do the right thing, but he didn't. I can't blame you when I wanted him to succeed myself." Martha sliced a bagel and put it in the toaster. "I bet you're starving. Sit down, and I'll get you some breakfast."

Jen took a seat, simply glad that Martha hadn't slammed the door in her face.

"So is Sky still sleeping?"

"How would I know, dear?" Martha set the bagel along with cream cheese in front of her.

"*What*?" Jen whispered, her appetite disappearing into the hollow pit of her stomach as black spots whirled before her eyes. "I thought—"

"Breathe, dear." Martha took the seat beside her and patted her hand. "Don't get upset, now. Eat your food, and I'll tell you what I know."

"How can I eat when my son—" Jen stared at Martha. "Is *where*?"

"When I told Dave I was coming to Florida early and he needed to take Sky, he freaked out and said he'd had a job offer and that he had to leave as soon as possible. I told him to make sure he had plans for his son as I was no longer going to be his full-time unpaid caretaker." Martha sipped her coffee. "I love Sky, but I have a life, Jen."

"Of course, you do." Jen nodded even though her brain was spiraling into a panic. "Dave said he'd just be using your address until he found a place for him and Sky to live."

"For all I know he might have found a place for himself, but he never officially moved in or collected Sky. It was extremely annoying."

"I can imagine." Jen tried not to apologize again.

"Eventually, when Dave worked out that I was serious, he said he'd been in touch with you and that he'd be able to drop Sky off as planned." Martha paused. "I was skeptical, but he assured me that he had it all sorted out, and that he'd be meeting you off the ship and then going to his new job."

"That's all news to me," Jen said. "He threw a fit when I told him I'd been delayed, and he's refused to talk to me ever since."

"He said he'd agreed to meet you on the East Coast and that the easiest thing to do was for him to drive us all here, and then he'd take Sky, and go and get you." Martha frowned. "I should have checked in, but Dave said you were unavailable."

Jen didn't want to call Dave a liar in front of his mother so went for a tactful reply. "I know I can be hard to get hold of, but I'm always contactable. We've skyped and facetimed in the past."

"I guess I was so pleased to see him taking some responsibility that I was willing to accept what he said at face value." Martha grimaced. "More fool me. He's my son. I should've known better."

Jen took a bite of her bagel and chewed slowly to give herself something to do to avoid her rising panic. She'd learned at an early age that she had to be the sensible one, and nothing in her life up until this point had persuaded her differently. But this—this was something else. She gathered all her resources.

"So where is he?"

"Dave?"

"Both of them. My ship docked in San Diego. Dave knew that beforehand, so why did he say something different?"

"I guess he wanted some time to come up with a solution and reckoned that taking me and Sky to Florida would stave off the fateful day."

"Dave always thinks something is magically going to turn up." Jen ate another small bite. "Where's his new job?"

"Africa."

Jen put down the bagel. "Which country?"

"He didn't say. I was just delighted he'd found a job."

"There's no way he could've taken Sky with him. He doesn't have a passport or any of the right shots. So where are they?"

Martha swirled her lemonade, making the ice clink. "Dave did send me a text a few days ago. He said he'd arrived safely, and not to worry about Sky, who was with your aunt."

"My aunt?"

"Why are you looking at me like that?" Martha slapped her hand on the table. "I'd strangle that boy myself if he was in front of me."

"I don't have any aunts. Well, I do, but none that I really know because I grew up in foster care when my parents couldn't cope."

"Oh my gawd." Martha's hand came up to cover her mouth. "What on earth has he done with Sky?"

"Do you have Dave's new cell number or employer's name?" Jen asked as a weird feeling of unease came over her. "I really need to talk to him."

"I have his number." Martha grabbed Jen's hand, her voice trembling. "I'm so sorry. I would *never* have let him take Sky if I'd realized what he planned. I love that little boy to bits."

"I know you do, and I bet Dave didn't even have a plan. He probably just went along until something happened to make it easy for him to leave Sky so he could go off to his new job."

"Dave wouldn't have abandoned him," Martha said earnestly. "He's a fool, but he's very fond of Sky, in his own way."

"I'm sure he is." Jen's mind raced through possibilities.

Should she contact the police? Was there a centralized missing persons bureau? Where in the vastness of the United States had Dave decided to leave their almost-one-year-old son? She should never have left them alone together. "As soon as I talk to him everything will become clear."

Martha shot to her feet. "I'll go and find those numbers for you."

"Thanks." Jen forced herself to finish half the bagel and stay calm. If her ship hadn't been delayed . . .

She gave herself a mental shake. It was definitely not the time for the "if onlys." Knowing Dave, the path to the truth would be long, often pointless, and definitely arduous, but she had to keep going. The safety and security of her son was on the line, and she couldn't afford to fail. When she had Sky in her arms, she'd allow herself to fall apart, but not until then.

Martha came back with a piece of paper in her hand. "He's in Nigeria. Does that help?"

"Anything helps." Jen took the information. "In my experience, he's more likely to respond to you than to me, so if you could just keep calling him that would be great."

"Oh, I'll be calling him all right." Martha's mouth set in a firm line. "And if he doesn't pick up, I'll be talking to his boss."

"I'll try his social media accounts as well. He hates to be called out in public," Jen said.

"True." Martha nodded. "He blocked me on all of those because he thought I made him look stupid."

"Not that he needed any help with that," Jen murmured as Martha went to refill their glasses. How she'd allowed herself to be charmed into bed by Dave still remained something of an embarrassing mystery. Even worse, she'd imagined having a future with him, only to find out she was one of many as opposed to "the one."

She plugged in her phone to charge and sent a text to Dave's new cell number—the one he'd mysteriously forgotten to share with her.

CALL ME RIGHT NOW.

She had no idea what time it was in Nigeria, but she didn't care if she woke him up. For once in his life, he was going to take responsibility for his actions and help her locate their son.

She switched to his social media accounts and saw a picture of him grinning and doing a shaka as he stepped off a small plane in what looked like the middle of a desert. She hit the reply button and typed in caps.

GREAT PIC! BUT DID YOU FORGET SOMETHING? CALL ME TO FIND OUT.

Jen finished her second cup of coffee and reminded herself that she had a huge network of friends all around the globe who would help her if things got complicated. If Dave had somehow gotten Sky into Nigeria, she knew people who could get him back. And some of them would have no qualms about how they achieved their goals.

"Why don't you take a nap, dear?" Martha said. "And when you wake up, we'll bombard Dave with questions until he gets his act together and replies."

"Sounds like a great plan." Jen went back into the hall to reclaim her backpack and headed up the stairs to the bedroom at the rear of the property. "Let's hope Dave's still scared of his momma."

Chapter Four

"Don't do that," Noah said to Sky, who immediately pushed out his lower lip, ignored the advice, and waved the corn stalk energetically in the air.

They were in the barn and Noah had set Sky inside a temporary hay fort so that he could get on with his work. Despite his protests, he'd ended up looking after the kid for two interminable weeks while the others tried to find out where the hell Sky's mom and grandma were located. They hadn't come up with anything, but they'd all been reluctant to call child services and have Sky taken away. The kid was strong willed, but he slept through the night, wasn't a screamer, and ate everything they put in front of him.

The weather had stayed cold, and the snow had settled, isolating them from the town and the rest of the world. Even if Sky's family got to Quincy, there was no way they'd get any farther without the help of the emergency services, and that wasn't happening while the county was locked down. Noah was surprised how easily he'd fallen back into the old routines of caring for a baby. His dad had walked out when Bailey, his oldest sister, was eight, and as his mom had to work to keep the family together, he'd basically brought his sisters up. He'd hated it and often loudly proclaimed to anyone who'd listen that he was never having kids.

Luke made some effort to help out, but he tended to over-analyze everything. Max was great at playing until Sky was wound up so tight, he wouldn't sleep, which wasn't helpful. For some reason, Sky seemed happiest when he was with Noah, which, considering he was big, bearded, loud, and, according to his sisters, should smile more, made no sense at all.

There was a wail from Sky, who had succeeded in jamming a piece of straw up his nose. Noah set his shovel to one side, walked over to the temporary pen and looked at the occupant.

"I told you."

He hunkered down and checked that Sky hadn't done any real damage before patting him on the head and resuming mucking out the stall. They'd heard nothing from Dave, which wasn't surprising when they all wanted to kill him. Luke had even checked with the cell phone company and found Dave's number was dead.

"Coward," Noah muttered as he dumped the last shovel-ful of manure into the wheelbarrow.

"Da." Sky patted the straw bale and lifted up his arms. "Da!"

"For the millionth time, I'm not your dad. I'd never have given you such a weird name for one thing." Noah decided it was time to take Sky in for his snack and morning nap. He wasn't sure which one of them was crankier and needed it most right now. "Come on, then. Let's go."

It was snowing gently, and the wind had died down, leaving the usual sounds of the ranch muted and indistinct. Strips of light streamed in diagonal lines between the trees, illuminating the greenish gloom. The faint noise from the highway that usually penetrated the forest when the wind was blowing from the west was noticeably absent. Nothing much was moving in Plumas County, and Noah was okay with that. They were well stocked up. The three of them had faced far worse conditions during their military service. If it wasn't for the presence of Sky, everything would be as good as it could be.

"Da." Sky patted Noah's beard as they walked back to the house. "Nono."

"Glad you're finally learning that one," Noah murmured. "I say it enough."

The house was silent and warm, and the kitchen was spotless because Luke had been in there last. Noah removed Sky's outerwear, sat him in the high chair, and made him a healthy snack Luke had researched on the internet.

While he was warming up his coffee, Noah noticed that Sky was happily eating the orange and dropping the bird seedy stuff over the side where Sally's two dogs, Winky and Blinky ate it up.

"Smart kid," Noah commented as he offered more apple. "Not sure what Luke's trying to feed you, either."

Sky grinned at him, his two front teeth shining white and proud. His cheeks were glowing. Noah hoped it was just from the cold and not because he was teething. He'd noticed a sharp increase in the rate of drool over the last couple of days, which was never a good sign.

He glanced out of the kitchen window and noticed the snow was getting heavier. There was a pile of laundry to do, and the ranch accounts, so he'd take the opportunity to stay inside and get stuff done. Luke and Max might think they were getting the last laugh leaving him with the baby, but at least he wasn't out there freezing his nuts off rounding up stray cattle.

Noah checked Sky's diaper, wiped his face and hands, and took him through to the farm office, where he'd rigged up a playpen full of toys Luke's nieces had left behind.

"Here you go, dude."

"Da." Sky picked up a doll and immediately started chewing on its hair.

"Yuck." Noah made a face and tried to take the toy away. "Not good."

Sky reluctantly let go of the doll, and Noah looked around for something the kid could chew on.

"Hold up, buddy."

He went back into the kitchen and found a new pack of plastic dog bones Luke's mom had left in the cupboard. He carefully disinfected and washed one with boiling water and returned to the study.

"Here you go."

Sky took the bone and examined it closely before jamming it in his mouth and energetically chewing. Drool ran down his chin as he grinned up at Noah.

"Good stuff, eh? Just don't think you can take the ones the dogs already own," Noah warned him.

The kid was already crawling and standing up. Noah guessed it wouldn't be long before he was ready to walk, which introduced a whole new set of problems. If Dave or his girlfriend didn't turn up soon, Noah might be the one having to deal with that, too.

"They'd better turn up," he muttered as he sat at the desk and opened Luke's laptop. "Or else."

Jen turned a slow circle so that she could take in the whole of Quincy's main street. She'd visited the area once before with one of her foster families and spent two weeks at a summer camp out in the park. Snow had settled everywhere and was at least a foot deep. There was very little traffic, and people were nonexistent. To her relief, the coffee shop had its lights on. She went inside and immediately appreciated the warmth.

"Hi! I was just about to give up and go home." The young woman behind the counter, who had red hair and the pale, freckled skin to go with it, greeted Jen brightly. "Did you get off the county bus? I thought they weren't running right now."

"They aren't." Jen set her backpack down. "I got a ride from one of the logging-company trucks."

She couldn't believe it had taken her two weeks to find out what Dave had done with Sky, and to make her way back across the country *again* to go and get him. It had taken the combined efforts of Martha, Jen, and Dave's social media supporters to finally guilt him into making the call. He'd been his usual breezy self, but this time Jen had really let him have it. He'd tried to turn it around and make it all her fault, which was fairly typical, but eventually she'd found out what he'd done with Sky.

"Would you like some coffee?"

"Yes, please. The biggest one you've got."

The woman chuckled. "I hear ya. It's cold out there." She handed over a large pottery mug full of coffee. "I'm Bernie, by the way."

"Hi Bernie, I'm Jen." She added cream and a ton of sugar to her mug. "This looks like a very cute town."

"It is when it isn't snowing or burning." Bernie made a face. "But that's northern California for you." She handed Jen a spoon. "Do you need a place to stay in town? My cousin Lucy owns a B and B right across the street, and she definitely could do with the business."

"That's great to know," Jen said. "But I was aiming to get to the Nilsen Ranch."

"Sally's place?"

"I guess."

"She's not there right now," Bernie said. "I think she's visiting her grandkids in Texas, or is it Florida?"

Jen had a sudden urge to laugh hysterically. Was this her life now? Had she somehow died and was now in purgatory, constantly running in circles only to be given the same answer at every port of call?

"But her son Luke's there," Bernie continued. "I saw him and his buddies in here a while ago."

"Was one of them blond and charming by any chance?" Jen asked.

Bernie looked thoughtful. "There was a new one. I couldn't see much of him, unfortunately, but he was blond, and he had a baby with him, which made him even cuter of course."

Jen's knees almost folded. "That's . . . great."

"Would you like to sit down? You look like you're about to bawl or something."

Jen took a seat and slowly exhaled. "You have no idea."

Bernie put her coffee in front of her, and Jen took a cautious sip.

"That's really good."

"I roast it myself. Would you like something to eat? I baked some great blueberry muffins, and it doesn't look like they're going to get eaten by anyone else."

"I'd love one," Jen said. "I'm starving."

She waited as Bernie warmed the muffins and took the seat opposite her.

"Here you go." Bernie waited until Jen had taken her first bite. "I don't mean to be nosey or anything, but does your visit have anything to do with Luke?"

"I've never met the guy."

"Okay."

Jen ate the whole muffin before replying. "I just need to get to the ranch. Is there a taxi service or Uber or something?"

"Um, not really. Nothing's operating." Bernie made a

sympathetic face. "You can't get up the road right now unless you're a county snowplow."

Jen mentally reviewed her options. "Is it possible to walk?"

"I guess you could hike up, but it's about four miles out. If we get another storm coming through, you could wander off the road and be lost forever."

Jen realized Bernie was serious and definitely not exaggerating. But she'd received training in navigating difficult terrain, and she didn't really have another option.

As if reading her mind, Bernie said. "You could stay the night at Lucy's and then see if the weather is better in the morning."

"Is it likely to be?"

"Not really." Bernie glanced out at the leaden skies. "This is actually a good day. It's supposed to get a lot worse."

"So I could end up being stuck in town for weeks."

"Yes, but at least you'd be safe and alive," Bernie countered.

Jen looked over at her backpack and sighed. "I can't wait any longer."

"Do you want me to call Luke and tell him you're coming?" Bernie asked. "Maybe he'd be able to meet you at the ranch gate off the highway or something."

"Call him if you like, but I'm quite happy to get there on my own steam."

Jen finished her coffee. She was so close to seeing Sky that a four-mile hike seemed like nothing.

"Do you have a flask?" Bernie returned to her position behind the counter. "I'll fill it with coffee and pack you a couple of muffins to go."

"Thanks, that would be great." Jen searched for her wallet. "What do I owe you?"

"Nothing. Just promise you'll let me know that you arrived safely."

"Sure." Jen handed over her phone while she zipped up her jacket and put on her knitted hat. "Put your details in there."

"Cell reception is spotty among the trees, but Luke will know the best places to make a connection." Bernie gave her the coffee and muffins. "I'll call him to let him know you're on your way."

"Thanks." Jen stowed the coffee and snacks in her backpack and hoisted it onto her shoulders. "I'd better get going before the light fades."

She reckoned that if she kept to the side of the road and made steady progress, she'd be there in three hours. Or five depending on the severity of the snow. But whatever it took she'd make it.

She had to.

Several hours later, Jen paused beside a barred gate that led off the highway. Her cell phone was no longer picking up a consistent signal. The helpful sign and mailbox proclaiming the gate belonged to the Nilsen Ranch was definitely a bonus. There was a keypad to open the gate, but it wasn't hard to toss her backpack over and climb the metal rails while praying it wasn't electrified.

She took a moment to drink the last of her coffee and eat a protein bar. A long gravel drive surrounded by tall redwood trees—it looked like an old logging trail—stretched ahead of her. It was deathly quiet, and the snow was deeper here than in town and had settled in steep banks. There were recent tire tracks on the path, which reassured her that someone was out there, even if she couldn't see a single building.

She shouldered her backpack and groaned as her body protested the weight. After two weeks of traveling on buses her fitness level was nowhere near where it needed to be, and it showed. She could only hope that the homestead was closer than it looked and that she wouldn't have to trek another two miles just to reach the front door.

She hiked on, trying to keep in one of the tire ruts, which at least gave her some traction and direction. The wind was a living, breathing thing out here, snapping at her face, singing in her ears, and gently buffeting her body. The deathly quiet was unnerving. If she was in a movie this would be the moment when she died a horrible death.

Her breath exploded out as she rounded another torturous bend and finally saw the ranch buildings laid out below her. There were two large barns, an old-fashioned timber-clad house, and miles of fencing. Fog was now rolling in off the trees and weaving its way toward her like more bad news. She wanted to increase her pace, but her legs weren't obeying her. She stumbled forward as fast as she could until she came to the edge of the paved drive.

There were lights on in the main house and the barn. If Sky was there, then hopefully someone had him safe in the house.

"Hallelujah," Jen murmured. "I made it."

Even as the words left her mouth, a huge, bearded figure stepped out of the shadow of the barn holding a weapon aimed right at her head.

"Stop right there and put your hands where I can see them."

"Oh, for goodness' sake. Knock it off."

The person Noah had his rifle aimed at took off their backpack and spun to face him.

"There's no need to be so dramatic, dude. Didn't Bernie tell you I was coming?"

Noah slowly lowered his weapon and made sure it was safe before he looked over at the tall woman who was now glaring at him.

"Who are you and what do you want?"

"I guess Bernie didn't call, or you're just making things difficult because this is a shitty situation all around." She met his gaze directly. "I'm Jennifer Rossi. I understand you have my son here."

"You're Sky's mother."

"Yup."

Noah strolled slowly toward her. "Nice of you to finally show up."

Her already pink cheeks flushed even more. "May I see my son?"

"It depends. Are you planning on sticking around for a while, because I don't want him being upset."

She blinked hard and looked away from him. "Okay, I suppose I deserved that. Can I see him?"

"He's taking a nap."

"Then I'll wait for him to wake up."

"I suppose you'd better come inside." Noah gestured reluctantly at the kitchen door. "I'll put my gun away and meet you there."

"Thanks." She nodded and turned toward the house. Just before she went up the steps, Noah called out to her.

"Don't steal anything or try to find Sky, okay?"

The filthy look she gave him was priceless, but he gave her credit for not slamming the door as she went inside.

He hadn't heard any vehicles and had only been alerted to the presence of a stranger by the dogs, who had come out to the barn with him while Sky slept. For some reason, she'd assumed he'd know she was coming, but he'd left his cell phone in the kitchen to recharge and hadn't checked it all morning. Besides, he didn't think Bernie from the coffee shop had his number, which meant she'd probably called Luke, who was way out in the hills and might not have gotten anything either.

Noah secured the gun in the safe and walked back to the

house. The afternoon fog had settled in early, and it was getting colder by the second. There was a storm forecast for the next day that looked like it was coming in already. He'd check in with Luke and Max and make sure they came back before things got bad.

He paused as he went into the kitchen to take in his guest, who was pacing in front of the fire in the adjoining family room. She'd unzipped her jacket and taken off her hat and gloves to reveal curly brown hair in a neat ponytail, brown eyes, and wind-chapped cheeks. She was tall for a woman, which meant he didn't have to crick his neck to look at her. She was nothing like Sky, who was all Dave.

Poor kid.

"I guess you'll be expecting an explanation, but are you okay if I warm up first?"

"Sure." His curiosity overcame him. "Did you hitch a ride up to the main gate and walk in?"

"No, I walked, period."

"All the way from town?"

He must have sounded as skeptical as he looked because her back straightened.

"There wasn't an alternative."

"You could have stayed in Quincy and called rather than risking your life walking in terrain you don't know and probably haven't experienced before."

"Wow, thanks for explaining how stupid I am," she said. "I had no idea."

He knew when someone was being sarcastic. "All I'm saying is that I probably wouldn't have risked it in these conditions, and I do know what I'm doing."

"Good for you. But maybe you shouldn't assume things about me, because you know what that makes you."

"An ass?" He shrugged. "Wouldn't be the first time

someone's called me that." He noticed she was shivering. "I'll get you some coffee."

"Thanks." She returned to pacing in front of the stone-fronted fireplace, her arms wrapped around herself.

He took the opportunity to check his cell while he made the coffee. Luke had tried to text him at some point, but it hadn't come through. He frowned at his phone. They needed to get out the radio system Max had developed that covered the whole ranch. It was invaluable in the winter months.

He checked the time and sent Luke a text telling him to start back asap. There was still no sound on the baby monitor. He wasn't going to wake Sky before he was ready. He'd learned that lesson on day two.

He took the two mugs of coffee and handed one to Jen.

"Cream and sugar are over there if you need them."

"Thanks, Luke." She helped herself liberally to both and offered him a hesitant smile. "It was quite a hike."

"Yeah, about that. I'm not Luke."

"But this is Luke's ranch."

"That's correct. I'm a friend of Luke's. My name's Noah."

"I'd like to say it's a pleasure, but you don't look very pleased to see me."

"Why would I be? You and Dave won't be winning any awards for parent of the year. He leaves the kid here, and you . . ." He shook his head. "Well, I guess you did turn up eventually."

"You think I did this intentionally?"

Noah shrugged. "Dave did say you weren't exactly reliable."

"Did he." Her tentative smile disappeared. "And you believed him."

"Dave's not a bad guy. He served in the same unit as Luke—saved his life at one point."

She cradled her mug in two hands and sipped her coffee

before looking up at him. "I guess that means he's infallible then."

Noah wasn't yet ready to concede that Dave could be a complete dick while he was still attempting to make Jen face up to her own parental failings.

"Everyone makes mistakes." Noah leaned back against the counter and drank his own coffee.

"But apparently Dave's are more forgivable because he's one of the boys."

Noah met her gaze. "I'm not a big fan of any parent who runs out on their kid."

"You think that's what I did?"

"Dave said you were off traveling around the world and that you got delayed."

"That's how he framed it?"

Noah frowned. "Yeah."

"Fine." Jen drank more coffee. "Is Sky awake yet?"

Great. So, according to Noah she was a terrible parent, and Dave was some kind of saint. She'd arrived willing to apologize profusely and thank Luke for keeping Sky safe, but now she knew what they all thought of her. Her tall, bearded, scowling companion had made his feelings abundantly clear, and she had to assume Luke would feel the same.

But it was Luke's house, and perhaps she'd wait until he turned up to explain herself rather than getting into it with his buddy. Noah didn't deserve to know anything, when he'd already made up his mind that she was totally at fault. If she was honest with herself, she understood why he was so angry with her. She wanted to apologize again, but something held her back.

He didn't look like the kind of guy who bent very easily.

She had plenty of guilt to go around and didn't need to feel any worse than she currently did.

'He's still asleep."

Jen made herself look calmly at Noah, who was well over six foot and had the body of a linebacker. Something about his stance screamed retired military, which made sense if he was a friend of Dave's. He gestured at the white unit on the countertop.

"Baby monitor."

"Great." Jen smiled. "Any chance I could have more coffee?"

His dark brows drew together as if he wasn't certain how to handle her being pleasant. "Sure."

"Thanks."

"Luke should be back soon."

"Good to know," Jen said sweetly. "I can't wait to meet him and thank him for taking care of Sky."

He walked into the kitchen to get the coffee, his blue plaid shirt stretching tight over his broad shoulders.

"Luke's a good man."

"So, I hear."

"Dave talked about him?" Noah looked over his shoulder at her.

"Dave only talks about himself."

"Yeah—" He stopped midsentence and frowned again. "Coffee coming right up."

Jen held out her mug and he refilled it. "I met Bernie at the café in town. She's the one who gave me directions to this place."

"I'm surprised she didn't tell you to stay put."

"Oh, she did." Jen stopped and took out her cell. "That reminds me: I promised to let her know if I arrived safely. She said there's a B and B in town where I can stay when I get back down there."

"I would've thought you'd be happy to wait another day before you had to take Sky again."

Jen met his skeptical gaze head on. "Then you would've thought wrong. You have no idea what I've been through to get here."

"I guess that if I had a kid, I'd like to think I'd be better prepared."

Jen opened her mouth to blast him, but as guilt overwhelmed her, thought better of it. Whatever Noah believed, he'd obviously done his best to look after Sky.

"Sometimes fate conspires against you. I thought I had all my bases covered and I made the mistake of believing Dave would rise to the occasion." She let out a breath. "Thank you for looking after Sky."

He studied her for a long moment before nodding and turning away. "Luke will be back soon. You can thank him."

"Oh, don't worry. I will." She sent a text to Bernie and received a smiley emoji back.

The sound of voices filtered in from the porch and Jen stiffened. How many people lived at the ranch? And how was she going to deal with a wall of masculine disapproval? She reminded herself that she was used to being underrated and outnumbered, and gathering her courage, turned to face the door.

"Hey." The first guy who came in smiled at her. He had kind, gray eyes and the look of a man who spent the majority of his working days outside. "You must be Jen. It's good to meet you. I'm Luke." He offered her his hand, which she shook.

"Hi, thanks so much for looking after Sky. You can't even imagine—"

"Oh, I'm sure we can." The second guy cut across her words as he also shook her hand. He had very blue eyes and black hair. "We've met Dave."

Jen glanced over at Noah, who was listening intently and didn't look too pleased about his friends being nice to her.

"Dave was supposed to meet me at his mom's in San Jose three weeks ago." Jen redirected her attention to Luke, who had the most sympathetic face. "When I got there, the place was empty. I almost had heart failure."

"I bet." Luke gestured for her to sit at the kitchen table and joined her. "We had a similar experience when we woke up one morning and discovered Dave had left for Africa without telling us he was leaving Sky behind."

Jen groaned and covered her face with her hands. "He didn't."

"He sure did." Max leaned up against the countertop and looked down at her. "Took Luke's mom's truck and left it at the airport. We had to go and rescue it before it was towed."

"I'll cover any costs you've incurred." Jen was mortified. "I can't believe he did that to his friends."

"I guess he thought three of us could cope with one baby," Luke said. "Although, to be fair, Noah did most of the work."

"That was kind of him."

Max snorted, and Jen looked at him rather than at Noah.

"Arkie wakes up first, so he got baby duties while Luke and I dealt with the rest of the ranch."

"That must have left you shorthanded." Jen grimaced. "I can't believe Dave didn't think things through."

"Really?" Luke raised an eyebrow. "In my experience of Dave, I'd say he'd behaved just like himself. He always had the blind optimism that things would work out in the end."

"Or that someone else would pick up the slack," Max chimed in.

Noah finally stirred. "And I guess they did. He got on his plane, and we ended up looking after his kid while Sky's mom was MIA."

Jen turned to Luke. "I can explain about that if you're willing to hear me out."

"Sure." Luke looked at his friends. "We have been wondering."

A faint sound came from the baby monitor, and Jen went still. Before she could get out of her chair, Noah was already on his way to the door.

"I'll get him. He'll want to see a familiar face."

Jen flopped back into her seat; her heart thumping so hard she imagined everyone could hear it.

"Sky's a great kid," Luke said. "Really nice personality."

"I'm glad to hear it." Jen took a quick breath. "I haven't seen him for months."

"That must have been tough."

"Yes." Jen nodded, her gaze fixed on the door. "It was."

Chapter Five

Noah took his time changing Sky and making sure he looked presentable before carrying him into the family room where Jennifer Rossi awaited them. Her gaze was fixed on her son, who appeared oblivious to her presence as he patted Noah's beard.

"Sky?" she said softly.

The kid turned at the sound of her voice and pointed his finger at her. "Da."

"Close," Noah murmured. "It's your mom."

He walked over and offered the baby to Jen. "Here you go."

Sky grabbed hold of his shoulder. "Nono."

"Yup, go to your momma." Noah gently untangled Sky's fingers and handed him over.

Sky looked up at Jen, who smiled so brightly Noah felt like he'd been hit directly by a sunbeam. Whatever her failings, her love and relief at being with her son shone through. How long it would last was another matter.

Jen's arms closed around Sky, and she sat down, her face hidden against the baby's blond curls, her voice muffled when she spoke.

"I don't know how to thank you all for keeping him safe."

"Not a lot else we could do at the time," Max said. "We're not the kind of guys who leave people behind."

"*Semper Fi,*" Luke said.

"Ooh-rah," Noah and Max echoed.

Jen raised her head. "You were all Marines?"

"Yes, ma'am." Luke gave her a sketchy salute. "That's where we met Dave."

Sky was examining Jen now, his expression intent as if he was trying to work out why this new person in his world seemed so familiar. Considering the kid was just about to turn one, his mom had been absent for almost half his life. Noah's sympathy for her diminished again.

"I've packed all his stuff," Noah said.

"That's great." Jen smiled at him over the top of Sky's head. "I'm amazed Dave remembered to bring anything with him."

"Some of the stuff Sky's been using belongs to my sister's kids," Luke said. "They use it when they come to visit, but Dave did bring diapers and clothes and all that kind of stuff."

"Martha probably packed it for him."

"Who's Martha?" Max had taken a seat close to Jen.

"Dave's mom. She has a place in San Jose. She's basically been looking after Sky since I left." Jen didn't seem bothered that Sky had now gotten a firm hold on her wrist and was gnawing at the cuff of her sweater. "I tracked her down in Florida to find out if she had Sky."

"Wait," Max said. "You arrived in San Jose and then had to hop on a plane to *Florida*?"

"It was worse than that. I had to go by bus. And then when I got there it took almost two weeks to contact Dave and get him to tell me where Sky was."

"Then you had to come all the way back out west again." Max whistled. "Hell, I know you're his girlfriend, but Dave can sometimes be a real dick."

"We're not together so you can say what you like. In fact, we barely ever were." Jen half smiled. "He didn't want to be a father, and I wasn't willing to share him with his other women."

"A girl in every port," Noah muttered to Luke, who was standing beside him.

"Sounds like Dave." Luke glanced at the clock. "We should eat."

"And I should go." Jen smiled at everyone except Noah. "You've all been amazing, but I've definitely outstayed my welcome. If one of you could drop us back to town, I'll be out of your hair."

"I can do that," Noah offered.

Luke frowned. "It's too late to drive these roads with a new storm front coming in."

"I'm fairly sure I could make it."

"And I don't want you risking your life, let alone Jen and Sky's. You haven't been out there today. It's not safe." Luke looked at Jen. "I don't know how you managed to get up here. There's a hard frost settling on the road."

"I hiked from town." Jen looked down at Sky and kissed his head. "I didn't have any other options."

"I already told her she was lucky not to wander off the road and get lost in the forest," Noah said.

"I bet she took that well." Max rolled his eyes. "I mean, women love men telling them what they're capable of."

Jen locked gazes with Noah. "I told *him* I was quite capable of making my own decisions, and we decided to leave it at that."

Luke stood up. "Well, no one is going anywhere tonight and that's my final word on the subject."

Noah opened his mouth to argue, but Luke was already on the move, his expression determined.

"Yes, sir." Max saluted and winked at Jen. "You can tell Luke was our team leader. He's still damn bossy."

Jen looked from Max to Noah. "Is there really no way I can leave? I feel terrible about imposing on you all."

"You could try hiking out with Sky on your back," Noah suggested.

The look she gave him was not friendly. "I get why you don't like me, Noah, but despite what you think, I wouldn't risk the life of my child."

Max stepped between them. "Hey, can we just cool things down here? No one's blaming you for anything, Jen."

"Noah is."

Jen wasn't letting it go, and Noah was happy to oblige her. It didn't seem right that Luke and Max had accepted her so easily when she was just as in the wrong as Dave.

"I guess I just don't appreciate anyone who abandons their kid."

Jen squared up to him, Sky in her arms. "*Abandoned*?"

"Yeah. Isn't that what you did?"

Max cleared his throat. "Hey, Noah, just hold up a minute there—"

Sky pointed his finger at Noah and shook his head. "No, no, shush, shush."

Max chuckled. "I think he's telling you to back off, bro."

Noah immediately took a step back. What had he been thinking, raising his voice in front of an innocent kid? He was acting just like his dad.

"Sorry, Sky. I'll keep it down." Ignoring Jen, he turned to Max. "I'll go and help Luke with dinner. Why don't you show Sky's mom where she can leave her stuff?"

Jen watched Noah stroll away as if he didn't have a care in the world.

"I'm sorry about that," Max said. "Noah's kind of blunt sometimes."

"So, I've noticed." Jen resettled Sky on her hip. She

couldn't believe how big he'd gotten. "He welcomed me to the ranch with a weapon pointed at my head."

Max blinked at her. "Holy shit." He grimaced. "I apologize for my language."

"It's okay. I did kind of creep up on the place because I hiked in."

"It's not okay." Max picked up her bag and walked toward the interior door. "Let me show you where Sky's been sleeping so you can get settled for the night before we eat dinner. The little guy's been eating the same stuff as us, but all mashed up, like a champ."

"That's good to know." Jen wasn't really listening as a wave of exhaustion flooded over her. She eyed the bed and the cot beside it. "How long until dinner?"

"About twenty minutes." Max nodded back at the hall. "Bathroom's next door. All Sky's diaper stuff is in there."

"Thanks." Jen sat on the bed, and Sky rested his face against her chest. "I really appreciate everything you've done for us."

"It's all good." Max winked at her. "I'd say don't fall asleep, but I don't think Sky will let you. He gets super vocal when he's hungry."

"Is he sleeping through the night now?"

"I guess so. You'd have to ask Noah. He's the expert."

Max departed, closing the door behind him, leaving Jen alone with Sky for the first time in five months. He regarded her seriously. Of course Noah would have to be the baby expert. The last thing she wanted to do was ask him anything, when he so obviously despised her. She smoothed a hand over Sky's well-brushed curls. But she wasn't being fair. By all accounts, Noah had basically raised her son for the last three weeks. She had to be grateful for that.

She wrapped her arms around Sky and hugged him as gently as she could while inhaling his scent. He didn't smell like her baby anymore, but that was okay. He was with her, and soon she'd be back at Martha's San Jose place while she worked out the rest of her life.

"Da?" Sky asked when she eventually eased away from him.

"He's in Africa, sweetie," Jen said. "But Mama's here now."

"Nono?"

Jen paused. "Are you asking after Noah?"

Sky beamed at her.

"Great, you're saying his name before mine." Jen sighed. "I guess I deserved that."

She put Sky in the crib to play and set about emptying her backpack. She didn't have much, but she always felt better when her possessions were in their right places. It was a routine she'd started as a kid moving from foster home to foster home, and she'd never quite grown out of it. She supposed it gave her the illusion of control, especially when she was stressed out like now.

She left a voicemail for Martha, brushed her hair, and used the bathroom before she heard Luke calling from the kitchen. She gathered up Sky and went back along the hallway, admiring the wide-planked flooring as she progressed. Max and Luke were in the kitchen and there was no sign of Noah. There was a high chair set at the head of the table that Jen put Sky in.

He immediately picked up his empty bowl and banged it on the tray.

"Hold up, youngster!" Luke said. "It's coming."

Jen went over to the kitchen area. "Can I help?"

"Sure, can you put some water glasses out on the table and make sure Max hasn't forgotten the serving spoons?"

"I thought we'd just put our hands in the pot like normal," Max said as he deftly removed a large casserole from the stove and walked it over to the table. He placed it as far away from Sky as possible. "I already took some out for the kid. It's cooling on a small plate if you want to put it in his bowl."

"Does he feed himself?" Jen asked, feeling awkward that she didn't know anything about her son's eating habits.

Noah spoke from behind her making her jump.

"He loves feeding himself, but not a lot gets in his mouth that way."

"Good to know." She kept her voice deliberately neutral as he tied a tea towel around Sky's neck and repossessed the spoon, which he handed to Jen before sitting at the table. "I think I can handle it from here."

"Knock yourself out." Max delivered the chopped-up food to Jen along with a pack of wet wipes. "Although watch out for that bowl flying around because you're more likely to go down than Sky is."

Jen took the seat nearest Sky and scooted as close as she could get. His eyes lit up when he saw the bowl of food, and he grabbed for it.

"Nope." Jen smiled at him. "I've got this. You can have a try when I'm done."

She offered him a spoonful of chicken casserole, which he accepted with great suspicion. He chewed slowly and then opened his mouth to allow two half-digested green beans to slide down his chin to the tray beneath. He poked them with his finger and definitely made a face.

"You don't like the beans?" Jen asked.

He spit out a few more green shreds.

"Okay." Jen sorted through the bowl. "I'll leave them to one side."

"My mom would've made me eat them," Max commented as he slid into the seat beside Jen and helped himself to the casserole. "She was tough."

"My feeling is that if he tries everything that's safe for him and there are foods he doesn't like, then that's okay."

Noah cleared his throat, and she looked over at him.

"What's wrong now?"

"I was going to agree with you." He nodded at the baby.

"He's not that picky, but when he doesn't like something, he lets you know real fast."

Even as he said the words, Sky spat out a piece of corn that hit Jen on the cheek. She burst out laughing while Sky smiled back and banged his fists on the tray.

"You like corn, buddy," Noah said. "What was that about?" He used his napkin to retrieve the corn from the floor. "Was it too much?"

"Nono," Sky said and pointed at Noah as Jen offered him another spoonful of chicken.

"Maybe he needs something to drink," Noah said as he straightened up. "I'll get his sippy cup. He's getting good at using it."

"I can do that," Jen said quickly.

Noah didn't answer as he went into the kitchen to dispose of the chewed corn, but she heard the faucet running, and thirty seconds later a cup appeared on the table beside her.

"Here you go."

"Thanks, but you didn't have to go to so much trouble."

"I was heading into the kitchen anyway."

"Aww . . . Noah's wishing he was still looking after the widdle baby." Max winked at Jen. "It's all so wholesome and cute."

"Wrong. I'm totally happy to hand over the reins to someone else." Noah retook his seat and helped himself to the food. "Sky's not going to notice one way or the other."

"Okay, I have to ask," Max said. "Whose idea was it to call him Sky?"

"Not mine."

"Then it was Dave." Max nodded. "Makes sense."

"He came to visit after the birth. While I was sleeping, he met the registrar and chose Sky's names." She spooned more goop into the baby's mouth. "When I woke up, it was too late to do anything except accept it."

"It's not so bad," Luke said. "It suits his sunny personality."

"I guess." Jen smiled at her son.

"You said names," Max asked. "What else did he pick?"

Jen sighed. "He's officially Sky Rainbow."

Max spluttered into his water. "The poor kid."

Even Luke had nothing positive to say about that as he helped himself to seconds. "Dave said you have an aunt who lives in Quincy?"

"Not that I know of." Jen wiped Sky's mouth, glad for the change of subject. "But I did come here to a summer camp once with my foster family."

"How the hell would Dave know about that?" Max said.

Jen frowned. "I remember mentioning the camp to him at one point because I'd just found out my foster mom Auntie Brenda had passed away. She was one of the good ones, and she brought me up here with her kids for one of the best summers of my life."

"Brenda. That's the name Dave mentioned." Max nodded. "It's a typical Dave tenuous connection with reality, which made sense to him at the time, and it fooled us into trying to help him. We walked all over Quincy looking for that woman."

There was nothing Jen wanted to say to that because it sounded just like her ex. She set the empty bowl on the table and wiped Sky's face again. "Does Sky have something to play with while we eat?"

"You could give him his bone." Max suggested. "I took it out of the dishwasher earlier, so it's clean."

"His *bone*?"

Noah shrugged. "Didn't have many things for him to chew on, so I went with that."

Jen's gaze fell to the two small, attentive dogs who sat by the table, hoping for falling scraps.

"It was a brand-new one," Max hastened to add. "Noah wouldn't just give him any old bone—would you, bro?"

"It would depend how desperate I was, because I think Sky might be teething. I'd rather he chewed the bone than my fingers." Noah shrugged. "Not that it's my problem any-more. If Jen doesn't like it, she's the boss."

"I think it was a great solution to a problem," Jen said before reluctantly raising her gaze to Noah's. "What makes you think he's teething?"

His cool expression didn't change. He'd decided he didn't like her, and she had to stop trying to make him change his mind. It had never worked with any of her foster parents when she was a kid, so she shouldn't be surprised.

"Mainly the amount of drool."

Jen had noticed that already. She leaned in and touched Sky's cheek.

"He's a little warm, and his cheeks are red." She eased her pinky finger inside Sky's mouth and gently ran it along his gums. "Definitely something going on."

"It's a shame my mom isn't here," Luke said as he offered Sky the bone. "She'd know for sure. She used to be the only doctor in a twenty-mile radius of this place."

"Your mom's a doctor?" Jen asked. "Did she practice in town?"

"Yeah, but she's gone part-time now, and she has a younger partner who does most of the work." Luke's pride in his mom was evident on his face. "I think she'd like to retire permanently, but a lot of people around here still won't take advice from anyone but her."

"She sounds amazing," Jen said. "I wish I'd gotten to meet her while I'm here."

"She is," Luke agreed before gesturing at the casserole dish. "How about you get something to eat while Sky's busy with his bone?"

Despite his best intentions to stay aloof, Noah kept a close eye on Jen as she dealt with Sky at dinner. What was he hoping? That she'd screw up and really be the worst mother of the year? That didn't sit well with him. He wasn't normally one to hold a grudge, but absentee parents had always been a sore issue for him. If he hadn't already decided not to like her, he might've been won over with her endless patience with Sky and the deft way she handled him.

"You're good with kids."

Noah didn't realize he'd spoken the words out loud until everyone around the table looked at him.

"I should hope so." Jen drank some water. "It's definitely a big part of my job."

"You're some kind of nanny?"

She set her glass down with deliberate care and turned to him. "Why would you think that?"

"I guess it pays better to look after someone else's kids than your own." Luke's sudden indrawn breath made Noah look over at him. "What? It's the truth. We all know that. Maybe Jen needed to take the job because Dave wasn't helping her financially."

"Maybe, you're getting this all wrong," Jen said sweetly. "And should stop talking about me like I'm not here."

"You don't think we have a right to know what's going on?" Noah demanded. "We've been looking after your kid for three weeks, lady."

"Because Dave screwed up. If he'd only done—"

"*You* screwed up," Noah interrupted her. "You didn't turn up when you were expected, and *he* was the one left hanging when he had a new job to go to and no one to mind your kid. Doesn't that make you the problem?"

"I got stuck in the middle of hurricane season in the Pacific." Jen was now glaring at him. "What was I supposed to do?"

"Find a way to get back!" Noah met her glare full on and returned it with interest. "Take a plane, a boat, find some means of transport, but get your ass back to the mainland."

"Noah—" Luke tried to intervene.

"It's okay." Jen was smiling now, which was somehow unsettling to Noah. "I'm more than happy to answer any questions you have about why I didn't get back in time for my son, even stupid ones."

"What's stupid about wanting to know why you couldn't find some way of getting back?" Noah asked.

She regarded him dispassionately, her fingers tapping against her water glass, her brown-eyed gaze steady.

"I was on a ship."

He raised an eyebrow. "So, get off at the next port."

"Without permission?"

"Presumably the kids you were looking after had parents. They could've managed without you for a while."

"Doubtful, and they weren't the people I needed to get permission from."

"Er . . . Noah," Max tried to speak. "I took Jen's stuff into her room, and I think you're way off base here—"

Jen smiled at him. "No, let Noah keep asking questions. If he tries very hard, he might eventually work it out."

"Work what out?"

"Why I couldn't leave," Jen said. "I mean, let's review. I was stuck on a ship, I couldn't just quit, and I was in the middle of a natural disaster. What in the world might Jennifer Rossi have been doing?"

"How the hell should I know?" Noah asked.

"Noah," Max spoke more insistently. "Trust me. She couldn't just leave."

Luke looked at Max and then at Jen. "Can someone just tell me what's going on?"

Max sighed. "I carried her ruck in. If I'm not mistaken, she's one of us."

Jen looked at him with approval. "You've got a good eye."

"Yes, ma'am," Max said. "Which branch?"

Her smile widened. "Same as you guys. Navy forever."

Noah blinked as he regarded her. "You were in the service?"

"Not quite. But I *am* in the Navy. That's why I couldn't leave, sweetie." She stood, picked Sky up, and settled him on her hip. "Excuse me while I go and change Sky."

She walked out with Sky, and Luke stared at Noah.

"Nice going, bro."

Noah leaned back in his chair. "How the hell was I supposed to know? She could've just told me upfront when she arrived."

"When you were holding her at gunpoint?" Max inquired.

"*What*?" Luke's attention swung back to Noah. 'Jeez, Arkie, what's gotten into you?"

"I didn't know who had turned up," Noah said defensively. "We had all that trouble with the illegal meth guys last year, remember?"

"I think you knew damn well who it was and just wanted to scare the crap out of her," Max said.

"That's bullshit." Noah scowled at him even as some demon in his brain wondered if his friend was right. "She snuck up on me, and I don't take that well from anyone."

"It's not her fault you think everyone's out to get you."

"As soon as I realized who she was I put the gun away and invited her in."

"What if it had been Dave's mom? The shock might have killed her." Max wasn't shutting up, which was usually Noah's job. "You overreacted, man. No wonder she wasn't willing to give out any information she didn't have to."

"For what it's worth, for once I agree with Max," Luke said. "You screwed up and you owe Jen an apology."

Chapter Six

After changing Sky, Jen debated not going back into the kitchen. She was tired enough to crash for a week, but she didn't want to make them worry about her or give Noah the satisfaction of knowing he'd upset her. She also didn't know Sky's sleep routine, and she had a horrible feeling she'd have to ask Noah about that.

"Come on, then." Jen picked Sky up and left her bedroom. "Let's see if your Noah is capable of admitting he might possibly have jumped to conclusions."

After being on a ship where she was outnumbered by men, her hopes weren't high, but that was even more reason to keep showing up and representing. She'd gone toe to toe with more than one male officer in her career, and the worst thing to do, in her opinion, was back down, especially in front of her team.

To her surprise there was no sign of Luke or Max, but Noah was still sitting at the table, his gaze trained on the door. He stood to attention as she came in and looked right at her.

"I apologize."

Jen waited for the rest of it, but he only looked at her as if those two words were enough.

"And . . . ?" Jen asked suspiciously.

"And what?" His dark brows drew together.

"An apology these days usually comes with a bunch of excuses. I was just waiting to hear what yours were going to be."

"I screwed up." He resumed his seat. "I don't know what else you want me to say."

Jen went to put Sky in the high chair, but he reached out his arms to Noah, who instinctively went to take him and then froze.

"Okay, if I hold him?" he asked.

"Sure." Jen handed him over. "He's been asking for you."

The skeptical look he gave her was no longer a surprise. "He says your name: Nono."

"Really?" Noah's face lightened up before he remembered to close it down again. "I thought he was echoing me telling him not to do everything."

"That's a single no. Nono is definitely you."

Jen wasn't sure why she was telling Noah something to make him feel valued, but she'd always been a peacemaker. It was one of the reasons why she loved her job so much.

"He's a good kid." Noah's gaze dropped to Sky, who was trying to undo the cuff on his shirt. "Dave did something right."

"Dave's had very little to do with raising him. That's mainly on Martha, who has been an absolute saint."

"And you, I guess." Noah didn't seem to mind that Sky was drooling all over his shirt.

"I looked after him for the first five months of his life, yes. Then I had to go back to work."

It had been the hardest thing she'd ever had to do in her life.

"Where are you stationed?"

"I work at the naval hospital and on the *USNS Mercy* out of San Diego."

Noah took a moment to digest that. "The hospital ship?"

"That's the one."

"Which was why you couldn't just get back."

"Correct." Jen grimaced. "The navy doesn't take kindly to deserters."

"Yeah." He paused, his attention on Sky. "That must have been tough."

"You can't imagine."

He finally looked up at her. "And from what I know of Dave, he wouldn't fill me with confidence that he would do the right thing while I was away."

"Dave . . ." She sighed. "I don't want to talk badly about him because he's Sky's dad, but—"

Noah interrupted her. "Knock yourself out. We all know what Dave is and what he isn't."

"I thought I'd covered all my bases, but Dave was barely around while I was away. Martha's been brilliant, but she wanted her life back. She's only in her fifties and didn't plan on being a full-time care giver to a child."

"Especially when she's still doing that for Dave," Noah added.

Jen almost smiled. "She's been nothing but kind and understanding about my career and its uncertainties, whereas Dave tends to make everything about himself."

"Dave should know better, seeing as he's retired military."

Noah was looking serious again. He obviously liked things done by the book, which in Jen's experience was way more common for a retired military guy than Dave's haphazard take on life. Before he remembered that he didn't like her much either, Jen decided to ask her questions.

"What time does Sky normally go to bed?"

Noah glanced over at the kitchen clock. "Around eight. He sleeps right through until six."

"Like, really?" Jen said. "That's . . . amazing." She smiled. "I haven't had a good night's sleep since we docked in San Diego and had to chase my ex and my child across the country. I'll probably turn in when he does. I'll be awake at six and ready to get out of here."

"Would you like something to drink?" Noah asked as he got up with Sky still in his arms. "I usually get this little guy a cup of warmed-up formula at this time of night."

"I'm good, thanks." She followed him through into the kitchen. The last thing she needed at this time of night was more coffee. "Where did Max and Luke go?"

"They're out in the barn making sure everything's secured for the night. It gets cold out here." He half smiled. "They also wanted to give you space to speak your mind after I apologized."

She sighed. "I appreciate that, but mainly I just have guilt because there's a lot of truth in what you said. What time do you guys normally turn in?"

"Early by most people's standards." Noah dealt with his tasks one handed as he continued to balance Sky on his hip. "We're up at dawn."

Jen glanced out of the window at the falling snow. "It's very dark out there."

"No city lights." He handed Sky a bottle. "Does it bother you?"

"Not at all. I've spent half of my career out in the middle of the ocean or in situations where electricity can sometimes be a bonus."

"I guess." He held Sky out to her. "Do you want to take him while I get myself more coffee?"

"Sure." Sky's smile turned into a yawn halfway through. He nuzzled against her shoulder, reminding her forcibly of when he'd been an infant. A wave of love for him washed over her so strongly she almost wanted to weep. She reminded herself that she was with him now and that she'd always be with him from that moment on.

"You okay?"

She looked up at Noah, who was regarding her carefully.

"I'm fine, thanks."

"Go sit in the family room. It's warmer in there."

She checked the time. She had half an hour before Sky went to bed. "I'll do that."

"There's a basket of toys if Sky wants them," Noah called out to her as she walked away from him. "His favorite thing right now is to cruise around the furniture. I don't think it will be long before he's walking."

Jen groaned. "Great."

She set Sky on the rug. He immediately pulled himself up to stand, patted the couch, and proceeded to side walk along to the other end of it before navigating the small gap to the coffee table with apparent ease. He turned to grin at her, obviously expecting applause.

"You've got this."

Jen clapped her hands as he headed unsteadily around the recliner to the stone fireplace. The fire was set way back, and as far as she could tell there was no danger of him burning himself, although he could crack his head. She kept a close eye on him. When he reached the other side of the fireplace, he completed his circuit around the old rocking chair and arrived back beside Jen.

"Good job," she told him.

Two seconds later he was off again.

Noah glanced back at the family room where Jen was now sitting with Sky. There was no sign of Max and Luke, who had told him to sort his shit out and left him to it. Should he join her until Sky was ready for bed? She might need some pointers as to how Sky liked to be put down to sleep. But would she even want him there after he'd been such an obnoxious dick to her?

Talk about making judgments before hearing the evidence. He'd allowed his own prejudices to color how he'd dealt with Jen from the moment he'd met her. He'd even pulled a gun on her, for God's sake. What kind of sane, balanced individual did that?

Maybe Sally was right, and he needed to talk to a professional about his current mental health. Just because he'd decided not to deal with some aspects of his military service didn't mean they'd disappeared from his memories or wouldn't turn up in some weird fashion to disturb him anyway.

He sent a text to Luke giving him the all-clear and continued to hang out in the kitchen, needlessly moving stuff around just to have something to do. Jen probably wanted some time alone with Sky before they turned in. She didn't need him trying to be polite when she wouldn't believe he meant it. Despite having three younger sisters, he'd never been good at the feelings part—something they'd jokingly reminded him about over the years. He'd been great at the taking-action part, but not so good at the listening.

The kitchen door opened bringing in a blast of frigid air to admit Luke, who was frowning. There was no sign of Max, but that wasn't unusual. He tended to keep odd hours and sometimes slept out in the barn despite the cold.

"It's getting worse out there. Thanks for rigging up that rope. I think we're going to need it."

Noah glanced back toward the family room and lowered his voice.

"What are the chances Jen can leave tomorrow?"

"Less than fifty percent right now." Luke took off his jacket and boots. "It could blow over tonight and be fine in the morning. We'll just have to wait and see."

He went through into the kitchen and called out to Jen. "Can I get you anything to drink?"

"No thanks." Jen picked Sky up and came toward them. "I'm going to turn in. Thanks again for everything you've done for us. I'll be ready to leave bright and early."

Luke smiled at her. "It's been fun."

Jen's amused gaze went to Noah, who obviously wasn't looking quite so enthusiastic because she smiled.

"Sure." She spoke to Sky. "Say goodnight, sweetie."

Sky waved his hand at Luke and Noah.

"'Night, kid," Noah said as Luke waved enthusiastically. "Sleep tight."

Jen was in the middle of some confused dream where she was running around the ship unable to locate her cabin when she flung out an arm and made contact with something hard.

"Crap," she whispered as her fingers fumbled to grab her phone. "Where am I?"

She opened her eyes and stared at the unfamiliar room and the empty crib.

Her door was slightly ajar.

"Dammit!" She sat upright. "What time is it?"

Her alarm had gone off at six. She'd either slept through it or turned it off so many times it had given up. Despite the darkness, it was well past eight, which meant she'd slept for twelve hours.

She scrambled into some clothes and rushed next door to the bathroom to clean up. The smell of coffee wafted down the hallway from the kitchen along with the deep voice of Noah talking soothingly to her kid—the one she was supposed to be in charge of. She exited the bathroom and rushed to the kitchen, where Noah was sitting with Sky.

"I'm sorry. I must have slept through my alarm."

He looked up at her. He'd rolled up the sleeves of his shirt to avoid the oatmeal splodges that splattered Sky's tray.

"It's all good. I heard Sky calling out when I walked by." He hesitated. "I shouldn't have gone in, but the door was ajar, and for one awful second, I thought we were getting a repeat of Dave and you'd be gone."

"I'm usually a light sleeper. I have no idea how I slept through that." Jen pushed her unruly hair back from her face. She couldn't believe she'd failed Mothering 101 on her first morning back, and right in front of her number one critic as well. "I feel like an idiot."

Noah didn't comment on that, which served her right, but he pointed at the counter.

"There's fresh coffee, oatmeal if you like it, toast, and bagels in the pantry."

"Thanks." Her stomach growled and she realized she was starving. "Are you okay to sit there for a few more minutes while I get sorted, or do you need to get going?"

He shrugged. "I'm kind of used to doing this now. It's no big deal."

"Well, consider it your last day on the job." Jen found a smile somewhere. He certainly couldn't be described as chatty. "I bet you won't miss babysitting one bit."

"I've done my fair share over the years," Noah said as he took the bowl and spoon away from Sky. "I can't say I thought I'd be doing it again."

"You have kids?" Jen asked as she poured herself a large cup of coffee and added cream and sugar.

"Hell, no. Just younger sisters." He shuddered. "That was enough to put me off kids for life."

Jen stuck a bagel in the toaster and alternated between watching Noah wiping Sky's face and hands and sipping her coffee. For such a big guy he was incredibly gentle. She already knew Noah had a good pair of lungs on him, but he always kept his voice down when dealing with her son.

She brought her bagel and coffee to the table and took the seat opposite Noah.

"Can you talk me through Sky's routine before we head out?"

"I have a spreadsheet." He paused. "If you give me your cell number, I'll send it to you."

"Wow, thanks! That's really helpful." Jen handed him her phone so he could input his number himself. "I guess you don't want me calling you every five minutes to check in."

"You're a smart woman. You'll work it out." He stood up. "I need to talk to Luke."

With a nod to Jen, he walked away, his expression stern. As usual she wasn't sure exactly what she'd said to set him off, but he was definitely unhappy about something, and her attempts to be humorous obviously weren't cutting it.

"Maybe it's because I exist," Jen murmured. "I just annoy him by breathing,"

She reminded herself that he'd apologized for getting her status wrong, not for disliking and disapproving of her in the first place. Apparently, she'd still never live up to the parenting skills of Dave. Speaking of her ex . . .

She found his new number and sent him a photo of Sky sitting in his high chair.

I found our son. No thanks to you but he's safe and well.

To her surprise he replied immediately.

I told you I left him in a safe place. They're great people, aren't they? See you soon.

Trust Dave to take the credit for his friends' willingness to look after his abandoned kid. Jen rolled her eyes as she typed a reply.

Not if I see you first.

Ha. We have stuff to discuss.

Now you want to be a responsible adult? Jen asked.

I've done a lot of thinking.

Jen considered what that might mean. With Dave it could

be absolutely anything from deciding to take a trip up Everest to marrying someone he'd just met. But he was still the father of her son, and she had to pay attention to him.

Then feel free to touch base with me when you return, and we can make some plans.

He sent the okay sign. Jen put down her phone and looked at Sky.

"That was your dad. He's been thinking. I hope it didn't hurt too much."

Sky grinned at her. "Dada."

"That's the one." She paused. "How about you try Mama?"

He stared at her. "Nono."

"Great," Jen murmured as she took him out of the high chair. "Let's get you ready to leave so that Noah can get his life back."

She was almost through the door when Luke came in from the outside, followed by Noah, and called her name.

"Bad news I'm afraid." He looked absolutely frozen through. "I just tried to get my truck through to the highway gate, and I couldn't get more than quarter of a mile. The snow drifts are too high."

Jen's gaze turned to Noah, who wasn't looking very happy.

"So we can't leave?"

Luke grimaced. "Not yet, and if the weather reports are right, you might be stuck here for quite a few days."

Jen clutched Sky to her chest. "Are you sure? Is there absolutely no way for us to get out of here?"

"Hold up," Noah said. "Luke's not running a prison here."

"It's okay, Noah," Luke said. "I don't think Jen's blaming me for the weather."

"I certainly am not." Jen hastened to agree with him. "I didn't mean to imply—"

"You didn't," Luke told her. "Noah's just being a mite overprotective." He shot his friend a look. "I totally get why you're concerned."

"I just feel like you must all be sick of me and Sky by now," Jen blurted out.

Luke came over and patted her shoulder. "It's okay, really. This isn't anyone's fault. We'll just hang here until the weather clears up, and then you can be on your way."

"Thank you." Jen hoped Luke realized she meant it from the bottom of her heart.

He winked at her and went into the kitchen to get himself a mug of coffee, leaving Jen staring at Noah.

He raised his eyebrows, and she braced herself for his next salvo.

"I usually give Sky a snack around eleven, lunch at one, and then he takes a nap for an hour."

Jen just nodded, and he turned toward the door and left without another word.

Sky waved as the door shut.

She fought the stupid desire to cry and hugged Sky instead. It wasn't like her to feel vulnerable, and she didn't like it one bit. She couldn't change the weather or the feeling that Noah was judging her every move, but she could do her best for Sky. That was all that mattered, and she refused to let anyone make her feel she couldn't handle it.

Chapter Seven

"Why are you still being so salty to Jen?" Max asked as Noah shoveled manure into the wheelbarrow. They'd been working together for an hour to clear out the stalls. "She's a good person."

"Just because she finally turned up?" Noah said, defending himself. "I mean, sure, that puts her on about level with Dave for parent of the year, but it doesn't mean much."

"Dave did his Dave thing for purely selfish reasons. Jen's active personnel and had no choice."

Max forked up some hay and put it into the feeder. There was nothing for the horses to graze on outside as everything was covered in snow.

"She's only been here for a day," Noah said. "Unlike you, I take my time deciding if I like someone. Just because she's got a great smile and a fit body doesn't mean jack."

Max grinned at him.

"What?"

"You checked that out then?"

Noah shrugged. "Hard to miss."

"She's tall, too," Max added. "And she can look you right in the eye."

Noah had noticed that, too, but he wasn't about to give his friend any more ammunition.

"As I said . . ." He picked up the handles of the wheelbarrow. "I care about what's inside a person more than anything else."

"Sure, you do." Max shut the door of the stall and came out still grinning. "You're all about the cerebral."

"Whatever that means," Noah muttered as he braced himself to leave the relative warmth of the barn for the freezing cold outside. He couldn't argue that Luke had made the right call. There was no way any warm-blooded being should be out on the roads today, especially not a baby.

When he returned to the barn, Max was in the feedstore putting stuff away. There was an open sleeping bag on the bench seat and an old velvet cushion that had once sat on the couch in the parlor. Noah frowned.

"You're still sleeping out here?"

"Sometimes." Max shrugged. "I get restless and like to see the sky."

"From here?"

"It's closer than my bedroom."

Noah studied his friend. "You know, Sally told me I should get some therapy. Maybe we could go together."

"Been there, done that," Max said. "I know what the issues are and what to do about them."

Noah considered how to get across that he was worried Max was getting worse without actually saying the words out loud. His friend would either crack a joke at his own expense or walk away to avoid the issue. Dealing with feelings definitely wasn't Noah's strong point. Maybe it would be better to take his concerns to Luke, who was excellent at people management.

"Now you're staring at me, which is freaking me out," Max said. "If you've got something to say, just spit it out."

"Anything I'd say wouldn't be something you'd want to hear." Noah washed his hands in the sink. "And I don't want to piss you off. Last time I did that, you disappeared for three days."

"I'm not going anywhere right now." Max looked out the open end of the barn, where snow was now steadily falling. "I don't have a death wish."

At the moment, Noah wasn't so sure about that, either.

"Luke was right to insist we all stay here," Max added. "And it gives us a chance to get to know Jen better, which is totally your thing."

"Yeah." Noah wasn't going to be drawn into that discussion. He glanced back in the direction of the house. "I hope she's managing okay with Sky."

"Dude, she works on a fricking hospital ship. I bet she's doing more than okay."

Jen had set up camp in the family room, where she could keep an eye on Sky and complete the reports due to her boss. He wasn't interested in the basket of toys. All he wanted to do was cruise around the furniture while taking the occasional experimental bite of anything that took his fancy. She'd already removed an embroidered cushion and distracted him from gnawing on a corner table by giving him his bone.

Sally's dogs had been relegated to the kitchen area with their own toys and bones, which Sky much preferred to his own. Jen reminded herself that a few germs never hurt anyone, and that she'd worked in far less ideal conditions than a cozy farmhouse in the middle of a pine forest.

After the tenth interruption in half an hour, she gave up any attempt to write and sat on the floor by the couch, keeping an eye on her son as he toured the room. How on earth had Noah dealt with the constant motion? She was worried Sky would fall, bang his head, or eat something he shouldn't. Not for the first time she wished babies arrived in a protective roll of bubble wrap.

When the outside door opened, she craned her neck to see who was coming in, but from her prone position could only see a pair of battered work boots.

"Nono." Sky held out his arms and bounced up and down on his toes.

"Dude." Noah loomed over Jen like a sequoia. "Okay if I pick him up?"

"Be my guest."

Sky's obvious delight in Noah's return was something to see. He'd been asking after Noah all morning, which hadn't done Jen's confidence much good. Jen scrambled to her feet as Noah allowed Sky to pat his beard and blow him kisses.

"I just came in to make some more coffee for my flask."

"Oh! I could do that for you if you want to hold Sky," Jen offered.

"I can do both." He turned toward the kitchen, Sky securely settled on his hip.

"Of course, you can." Jen hurried along behind him. "How's the weather looking?"

"Crap." He handled the coffee machine expertly and set a metal flask beside it. "We were right not to go."

"I thought you were all for it."

"I guess I just like things to be clear."

"As in?"

He shrugged. "Defined parameters, clear objectives and solutions."

"And I'm a problem you can't currently solve?"

"Something like that."

"You'd prefer dealing with a military operation than a living human being."

His sudden smile was a revelation. "Like you can separate them out. We both know that's not how it goes."

"Tell me about it. Some years I spend my life going from crisis to crisis."

"Personal or professional?"

"Apart from the Dave debacle, my personal life is very straightforward. My job is another matter."

"What do you do on that medical ship?" He spooned out some coffee.

"I'm a midwife."

Noah turned to look at her. "People give birth on those boats?"

"Not if we can help it." She smiled. "Most of what I do is community outreach in underserved populations, but I also deal with onboard staff who need our services."

"That explains why you're good with Sky. You're used to dealing with kids."

She was so surprised at the compliment that she forgot to consider the source.

"All Sky wants to do is walk around the furniture. I'm scared to take my eyes off him," Jen confessed. "Somehow it's much easier dealing with other people's kids than my own."

"I guess." Noah went to pour his coffee into the flask and handed Sky back to Jen. "All this activity should wear him out nicely for his nap."

She watched him depart and wondered why she'd expected him to sympathize with her when he'd obviously managed perfectly well with Sky on his own. He wasn't into giving her advice either, which was just fine and dandy. She reminded herself that she was a well-qualified medical professional who'd dealt with hundreds of mothers, babies, and children at clinics all over the world.

One small baby should be easy, just like Noah said. She

looked at Sky, who was still waving at the closed door, and went back into the family room. She closed the gate across the doorway and set him down beside the couch.

"In half an hour you can have a snack, and then in two hours it will be lunch, and then your nap." She glanced at the kitchen clock, which seemed to be moving way too slowly. "And then maybe I'll get some work done."

"Hey." Noah approached Luke, who was sitting in what passed for the ranch office, apparently staring into space. He'd just come in to get some lunch, leaving Max in the barn. "Have you got a minute?"

"Sure. What's up?"

Noah shut the door behind him, and Luke's eyebrows rose.

"This must be really serious."

"It's about Max."

Luke sighed. "Yeah. He's not doing too well, is he?"

"I tried to suggest we both get some therapy, but he wasn't having it."

"I'm surprised he stayed around long enough to hear the suggestion. Every time I open my mouth to say something, he bolts."

"Damn, I was hoping he'd listen to you."

"Not a chance." Luke shook his head. "I guess this is one of those situations where we're just going to have to catch him if and when he falls."

"Yeah. I was thinking the same thing." Noah frowned. "It sucks."

"Right back at you." Luke rose to his feet and stretched. "How are things going with Sky and Jen?"

"Why are you asking me?"

Luke gave him the side-eye as he approached the door. "Because you've been watching her like a spy satellite."

"I . . . just don't want her to be another Dave."

"She's nothing like Dave," Luke said. "In fact, she's like his polar opposite, which makes the whole idea of why she was ever attracted to him even weirder."

Noah tried to think about that and really didn't want to. "She had a kid with him."

"Yeah, that's a kicker. But we both know Dave was always good at charming the ladies."

"Fooling them, you mean."

"Exactly. Didn't Jen say he had other women on the hook when she thought she was his one and only?"

"Sounds like Dave."

Noah opened the door and headed back across the hallway to the kitchen, where he could already hear Sky banging his spoon on his tray. Jen was rushing around the kitchen randomly opening cupboard doors.

"What are you looking for?" he called out as he came toward her.

"Sky's bowl."

"I think it might still be in the dishwasher." Noah retrieved the bowl. "What are you giving him for lunch?"

"I was thinking of more of that chicken from last night." She flashed him a constrained smile. "De-beaned of course."

"Sounds good."

Noah got out of her way and helped himself to two bagels, which he stuck in the toaster while he continued to monitor her progress.

"He doesn't like his food too hot," he said as Jen retrieved the bowl from Noah. "You don't want him to burn his mouth."

"I know."

"And you'll definitely need to put a bib on him because he loves to smear everything on his face."

"Noah . . ." Luke came up beside him. "I think Jen's got this. Would you like some coffee, Jen?" Luke asked.

"Thanks, but not quite yet." She was carefully mashing Sky's food with a fork.

"Watch out for chicken bones," Noah advised.

She slowly raised her gaze to meet his. "Would you like to take over?"

He frowned as she rushed past him, the bowl in her hand as if she wanted to throw it at his head. "No thanks."

"Then perhaps you could just get your own lunch and not worry about ours?"

"Sure."

He retrieved his bagels, slathered them with cream cheese, and sat as far away from Sky's end of the table as possible while Jen fed her son. Sky wasn't in a cooperative mood. He insisted on taking a spoonful and then spitting it out on the tray to examine it with one finger before scraping it back in his mouth. It was a practice that had driven Noah crazy.

"Sky!" he called out sharply. "Stop that."

Jen slowly swiveled to face him, her expression calm but not entirely friendly. She slid the bowl down the table until it was in front of him.

"If you think you're so much better at everything, Noah, why don't you do it?"

She stood up and walked out, shutting the door firmly behind her.

Luke whistled. "Man, you so deserved that."

"Why?" Noah scowled. "I was just trying to help." He scooted up his chair to Sky, who was staring after Jen. "He shouldn't be allowed to do that."

"And you're not his parent to make that decision," Luke reminded him. "You're acting like the worst mother-in-law in the world right now."

"I am *not* apologizing to her again."

"Why not? You have a weekly limit on your spreadsheet

for how many times you admit you're being an ass?" Luke snorted.

"You're beginning to sound like Max." Noah gave Sky a spoonful of food and stared hard at him until he swallowed it down. "See? All it takes is a bit of encouragement."

"Still not your job," Luke said. He picked up his plate and put it in the sink. "I'll be in my office if anyone needs me."

Just as Sky finished up, Jen came back into the kitchen and faced Noah, her arms crossed over her chest.

"I'm sorry. I guess I'm a little more sensitive about my lack of mothering skills than I realized."

Noah looked at her slightly red eyes and realized she might have been crying, which made him feel like a heel.

"I overstepped," he said abruptly. "I have no right to tell you what to do with your kid."

She sank into the chair opposite him, her hands clasped together on her lap. "But maybe you do. You have way more experience about what he's doing right now than I have."

Her ability to admit that out loud, coupled with her honesty, took him aback.

"I know you want the best for Sky, so if there's anything you need to share with me, please go ahead and say it." She held his gaze. "I might not always agree with you, but I'd appreciate your perspective."

"I should've phrased it better," Noah added gruffly. "My sisters always tell me that."

She shrugged. "I'm in the navy. I'm not exactly a sheltered flower. I've heard far worse."

Noah didn't doubt that, but it still didn't make him feel any better. Her attempt to make things right between them spoke of a much better person than he would ever be.

"I guess I'm overprotective." He finally got the right words out. "Can't seem to get ordering people around out of my system."

She looked him up and down. "Let me guess—gunnery sergeant?"

"Master sergeant. You?"

"Lieutenant."

"Ma'am." He offered her a quick salute.

"Comes with the job." She shrugged. "I bet you earned yours."

He didn't want to think about that and rose to his feet. "Can I get you that coffee now?"

"I can get it." She was way quicker off the mark than he was. "Has Sky had any fruit yet?"

"Nope. I just finished with his main course."

Jen tossed a box of wet wipes at him, which he somehow managed to catch. "Why don't you sort Sky out while I get us both some coffee?"

Noah looked down at Sky, who was licking his palm with great attention. He had mashed potato in his hair and a piece of carrot in his ear.

"Come on youngster." Noah pulled out a bunch of wipes. "Let's get you cleaned up before you smash into your banana."

Jen brought the coffee over to the table. "I know it doesn't make any sense to wash him when he's just going to get all messy again, but the thought of chicken dinner and banana all squished up together makes me feel nauseous."

"I hear ya," Noah said as she handed Sky a chunk of very soft banana. "I made the mistake of setting a whole pot of rice pudding on his tray once while I went to get a spoon. By the time I got back he'd poured the whole thing over his head."

She burst out laughing, and Noah couldn't look away from the vibrancy of her face as he warily smiled back. If things hadn't started so badly between them, he'd be all over asking her out. He hastily repressed that stupid idea and continued.

"After I scraped the worst of it off both of us needed a shower."

Max came into the kitchen. "Nice to hear you two getting along. What did you do, Jen? Threaten him with his own gun?"

"Now, there's a thought." Jen gave Sky another bit of soft banana. "I'll keep it in mind if he gets out of hand again."

She had a dry sense of humor that appealed to Noah, and a calmness about her that drew him in, whether he wanted it or not. He could understand why she liked being involved in community outreach—something that filled him with horror. She was probably good at it as well.

"Has anyone heard from Dave?" Max asked as he joined them at the table.

"I texted him to let him know I was finally with Sky, and he took all the credit for bringing us together," Jen said. "Like he'd done me a favor."

"Right . . . ," Max said. "It was all done deliberately to get his favorite people under one roof."

"In Dave's mind, probably yes. He's always been great at rearranging the past to suit his present."

"That's a good way of putting it," Noah chimed in.

He noticed Jen smiled a lot more at Max than she did at him, which was hardly surprising. Max had been on her side before he'd even met her. She'd be good for Max.

He snorted. Like that was any of his business. Jen wasn't going to be here long enough to want to get involved in any of their lives.

"What's so funny?" Max asked.

Noah realized they were both looking at him.

"Nothing."

Max turned to Jen. "You might have noticed that our Arkie isn't much of a talker."

"Arkie . . . ," Jen mused. "I get it now. Noah's Ark."

"Yup. And because of his determination to herd us all into two straight lines and march us anywhere he felt like going."

"It was my job—to keep you alive," Noah reminded him.

"Yeah." A shadow passed over Max's face. "I suppose I should be grateful for that."

"I would be." Jen's gaze flicked from Noah to Max. "It's way better than the alternative."

"How's the weather looking?" Noah asked quickly when Max looked over at the door as if planning his escape. "Any break in the storm?"

"Not so far." Max grimaced. "I hate to be the one to break it to you, Jen, but I think you're stuck here with us for at least another night."

"That's okay," Jen said. "I'm used to being held hostage by the weather. I'm just embarrassed that you guys have to put up with me."

"We love having you here, don't we Noah?" Max said and turned to Jen. "He was just telling me earlier that he loves the chance to get to know you. Underneath that salty exterior he's a real people person."

"It's all good." Noah made sure Sky had his last piece of banana and turned to Jen. "I'll get a washcloth. He'll be ready for his nap soon."

He didn't appreciate Max putting him on the spot like that when Jen was obviously uncomfortable. Max's jokes sometimes weren't that funny anymore. He washed up and handed the washcloth to Jen.

"I've got work to do outside."

Max finished his coffee and stood up. "I'll come with you."

"No need." Noah met Max's eyes. "I can manage by myself." He nodded at Sky. "Behave yourself, kid."

"Bye, Nono." Sky waved at him.

"Wait, did he just say a complete sentence?" Jen asked. "Wow!"

Noah shrugged as if it didn't mean much and turned to the door where no one would see that he was actually smiling like a fool. The freezing cold would soon wipe that off his face, and maybe that was for the best.

Chapter Eight

Twelve days . . .

Jen leaned in to look out of the frosted windowpane, her breath condensing on the cold glass. It was midmorning, but she wouldn't know that from the gray gloom of the sky. The forest mists, the constant snowfall, and the wind had barely let up since the night of her arrival. It was hard to distinguish between what was a building and what was a snowbank now. She didn't know much about ranching, but this had to be bad.

The grim expressions on her three hosts' faces every time they came into the house from performing yet another impossible task in the rapidly deteriorating conditions spoke volumes. But none of them complained except Max, who did it in such a sarcastic way that it was hard to take him seriously. Jen just wished there were more she could do to help. She'd taken on most of the cooking duties and obviously cared full-time for Sky, freeing the guys up to accomplish what needed to be done. She also made sure there was fresh coffee brewing and that the fires stayed lit.

Luke was always optimistic and positive about everything as a good officer should be. Noah kept his thoughts to himself, and Max generally complained about everything. In the last day, she'd noticed some tension developing between

Max and Noah, but so had Luke, and he usually stepped in to defuse it. She was glad it wasn't on her. She'd spent way too much of her childhood negotiating between her mother and her family to avoid getting a sick feeling in her stomach at the very thought of being in the middle of anything.

Her cell buzzed and she took it out of her pocket. Sky was in his high chair finishing up his snack, so she had a minute to herself.

Hey stranger!!!!

Jen smiled as she typed back to her onboard boat roomie Heather, who was a pediatric nurse.

Hey! What's up?

Where are you? I've been expecting you back in San Diego!

I'm stuck in the middle of a forest in a snowstorm with Sky and three cowboys. Jen typed.

Seriously?? Are any of them hot?

Trust Heather to go for the most relevant information. Max was definitely hot, Luke's personality made him very attractive, and Noah . . . made her want to climb him like a tree. A prickly, stubborn old pine tree, but still.

She almost dropped her phone at her own admission. Trust her to go for the guy who didn't like her. It was almost as if she craved being rejected. Her therapist said she chose men who weren't interested in her to reinforce her own belief that she was unlovable, which kind of sucked, but had a horrible ring of truth to it. She'd known Dave was bad news five minutes after meeting him, but she'd still gone ahead and allowed herself to be charmed into bed.

She stared at her blinking cursor. The good thing was that Noah never had to know her secret because he was absolutely, one hundred percent not interested in her. She typed her reply.

One of them is super-hot but complicated.

Dammit. Why do those two things always come together? Anyways, when are you leaving?

I literally can't get out. We're cut off by a massive snowstorm that doesn't want to end.

Like, really?

Yes. Jen added a sad face.

Then you've got time to work things out with the hot one while you wait.

These are Dave's friends.

Crap . . . Leave them well alone, babe. That man was bad news.

Tell me about it. Jen looked up as the outside screen door banged shut to find Noah had come into the kitchen. I've got to go. Will keep you updated on my movements.

Love you x

Noah stripped off his heavy coat, gloves, and scarf, and shook himself down like a horse. "It's cold out there."

"That's an understatement if ever I heard one." Jen set her phone down. "I guess we won't be getting anywhere today."

"Or for a while." Noah grimaced. "We can't get any of the vehicles to function."

"It's fine." After her last thought about him being the cowboy she'd like to get up close and personal with, she was having difficulty meeting his eyes. "I don't want anyone to put their lives at risk just to get us to town. We're perfectly safe here."

"True." Noah waved at Sky and then turned to get some coffee. "Shit."

Jen looked up just as the mug slipped from his grasp and crashed on the floor. Sky cheered as Jen rushed over to help Noah.

"Sorry. My fingers are freezing." Noah tried to flex his hand and winced.

"Let me see." Jen grabbed his hand and slowly massaged each joint, bringing her warmth and strength into his scarred flesh. "Does that help?"

She looked up just as he looked down, and she couldn't stop staring into his whiskey-brown eyes.

"That's great," he said hoarsely. "Thanks."

Jen hurriedly returned her gaze to his fingers and continued her work until he was able to move all his digits freely. He smelled like pine and the barn, a combination that she'd never imagined might be attractive but apparently was. She was tall for a woman, but she still fit neatly under his bearded chin. She reminded herself that he was Dave's friend and definitely off limits for too many reasons to even bother to list.

Number one being he didn't like her.

But that wasn't the vibe she was getting off him while they were so close. He seemed to be leaning into her touch rather than pushing away.

"Other hand?"

He silently offered it to her, and she worked on it as well. His palm and fingers were as big as the rest of him—strong, capable, and rugged. She'd never thought those were qualities she'd be panting after either. Maybe the isolation was getting to her.

He eased his hand free and slowly fisted his fingers.

"Thanks. That really helped."

He was crowding her against the countertop, his long, jean-clad thigh aligned with hers, his uneven breath warm on her neck. For a crazy second, she thought he was about to drop his head and nuzzle her throat. What she would do if he did, she wasn't sure.

He stepped back. "I'd better clean up this mess."

"I'll help you."

She crouched down just as he did and they cracked heads, sending Jen falling backward on her ass, clutching her forehead.

"Ouch."

He reached out and cupped her neck bringing her easily upright again. "You okay?"

She frowned as his thumb gently caressed the side of her throat. "You're built out of steel, aren't you?"

His half-smile was almost a grimace. "Hard as a rock."

She made the mistake of glancing at the zipper of his jeans.

He eased away from her and hastily stood up. "I'd best get on."

"Yes, of course." She stayed where she was and picked up the pieces of the broken mug. "You must have a lot to—"

The door slammed behind him before she finished her sentence.

"—do."

She put the pottery shards in the trash and brushed up the smaller pieces before turning to Sky, who was watching her with great interest.

"Sorry about that, little one."

"Nono, bye-bye?"

"Yup." Jen ruffled his hair. "The sooner we can say bye-bye to Noah the better."

Jeez . . . Noah stomped over to the barn. He'd got a hard-on right in front of Jen, and she'd definitely noticed. And why that had happened when she'd just been massaging his *fingers* in a thoroughly professional and unsexy way he didn't even want to think about. He'd wanted to nuzzle her hair and lick and bite his way along the column of her throat until she wrapped her arms around him and kissed him back.

"She's Dave's girlfriend," he reminded himself as he stepped into the barn and shook off the snow.

"No, she isn't." Unfortunately, Max was right there in the doorway of the feedstore. "She hates Dave like every sane person should."

Noah scowled. "I wasn't talking to you."

"Doesn't matter. It's been obvious for a while that you've got the hots for her."

"I don't." Noah went to push past Max.

"Great, because if that's true, I'll take a pop at her."

Noah pivoted on his heel and got right up in Max's face. "Shut your mouth."

Max continued to stare at him. "What's it got to do with you?"

"You're being a dick."

"So what?" Max shrugged.

"I'm not having you messing with Jen, okay?"

"You're her keeper now?"

"Hell, Max, we all are. She's stuck here with us. The least we can do is not make her feel obligated to put up with any crap from you."

"Maybe I really like her."

Noah stepped away, shaking his head. "You're just out to make trouble."

"Why would you say that?"

"Stop with all the stupid-ass questions, okay?" Noah only realized he'd raised his voice when Max winced. "Just because your life isn't working out doesn't mean you have to bring everyone else down. You're being a complete douche."

Max stared at him, his expression curiously blank.

"*I'm* the ass? You know why you're being so cranky, bro?

Because I called you out about how you want to get in Jen's pants. Everything else you said about me was what we call 'projection,' so screw you."

He gave Noah the middle finger and walked out of the barn, leaving Noah staring after him.

"*Shit.*" Noah kicked the nearest bucket. "Luke's gonna kill me."

When it came to the delicate nature of personal relationships, he had all the finesse of a bucking bull. Max was pissed with him, and that was never a good thing. Even when he was feeling good Max never let anything or anyone get the better of him. Noah stared around the barn as if he'd never been there before. What had he come out for? Between Jen and Max, he was totally turned around.

He'd run out of the house because he had the hots for Jen. Everything that had come after that had been a disaster. Maybe Max had a point, and it really was all on Noah.

He sighed and gently banged his head against the wall. He hadn't given Jen any reason to like or trust him, so why would she ever be interested in dating him? She was still involved with Dave and, as he'd pointed out to Max, she was a guest at the ranch.

She was off-limits.

Noah took in a breath and went to look for Luke. Better to give him a heads-up before Max got to him first. He also needed to work out how he could apologize to Max without actually admitting that his friend had been right about anything.

Jen set the big platter of fried chicken on the table and tried to ignore the weird vibe between the guys. Max had turned up early and had helped her make dinner with his usual charm and efficiency. She'd been laughing at something he'd said when Noah had come in, and the atmosphere had taken a nosedive from there. She'd lived in very close quarters with a diverse group of people for months onboard ship, and she was attuned to the potential for conflict coming out of nowhere.

Luke was the calm at the center of every storm, Noah was his enforcer, and Max was like the unexpected glitch that threw everything out the window.

"Can I help?" Noah asked.

"Sure, you can get the corn and beans out of the oven and put them on the table if you like."

Jen offered him a casual smile. She would not think about how unexpectedly hot and heavy they'd gotten earlier, especially when he seemed okay about it. It wasn't uncommon for people to have unwanted physical reactions to medical personnel in certain circumstances, and she had been working on his hand . . . his big, strong, scarred hand.

"Evening all." Luke came in. He looked exhausted. "No letup in the weather yet, Jen."

"It's okay." Jen gave Sky a tiny piece of softened cornbread, which he loved. "At least we're all safe."

"True." Luke paused, his gaze traveling from Jen to Noah and Max. "You guys doing okay?"

"Why wouldn't we be when our kitchen goddess made fried chicken from scratch for dinner?" Max smiled. "Anyone want a beer? Not you, Sky."

"I love fried chicken." Luke washed his hands and went to the refrigerator. "Not sure I need cold beer when my body wants hot chocolate, but I'm going for it anyway."

"How are the cows?" Jen asked as she set the warm plates on the table in front of everyone. "Max said you were having some problems getting out to them today."

"Yeah." Luke sat down and shoved a hand through his blond hair. "We need to feed them right now, but we can't get out there in any of the vehicles."

"We'll have to use the horses." Noah spoke for the first

time since he'd come into the kitchen. "We can drag the feed behind or pack it on the horse."

"It'll take forever, but it might end up being the only way," Luke agreed. "I'm glad we brought all the cattle as close to home as possible."

"I can ride," Jen said as she put some mashed potato and pureed chicken in Sky's bowl. "If you need an extra pair of hands."

"That's good to know," Luke said as he helped himself to the chicken. "But you're also doing a great job looking after Sky and running the house right now, which we all appreciate."

"We sure do." Max winked at her. "This chicken is almost as good as Sally's, Luke."

"It's better, but don't tell Mom I said that." Luke grinned.

Max got up to fetch the napkins Jen had left sitting on the countertop, and took another beer from the refrigerator. He'd already finished the first one. Jen saw Noah glance at Max and then at Luke, who gave a tiny shake of his head. Whatever was going on she'd rather not be part of it.

She started feeding Sky, patiently spooning the mashed potato into his mouth, scraping up the bits he discarded on his chin and offering them again.

"It's like spackling a wall," Max said.

Jen half turned to look at him, and he raised his eyebrows. "Feeding the kid; you're constantly filling in the holes."

"I suppose you're right." Jen considered the potato. "It certainly feels like spackle."

"Doesn't taste like it," Luke added. "I can't tell you how good it is to come home to a hot meal right now."

"Well, thank God for Jen, then," Max said as he finished his second beer. "I suppose we should really be thanking Dave because you just know he'd be taking all the credit for getting us together right now."

"He would," Jen agreed as she finished scraping out the bowl and put another bit of cornbread on Sky's tray.

"Having gotten to know you a bit, Jen, I can't imagine what you saw in that loser," Max continued. "I mean, I would've thought you'd go for someone more like our Noah here—you know, a solid, reliable Dudley Do-Right kind of guy."

"Max . . ." Luke stirred in his seat.

"Nothing wrong with asking, Luke. We're all friends here, right?" Max's smile held a hint of something Jen didn't like. "I just can't imagine Jen taking any of Dave's shit. We had to work with him because he was seconded to our unit, but Jen made an actual choice."

"And Jen doesn't have to answer your incredibly insensitive questions about her personal life over the dinner table," Noah growled. "I know you're mad at me, Max. Don't take it out on the wrong person."

"Why would I be mad at you?" Max asked. "Nothing you accused me of had any basis in reality." He turned back to Jen. "As I was saying, Noah would be . . ."

"That's enough," Noah said sharply. "Eat your food and shut the hell up."

Max's eyes widened. "You see how defensive he gets when I mention you, Jen? Why is that?"

Jen held his stare. "I don't need Noah to stand up for me, Max, and I don't owe you any explanations as to my personal life."

"Yeah, shut up, Max," Luke added.

"Suit yourself." Max shrugged like it was no big deal. "I just wanted to give you the opportunity to answer a question we've all been wondering about, Jen."

Jen tried not to let her gaze sweep over the other two silent men at the table. Did they talk about her behind her back? It wouldn't be the first time she'd encountered that kind of male culture. Sometimes on the ship it could get out of hand and become toxic. For the first time in a while, she really wished she could just pack her bags and leave. She'd allowed herself to get comfortable and complacent. Every time she'd done that as a foster kid, everything had changed, and usually not for the better.

Max stood and picked up his plate. "Thanks for the food."

He walked over to the refrigerator and got out two more beers before exiting the kitchen.

Luke exhaled. "Sorry, Jen. Sometimes he gets a bit salty."

"A bit?" Noah said. "His behavior sucked." He met Jen's gaze. "I'm sorry. I riled him up today, and he tends to lash out, and not necessarily at the right person."

"It's okay," Jen said, even though that wasn't true.

"And, for the record, we don't all sit around wondering about your love life," Luke added. "Max is just stirring the pot."

Jen had forgotten that Luke noticed everything and must have seen her discomfort.

"He'll get over himself." Noah reached for more chicken. "Tomorrow it'll be like none of this ever happened."

Jen wished she shared their optimism. From where she was sitting, and with her experience dealing with military personnel, Max needed help, and there was currently no way of getting him any. Luke took Sky's bowl and his plate over to load the dishwasher and started cleaning up, leaving Jen facing Noah, who was carefully feeding Sky mashed up chicken from his plate.

"Don't worry too much about Max," Noah said. "We'll take care of him."

"It's really none of my business," Jen tried to sound neutral.

"It is your business when he drags you into it," Noah countered. "I bet you wish you were out of here."

"It's okay."

He put his hand over hers and gently squeezed her fingers. "Nah, it's not. You're all tense."

"I'm just not good at dealing with conflict sometimes," Jen confessed. "It makes me want to curl up and hide."

"Shame you ended up sharing your space with three retired Marines, then." Noah finished feeding Sky and wiped his fingers on his napkin. "I bet you get enough of that shit at work."

"It can get a little testosterone heavy sometimes." Jen cleaned Sky's face as Noah dealt with the tray. "I'm good at being a peacemaker."

"Then you picked the right line of work. Bringing new life into the world is about as far away from what I used to do as you can get." Noah nodded at her. "I'll rinse out this washcloth and get some applesauce for Sky while you finish your dinner."

Jen glanced down at her almost uneaten food. Stress did that to her.

"Eat," Noah said as he stood up. "Don't let Max being an idiot get to you."

He didn't wait for a reply but headed into the kitchen, where he started talking in a low voice to Luke. Jen considered the fried chicken she'd made from scratch. She picked up a piece, bit into it and chewed thoroughly. Noah was right. It was definitely too good to waste.

Five minutes later, he set a mug of coffee at her elbow and lifted Sky clear of the high chair. "I'll get him washed."

"I can—"

"I know you can, but you don't have to." Noah settled Sky on his hip. "Come on little buddy, let's give your momma five minutes peace."

She watched them both disappear through the door, Sky chattering away as he patted Noah's shoulder with a very sticky hand. Noah might not be good with words, but when it came to action and doing something to actually help out, he was a champ.

Luke finished in the kitchen and came back to the table, wiping his hands dry on a towel. He gestured at her coffee mug.

"Go sit in the family room and finish that. It's way more comfortable in there."

"Will do." Jen stood up. "And Luke, I still appreciate you putting up with me."

"You're pulling your weight, which is way more than most people would do, and I appreciate that. Dave put all of us in an uncomfortable situation. *Most* of us are making the best of it." He paused. "Max's issues aren't really about you—you know that, right?"

Jen nodded. "He's retired military and fought in active combat. I understand how that goes."

"Exactly." Luke sighed. "And the resources around here aren't great to start with, so finding someone to help him isn't easy."

"I can ask around if you like," Jen offered. "I know a lot of medical retirees in the state."

"That would be awesome." Luke smiled at her as he headed toward his office.

As Luke left, he passed Noah coming in with Sky already in his pajamas. There was no sign of Max.

"I ended up giving him his bath early." Noah set Sky on the couch beside Jen. He immediately got down to stand on his own feet. "There was a lot of food in a lot of places."

Jen had to laugh as Noah took a seat on the recliner across from her.

"Thanks."

He offered her a brief smile but appeared to have gone back to guarded mode, which was somewhat depressing. "It was kind of nice not to be staring at a cow for a while."

"I thought all cowboys loved cattle."

"Not when it's like this." He glanced out of the window and then got up to shut the drapes before sitting down again. "No point in looking at it when it's not going to get better any time soon."

Jen shuddered as Sky cruised past her tucked up feet. "Amen."

Noah took a deep breath and leaned forward. "I wanted to talk to you about what Max said about me—"

"Look!" Jen gasped. "Sky!"

"Whoa."

Sky had let go of the couch and toddled toward Noah, his arms outstretched as he launched himself optimistically across the divide.

"He's walking!"

"Oh my God!" Jen jumped to her feet as Noah picked Sky up and tossed him into the air. The next minute she was hugging them both like crazy. "I got to see his first steps!"

Noah's arm came around her, and for a moment they were all united in one giant excited hug, with Sky squealing between them. Jen looked up at Noah.

"I'm so glad we both got to see this first."

"Yeah." His slow smile made her want to kiss him silly.

Luke ran back in the room. "What's wrong?"

"Nothing." Jen grinned. "Sky walked by himself."

"Really?" Luke took a seat on the couch and held out his hands. "Come on then, walk to Uncle Luke, buddy."

Noah set Sky on his feet in front of the recliner, and he immediately set off toward Luke, who whooped his approval.

Jen leaned into Noah's side, her arm still wrapped around his waist and watched with great pride.

"He's really doing it!"

Luke turned Sky around like one of those wind-up toys and sent him back her way, which meant she had to move away from Noah and crouch down to receive him. She hugged him hard, and he toddled off again, his expression determined, toward Noah.

"Now the fun begins," Luke commented. "You'll never be able to stop him."

Jen mock groaned.

"Nothing wrong with leading strings," Noah said. "I used them with my sisters sometimes because wrangling twins was hard work."

"Lots of the mothers I met in other countries used them," Jen agreed as she glanced around the room. "Luckily, this place is pretty childproof already, so I don't think there's too much to worry about."

"Yeah, my sister and mom were very hot on that," Luke said. "But the little munchkins still found things to fall off, fall over, and generally scare the shit out of us with."

"That's kids for you." Jen smiled at Sky, who was now determinedly walking between her, Luke, and Noah. "Hopefully he'll sleep well tonight."

It wasn't until she was putting Sky to bed later that evening that she wondered what Noah had been about to say before she'd interrupted him.

Chapter Nine

"Where the hell is Max?" Luke asked as Noah came into the barn.

"He didn't sleep out here last night?"

Noah poked his head into the feedstore, where the sleeping bag and pillow lay undisturbed. The temperature had remained well below zero all night, setting off a hard frost that, coupled with the biting wind, made all his hackles rise. It was one of those rare times that the sense of isolation really got to him—what with the trees creaking under the weight of the snow, the sunless sky, and the dark clouds that grazed the soil like creeping fingers.

Luke was walking down the center of the barn, checking the stalls. "All the horses are here."

"Even Max isn't stupid enough to go out in this and risk the life of his mount."

"I dunno." Luke wasn't smiling. "He's acting like he doesn't want to be here right now."

"You think he's backpacking it out on foot?" Noah grimaced. "Hell, it would be just like him, wouldn't it? Should I go and check his room and see if he's taken anything important?"

"You know Max—he'd leave with just his wallet if he had

to." Luke sighed. "We'd best get on. I'll call him in a while and see if he responds."

"And if he doesn't?"

"Then we'll try something else."

As he shoveled muck out of one of the stalls, Noah admired Luke's quiet optimism. He never gave up on anyone or anything, which had made him an exceptional team leader. Even in their darkest moments in Afghanistan, Luke had kept them focused and confident while Noah kept them physically together and in motion. They'd been a great team, which was why when Luke had suggested Noah join him to work the ranch, he'd gone for it.

"How about Sky walking?" Luke said as they passed each other on his way out of the barn.

"I'm glad Jen got to see it. She's missed a lot of milestones."

"Yeah, I noticed you two hugging like proud parents." Luke winked. "She's a good person, Noah. You know that, right?"

"She's okay," Noah conceded.

"Dude, you don't have to fake it with me. I know you like her."

Noah shrugged. "It's hard not to."

"You look good together."

"And she had a kid with Dave, who will be stateside soon."

"She doesn't want Dave."

"Neither do I, but he's still front and center, isn't he? Just like Dave always wants to be."

"So you're not going to do anything?"

"Now you sound like Max."

Luke held up his hands. "Hey, if both Max and I noticed you're crushing on Jen then that should tell you something."

"That my friends are hopeless romantics?" Noah picked

up the handles of the wheelbarrow again. "You read too many romance novels while we were on tour."

"They taught me a shitload of useful stuff about what women want in bed," Luke said. "I mean—*invaluable* stuff. That's why I started reading them out loud to you guys. At least two of my team privately reported back to me that their partners were super impressed by their new skill sets."

Noah shuddered. "TMI." He headed out into the freezing cold with the load of manure.

When he came back there was no sign of Luke, but he could hear him chatting away to one of the horses, which was fairly typical of his boss. It was good Luke didn't know that Noah had been about to try and explain Max's pointed comments to Jen just before Sky started walking.

And then they'd shared that moment over Sky's achievement like proud parents. . . .

Jeez . . . what was wrong with him?

He glanced at the leaden sky. The thing was, Jen wasn't going anywhere anytime soon, so maybe it was a good thing he'd kept his mouth shut and his pants zipped. He might have ended up saying something stupid, and then he would've been kissing her, and . . . Noah mentally gave himself a shake. He was a grown man. He had standards, and seducing a woman who was unwillingly stuck in his place of residence and had a kid with an old comrade was not on his radar. The fact that he genuinely liked her and thought she was hot was irrelevant. He glanced down at his Wranglers. Now, if only his dick could get that message, everything would be great.

His cell buzzed and he accepted the call, which his sister Bailey immediately turned into a screen of her vibrant face. Reception wasn't great at the best of times, and she kept fading in and out.

"Why haven't you called?" Bailey asked. "We've been worried."

As the older of his three sisters, she was usually the one who hounded him the most.

"It's been a bit hectic here what with the snow and—"

She interrupted him, which was usual, as she ran and talked at twice his speed. "I called Sally because you didn't answer my last five texts. She said you had a *woman* staying there!"

"It's a long story."

"I know! Sally told me! What's she like?"

"Jen? She's great." Noah managed to get a word in.

"Do you like her?"

"As I said, she's great," Noah repeated, aware that any sign of weakness would immediately be pounced on and relayed to the twins, who would be added to the call in an instant. "She serves on the USNS Mercy."

"I saw a thing about that on CNN. It's like a floating city," Bailey said. "She sounds awesome. What's it like having a kid around again?"

"He's a lot easier to manage than you lot," Noah said.

"You've just forgotten how sweet we really were."

"Nah, I remember you were all little devils."

She pouted and then grinned. "But you still love us, right?"

"Sure. You're my family."

Bailey sighed. "Then be nice to her, won't you?"

"Of course."

"You're not being all judgypants? Because I know how you can get when someone doesn't do something just like you would."

"He's not my kid, or part of my family, so I can respect those boundaries," Noah said. Especially now that Jen had told him to back off. "I do my job and try not to get in her way."

That wasn't true either, but he hoped Bailey wasn't picking up on it. She was way too smart for her own good.

"How's Will?" he asked as a diversionary tactic.

"He's just got promoted."

"Good for him."

"He wants us to move to New York."

"Okay." One thing he'd learned over the years was to wait for direction from his sisters as to how he was supposed to react to a crisis before jumping in and trying to fix it for them. "How do you feel about that?"

She made a face. "Not sure."

"Then make sure you talk it out until you are sure one way or another."

"Will do." She glanced over her shoulder. "Okay, I have to go now. Don't make me have to chase you down again, okay? Be nice to Jen and that baby!"

She ended the call, and Noah slipped his cell back in his pocket. Bailey had no idea how nice he wanted to be to Jen, but if he had his way, neither of them would ever know that. He rarely reacted to a woman so strongly, and he wasn't sure how to deal with it, especially when the situation was so damn complicated. He sighed and returned to the endless task of shoveling shit. With Max AWOL, he'd have twice as much to do.

But it would keep him out of the house and away from Jen. Maybe that was a good thing while he worked out how he was going to keep his hands off her for the foreseeable future. He was the kind of guy who liked to find solutions to problems, but this one was beyond even him.

Jen handed Noah a mug of coffee and made sure Sky was eating his sandwich and not tossing it over the side of the tray for the dogs. He'd developed a fascination with dropping things, which meant Jen was constantly picking stuff off the floor. She knew it was an important developmental milestone, but her back was already complaining from all the stooping.

"Is Max all right?" Jen asked as she took the plate of sandwiches she'd made out of the refrigerator and heated up a bowl of soup for Noah, who looked chilled to the bone. It was almost two and no one had been in the house all morning, "I haven't seen him today."

"Neither have I." Noah frowned. "Luke's out looking for him."

Jen stared out of the window at the silent, frozen landscape. "Where could he go in this weather?"

"There's another barn closer to the county road he might have trekked out to check for stray cattle."

"Why would he do that?" Jen asked cautiously. "I didn't think it was safe to leave."

"It isn't safe, and Max . . . ." Noah sighed. "Let's just say that Max isn't in a good headspace right now."

"Down!" Sky called out to Jen.

She turned to see Winky, one of the dogs, making off with Sky's lunch, closely followed by his brother, Blinky.

"I'm not making you anything else, Sky," Jen told him. "You can finish your juice instead." She handed him his sippy cup and waited until he started drinking. "Good boy. When you're done, you can go back inside and walk around a bit more."

"He's still doing that?" Noah sat at the table next to Sky and offered him a fist bump.

"Never stops," she said. "He's making me dizzy." She paused and then continued. "I know you won't mind me being blunt: Is Max's behavior something to do with me?"

"Not entirely." Noah smoothed a hand over his bearded chin. "He's been struggling for a while now. Being confined here with all of us might have exacerbated things."

Jen appreciated his straightforward reply.

"He's always been nice to me."

"He's a good guy." Noah shrugged. "Like most of us, he has his demons, and sometimes they get out of the box. What I don't appreciate is him disappearing during a storm and making Luke have to chase after him."

"Understandable."

Noah started on his soup. "This is good."

"I found it in the freezer and stuck it in the crockpot this morning. I guess Sally made it."

"She left us loads of stuff because she knows how it gets out here."

"How long have you lived here?" Jen asked, willing to risk a Noah rebuff because she'd only had Sky to talk to for hours.

"Three years."

"And you like it?"

"Yeah, although I miss my sisters, who are based in San Diego." Noah ate half a sandwich in two bites and chewed slowly.

"The sisters you brought up, who soured you on having kids?"

"That's right. Bailey's the oldest, and then Cameron and Maya are two years younger. They're twins."

"That's a lot," Jen said. "I once assisted at a birth of quadruplets. I couldn't even imagine dealing with that."

"Being a midwife didn't put you off having kids?"

"Nope." Jen smiled. "Bringing new life into the world is amazing. And helping someone achieve that safely? Magical."

Noah studied her. "You're an optimist."

"You say that like it's a bad thing."

"I guess I take a more cautious approach to life." He held her gaze. "I like to plot out every move. I hate screwing up."

"Don't we all," Jen agreed. "I mean, apart from my monumental mistake with Dave, I usually try and stay on the right side of life."

She waited to see if he was interested in getting into it about Dave, but he simply nodded and kept eating. The silence between them was remarkably comfortable and only broken by Sky dropping his cup on the floor and nearly braining one of the dogs. When he'd finished all his food, Noah finally looked over at her.

"Have you heard from Dave?"

"Not for a few days. Why?"

"Just wondering." He stood up and pushed in his chair. "Do you have his new phone number?"

"Yes, do you want it?"

He stopped to consider her and then grimaced. "Nah, he's really Luke's problem, not mine."

"I already gave his number to Luke if you need it. Are you expecting him to come back here?"

His brows drew together. "If you and Sky are here, then sure."

"As long as he knows I've got Sky, Dave won't do that." Jen held his gaze. "We're not together anymore. We parent separately, and it's my turn to stay put."

"How's that gonna work when you're back at sea?" Noah didn't sound any happier.

"I'm working on that," she assured him, despite her own doubts.

"Do you have family who could help out?"

"No." She almost kept it at that, which was a Noah-like response he should appreciate. "I don't have much contact with them, and I'm not expecting Martha to step up after Dave basically left her on her own."

He slowly rubbed his hand over his mouth as he considered her.

"That's tough. It's not like you can just quit."

She couldn't stop imagining what it might feel like to pet him like that—to feel his beard against her skin . . .

"Jen?"

"What?" She blinked at him.

"Have I got something on my face?"

Damn she wished she were sitting on his face at that moment. She blushed as she stuttered out a reply.

"No! I mean you're fine, you look great."

He leaned forward, his hand extended, his expression intent. She almost forgot how to breathe as his callused thumb brushed the corner of her mouth.

"Mayo."

"Thanks," she whispered and automatically licked the spot he'd just touched. She hadn't had sex for a very long time, and everything female in her body was currently screeching at her to jump Noah while she had the chance. He stayed close, his gaze fixed on her mouth. She didn't dare move as he studied the rest of her face.

"All good."

God, she wanted to reach out and plunge her fingers into his thick, dark hair and drag him so close there was no air between them and he'd have to kiss her.

He cleared his throat. "We can't do this."

"Do what?" Jen tried to sound innocent.

"You're a guest in our house."

"And?"

"I respect that, and I respect you." He straightened and stepped back.

"What if I told you I'd still feel respected whatever you wanted to do?"

He groaned. "Don't."

"Why not?" Jen wasn't sure why she was getting argumentative, but she couldn't seem to stop herself.

"Because—" He sighed. "I'm not a saint, Jen."

"I've always preferred the sinners anyway," she hastened to reassure him.

"Okay, then it's not fair."

"To you?" She opened her eyes wide.

He glanced over at Sky. "To all of us."

Jen took a deep, steadying breath. What the hell was she doing flirting with a man in front of her kid anyway? What must Noah think? She never took risks like this. Was she turning into someone she didn't know? Had dating Dave destroyed her common sense forever?

She walked past Noah and picked Sky up. "Time for this little guy to get cleaned up. Let me know if you find Max, won't you?"

"Jen . . ."

She closed the door behind them before he could say anymore. Half an hour with Sky would remind her where her priorities lay. Just because Noah was the most attractive guy she'd ever lusted after didn't mean she should rush into another disastrous relationship like she had with Dave. She hadn't dated anyone since because she didn't trust her instincts anymore, and she'd do well to remember that.

She smiled brightly at Sky as they went into the bathroom.

"I'm sorry you didn't get more time to play, sweetie. But let's get you ready for your nap, okay?"

Noah stared after Jen in frustration. He'd done the right thing, but somehow it didn't feel like it. In fact, it felt like he'd lost something important, which was ridiculous, as he'd only known her for two weeks. But once he'd gotten over his decision to dislike her on sight, he'd quickly realized that not only was she easy on the eyes, but she was smart, funny, and a great mother as well—everything he'd always looked for in a woman and never yet found.

Trust him to find himself right in the middle of an estranged couple. He'd had this bizarre idea to call up Dave to clarify his position on his relationship with Jen, which as soon as he'd mentioned getting the new phone number had seemed presumptuous as hell. He had no claim on her, and her relationship with Dave was her own business. But he craved clarity because if he didn't have that it made it impossible to plan.

He wanted her, he couldn't have her, and that should be the end of it. Except now he'd panicked, taken the coward's way out and made her feel bad about Sky, which wasn't playing fair. He knew she was worried about her long absence from Sky's life and pointing it out, even obliquely, hadn't helped.

"Dammit!" Noah was halfway to the door before he thought better of it. If he followed Jen and apologized, they'd be back at square one. Maybe making her dislike him again was better in the long run for both of them.

He changed direction and went through to the farm office before he remembered Luke was still out looking for Max. At least he'd reactivated the radios that gave them way better coverage on the ranch than the cell network. Noah picked up the radio on Luke's desk and tried to get hold of his friend, his troubled gaze settling on the worsening conditions outside.

He heard someone whistling in the kitchen and walked back out there to discover Max helping himself to coffee.

"Where the hell have you been?" Noah demanded.

Max's eyebrows rose. "There's no need to yell, you're not my mom. I noticed the hen house roof needed patching. I fixed that and added a whole new layer of insulation. It took quite a while."

"Without letting anyone know where you were?" Noah wasn't giving an inch. "Come on, Max. You know better than that."

"It's not like I wandered far from the house. I'm not that stupid." Max paused, his gaze fixed on Noah's. "What's up?"

"Luke's been out looking for you for the last two hours, and I can't raise him on the radio," Noah said evenly. "You'd damn well better pray he's okay, or we'll be circling back to this discussion later."

"I'll go look for him." Max set down his mug. At least he wasn't smiling anymore.

"You've done enough for one day." Noah pushed past him. "Stay here and keep an eye on the radio while I go and find Luke."

Chapter Ten

"What's wrong?" Jen peered around the door of Luke's office to see Max sitting in the chair, his feet on the desk and his expression grim. "Are you okay?"

She'd put Sky down for his nap and decided it was time to come out and face Noah like a grownup. But he wasn't in the kitchen, and there was still no sign of Luke.

Max looked over at her. "Before you ask, I was fixing the hen house."

"Luke thought—"

"I know what he thought," Max interrupted. "And I also know he's gone out looking for me. If he'd just hollered from the front porch, I would've come running. I was just behind the fricking barn."

Jen gave him a skeptical look, and he shrugged.

"Well, maybe not running, but I would've come. There was no need for him to go haring off out there in this weather."

Despite what he was saying, there was a thread of anxiety in Max's voice that Jen couldn't ignore.

"Where's Noah?"

"He's gone to find Luke after chewing me a new one." Max held up a clunky radio. "If I hear anything I'll let you know."

"Are they in actual danger out there?"

"Snowstorms are unpredictable, but Luke knows every inch of this place, so if anyone can navigate himself safely back it's him."

"What about Noah?"

"He's the best tracker I've ever known."

Despite Max's reassurances, Jen was still worried, but one thing she'd learned in her professional life was never to let that show.

"Okay, let me know if you need anything."

"Will do."

Jen went back into the silent kitchen and spent a while tidying up, filling the dishwasher, and deciding what to cook for dinner. She was anxious enough to make a casserole, just in case the guys needed something warm when they got back. She kept an ear out for the baby monitor while simultaneously listening for the crackle of Max's radio.

Another hour crawled by, and she had just gone to fetch Sky when Max abruptly left the house and ran toward the barn. Jen watched him disappear into the snow. Surely Luke and Noah should be back by now? The ranch was large, but not the size of a small country. She fed the dogs and then Sky, stirred the casserole, added potatoes, and sat down to wait in the family room. In her line of work, she'd learned to be a champion waiter, but even her nerves were straining to hear any sign of activity outside.

The wind picked up, battering against the windows until the glass shivered like a living thing and gusts howled down the chimney. The electricity flickered, and Jen prayed that the generator would hang in there. Sky played on, oblivious to both Jen's increasing anxiety and the gathering threat of the weather.

Suddenly there was a rumble of noise from the front porch. Jen made sure Sky was secure in the playpen and ran to open the door. It slammed back on its hinges as the wind took it, and she barely got out of the way.

"Help me." Noah shouted through the rising storm as he stumbled up the steps with Luke in his arms.

She ran out, oblivious to the freezing cold, and helped him drag an unresponsive Luke through and onto the mudroom floor. She crouched beside him, and Noah went to his knees as if all the strength had suddenly gone out of him.

"You okay for a minute?" Jen looked over at him as she cupped Luke's chin. He was pale and cold to the touch, his lips almost blue.

"I'm good. Just give me a sec," Noah said hoarsely, his breathing harsh. "Max will be here in a minute. He's just stabling the horses."

Jen removed Luke's sodden gloves and pushed her warm fingers against the pulse point at his neck. He was still breathing, which was good, but his skin was freezing and his pulse was sluggish.

"Do you have a medical kit and a thermometer?" Jen asked.

"Yeah." Noah heaved himself back to his feet, swaying slightly as he fought to remove his soaked jacket. "I'll get it."

After carefully checking Luke's neck for any obvious damage, Jen rushed over to the couch and got one of the pillows to put under his head. His eyes remained closed, his breathing shallow. His chest was barely moving. Even though she was a midwife by profession, she'd dealt with countless other problems during her working life. Frostbite and hypothermia were common, and she'd learned how to deal with them.

She continued her examination as Noah returned with a substantial medical kit, which she assumed belonged to Sally

"Where did you find him?" she asked Noah as she carefully unbuttoned Luke's jacket and removed his snow-packed boots.

"Out toward the county boundary. I think he came off his

horse, but he had the sense to crawl into the shelter of the trees."

Jen spent a while examining Luke's skull but found no obvious injuries—not that she could rule out concussion while he was still unconscious. It wasn't until she resumed her examination and moved lower that she discovered another issue.

"I think he's damaged his lower left arm. If he was tossed, he probably used it to break his fall. Happens all the time." She held her breath as her fingers gently probed the bones. "Yeah, his radius and ulna aren't in line, but it looks like a straightforward break."

Max came in, brushing snow from his hat, his expression tight as he glanced down at Luke.

"What can I do?"

Noah opened his mouth, and Jen quickly spoke over him.

"I think we need to get him off this cold floor and into bed. Can you guys help me lift him?"

"Sure." Max crouched beside her. "I'll take his feet."

Noah moved to the center and Jen took up position at Luke's head, her hands gently cradling his skull and supporting his neck.

"Okay, on my count. One, two, three."

With two big guys helping it was easy to get Luke settled onto his bed. Jen went back to get the medical kit and to check on Sky, who was happily chewing his bone and singing to himself.

When she got back into the bedroom, Max and Noah were facing off across Luke's bed, and neither of them looked happy.

Jen cleared her throat and they both stared at her.

"One of you needs to stay here and help me, and the other is on Sky duty."

"I'll stay. I'm a trained field medic," Noah said. "The last thing Luke's gonna want to see when he wakes up is Max's face."

"That's not—"

"Guys." Jen held up her hand. "This is neither helpful nor relevant. If you can't drop it down a notch, both of you can get out."

Max gave Noah another scathing glare and went to the door. "I'll keep an eye on Sky."

"Thank you, and while you're out there, can you put the kettle on and see if there are any heating pads, hot water bottles, or thermal blankets around? I'm betting we'll need to get Luke's core body temperature up." Jen waited until Max closed the door before turning to Noah, who shrugged.

"I'll behave I promise."

"Then let's get him undressed." Jen started on the buttons of Luke's shirt. "His coat kept most of the snow out, which is good, but he's still cold and damp."

Noah moved to the end of the bed and eased off one of Luke's socks. "His feet are freezing."

"You can start a gentle massage if you like," Jen said as she took Luke's temperature. "It might help get his circulation going."

"How do you know all this stuff?" Noah asked as he did what she suggested.

It was her turn to shrug. "You pick things up on a ship like ours. If there's a problem, we all help out." She checked the thermometer and frowned. "Ninety-three point five degrees isn't great. We definitely need to get his core temperature up."

Max knocked on the door and deposited a couple of electric blankets, a huge quilt, and two old fashioned hot water bottles he'd already filled.

"Luckily Sally never throws anything away. She used them to warm the bottom of her bed in the winter."

He retreated, and Jen turned back to Luke.

"Did he still have his phone?"

"Yeah, but I'm not sure if it's working." Noah had just retrieved it from the pocket of Luke's jeans. The screen was cracked. "Why do you need it?"

"I thought it might be a good idea to check in with Luke's mom. She's the doctor. She might have info about Luke's medical history that can help us deal with this problem."

"I'll call her." Noah tapped a few times and then frowned. "I'm not sure if Luke's phone is broken or there's no cell network." He got out his own phone and tried it. "Dammit, the network's down."

Jen met his gaze. "Then it looks like we're on our own. Once we get him warm, the next task is to set his fractured arm."

"Without an X-ray?"

Jen pretended to look around. "Unless Sally's got an X-ray machine hidden away somewhere I guess I'll just have to do it myself."

Noah stared at her for a long moment. "Tell me you've done this before."

She smiled at him. "Loads of times. All I'll need you to do is hold his arm steady and in position, and I'll take it from there."

Noah stared at Jen. He'd thought she was strong before, but seeing her in professional mode made that even clearer. She was calmness personified as she faced fixing his friend's arm without the aid of modern medicine. He had this weird sense that he'd slipped back in time and they were reenacting the kind of shit Luke's great-grandparents must have gone through back in the day.

"What do you need to get this done?" Noah asked.

She gave him a nod of approval. "Something to make a splint for his arm and a decent size bandage." She glanced down at Sally's medical kit. "Those things might be in there, but any kind of straight wood would do in a pinch, and you can always rip up a sheet for bandages."

As she talked, she was gently moving her fingers along Luke's left arm. "It's probably best if he's still out for this part. It's going to hurt."

Noah crouched beside the medical kit and rummaged inside. Because Sally was the local doctor and still made house calls, she had an impressive amount of stuff. Noah set a series of bandages on the side of the bed.

"Will any of these work?"

"Yup." Jen pointed at one of the wider ones. "That'll do nicely."

"What else?"

"A splint. It needs to be about the length of Luke's forearm."

Noah checked again, taking things out as he went and spreading them on the rug next to the bed. "I can't see anything."

"Can you make me one or improvise? Chopsticks might work," Jen asked as Luke stirred against the pillows and frowned deeply.

"I'm on it." Noah rose to his feet and headed for the kitchen.

Max was sitting with Sky in the family room watching some kid's thing on TV.

"Everything okay?"

"Fine. I just need a splint." Noah jerked open the drawer full of kitchen utensils. There weren't any chopsticks, but he grabbed a few wooden spoons and measured them against his forearm. "These two will work."

"I could run over to the barn and saw the spoon part off," Max offered.

"No need." Noah said. "There's a small hacksaw in the office."

He kept moving. It didn't take long to get through the

wooden handles, but by the time he got back to Jen, Luke was definitely waking up, which was both a blessing, and a curse.

"Do you have something to help with the pain?" Noah murmured as he handed over the two sticks.

"Yup, already prepped and ready to go." Jen smiled down at Luke who had just opened his eyes. "Hey, sleepyhead. It's Jen. You're back home, and Noah and I are going to take care of you."

"Max?" Luke whispered.

"Keeping an eye on Sky while I get you patched up," Jen said, her voice soothing, "You lost consciousness, and you've fractured your left arm."

"Horse stumbled and I went over his head like a newb."

"Happens to the best of us, bro," Noah said, giving him a reassuring smile. "But you're safe now and in good hands."

Luke frowned. "Where's Salinger?"

"He's not on the ranch," Noah kept his voice calm.

"Can't leave him behind."

"We won't."

Jen glanced at Noah and then back to Luke. "I'm going to reset your arm now, Luke."

"Okay." Luke had already closed his eyes and his voice was a whisper. "Go for it."

For the next few minutes Noah tried not to remember that it was his best friend Jen was working on and just did what she told him without hesitation. To her credit, she worked at a speed he could never have managed while simultaneously checking that Luke was doing okay. It didn't occur to him until she'd finished and told him he could step back that the only thing stopping him from keeling over had been her calm presence.

She glanced up at him as she settled Luke's splinted arm onto a pillow.

"You were awesome. Can you get me some warm water in a bowl and a towel?"

"Sure." He nodded, his gaze fixed on Luke's pale face.

"And Noah?"

"Yeah?"

"There's no rush. Take your time."

Noah was already in the hallway before the shaking hit him. He had to stop and breathe hard. PTSD was a weird thing that crept up on him when he least expected it. For a moment, he'd been transported back to Afghanistan, dealing with the aftermath of an attack, where he'd been the one patching up a fallen team member. He could still smell the blood, even though there hadn't been any.

"You okay?" Max stared at him from the family room.

Noah pushed away from the wall. "I'm good. Jen needs some hot water."

"Kettle's already on the stove." Max checked that Sky was busy watching the cartoon and walked into the kitchen. "What else does Jen need? I made a fresh pot of coffee."

"Great. We could both do with some of that." Noah didn't have the energy to argue with Max at that moment, when his hands were still shaking. "How's Sky doing?"

"He's awesome." Max glanced at the clock. "I'll get him something to eat soon. I checked the stove and there's a beef casserole cooking away in there. Jen must've been busy."

"She's multitalented." Noah leaned against the counter and took a long slug of coffee that helped calm his jittery nerves. "You should've seen her setting Luke's arm like a pro."

"She could probably do it in her sleep." Max checked the kettle. "Where do you want this?"

"In a washbowl." Noah finished his coffee and refilled the cup. "I'm not sure when we'll be done, but at least dinner won't spoil."

"True." Max set the filled bowl on the table in front of

Noah and put a towel by the side. "Let me know if I can do anything else, okay?"

"Will do." Noah stood up, shook off his past demons, and focused on the present. "Thanks."

He set the towel over his shoulder, wrangled the two mugs of coffee and the bowl, and made his way back to Luke's bedroom. Outside, the wind battered against the solid walls of the house. It felt like they were under siege.

In Luke's room all was quiet and serene. Jen had closed the drapes and drawn a chair up beside the bed so she could observe her patient. She sat next to Luke, her fingers lightly clasping his wrist as she took his pulse. Noah paused to stare at her, struck by the beauty of her face in the lamplight. She looked up and smiled but didn't speak as she consulted her watch.

He set the bowl of water on Luke's chest of drawers and placed the towel beside it.

"How's he doing?"

"Good so far. He's warming up nicely."

"Did you give him something or is he unconscious?" Noah asked as he came to stand on the opposite side of the bed.

"He's very lightly sedated. I need to make sure his body temperature returns to normal and that he's not suffering from a concussion."

"Makes sense," Noah spoke as softly as he leaned over to set the coffee on Luke's nightstand. "Thought you might need this."

"Thanks." Jen picked up the mug and cradled it between her two hands as she took a sip. "Did you have some?"

Noah pointed over his shoulder at his cup. "Yeah. Max made a fresh pot."

Jen lowered her voice even more. "Who's Salinger?"

"One of our unit who didn't make it out of Afghanistan."

Noah grimaced. "Luke often has nightmares about that whole fiasco."

She nodded. "That's not uncommon. How are you holding up?"

He reached behind him to grab his coffee. "I'm good."

She studied his face. "Okay."

"Don't try that noncommittal shrink talk on me." Noah met her gaze. "I'm the guy whose job was to get my people out. I'm not allowed to crack up."

"And I bet you did your job well." She paused. "Doesn't mean you don't have your own issues to deal with, though."

Noah thought about his intense reaction in the hallway. Had she noticed his stress levels rising and sent him out to get a hold of himself? He gave a nonchalant shrug. "As I said, I'm good."

Her sigh was as eloquent as a long lecture. She set her coffee down and returned her attention to Luke. "I took his temperature and it's at ninety-four now."

"I'm just glad I found him." Noah exhaled. "It was rough out there. Visibility was down to zero in some places. The only good thing was that he was riding my gelding, Sunset, and I heard him neighing."

"Luke or the horse?"

Noah smiled, pleased she'd let him off the hook about his emotional shit and happy to explore another topic.

"Definitely Sunset. He'd hung around with Luke, which was a damn good thing."

"Yes, I should imagine it's way easier to spot a horse than a person in all that snow."

"Especially if the horse is red."

"Sunset, right." She smiled at him. "Is he okay?"

"Max took care of him. I haven't had a chance to ask about that yet." He glanced over at Luke's still face. "But he's a damn fine horse."

* * *

Jen was happy to let Noah talk as she continued to monitor Luke. Despite what he'd said, she'd noticed him looking a little rocky earlier, and rather than having him keeling over on top of her patient, she'd sent him off on a relatively unimportant errand. In typical Noah fashion, he was shrugging off her concerns and pretending everything was great. Sometimes she had this strange urge to bash his and Max's heads together and tell them that asking for help was a sign of strength, not weakness. But she'd been singing variations of that song for years, and it rarely made any difference. In her experience, most people waited until they were in crisis mode to act.

Her gaze passed over Noah, who was drinking his coffee, to focus on Luke's bedroom. She hadn't had time to take it all in before. The walls were covered with photos of Luke excelling at things—sports, social activities, academics. She wasn't surprised to learn he'd been officer material from the start. There was also a huge poster of Pikachu from Pokémon, and one of the Sailor Moon cartoon girls. His bed was covered in handmade patchwork quilts, and the rug under her feet was made of rags.

There was a sense of home and longevity in Luke's room—something Jen had never had and always yearned for. And Luke had used that security and love to find the courage to serve his country in the most dangerous of theaters.

"What happened to Luke's dad?" The question escaped her lips before she realized it.

"He died about four years ago. Cancer," Noah said quietly. "Sally was gutted. They'd been married for forty years."

"Ouch," Jen winced. "I can't imagine how that must feel."

"Me neither. My parents split up when I was a kid. It was ugly."

"My parents were never really together at all. My dad kind of drifted in and out, which made it hard for my mom to cope," Jen confessed. Something about the quietness of the room in the center of the storm made her feel able to talk about the difficult stuff. "The problem was that when he did come back, she'd drop everything and just disappear, leaving us to fend for ourselves."

"That sucks." Noah said, frowning.

"We ended up in foster care a few times. That's how I came to spend a summer up here."

"It's a beautiful part of the world." Noah paused. "How come you ended up going for someone like Dave, then? I mean—"

Jen raised a hand. "You mean he sounds just like my dad?" She smiled. "Maybe at some level I thought I didn't deserve any better, I don't know." She shrugged. "He was funny, he was charming, and he was one hundred percent totally into me, which made me feel very powerful. Of course, by the time I realized he was like that with every woman he wanted to sleep with, it was too late."

Noah didn't say anything, and Jen found herself carrying on.

"It's also embarrassing that someone who spends hours of her day working with women all over the world to promote female health and hygiene ended up pregnant." She glanced over at her silent companion, who was now looking at anything but her. "It's okay, I know you must have wondered. It was a terrible combination of having the flu and changing my birth control meds—something I knew could happen, but I didn't really believe would happen to me."

He nodded and sipped his coffee, his gaze now fixed on Luke's face. Had she embarrassed him? She'd certainly given him enough personal information for one night. She rose to her feet.

"Can you keep an eye on Luke while I go and check in on Max and Sky?"

"Sure."

Jen skedaddled for the door, aware of a flurry of conflicting emotions. Had she wanted Noah to tell her he understood what had gone down with Dave, or was his silent acceptance of what she'd told him enough? She closed the door and went down the hallway toward the kitchen. More to the point—why had she decided to share such a personal thing with a friend of Dave's in the first place?

She stopped walking and pressed her hand to her heart. Maybe Noah's lack of interest in engaging meant he was disgusted by her behavior. She couldn't blame him. Of all the people to completely screw up and get pregnant she should've been on the least-likely list.

Jen took a deep, steadying breath and continued down the hallway. She wouldn't change her life now for anything. Sky was a blessing. What Noah did or didn't think about her made no difference at all—did it?

Chapter Eleven

The wooden clock that looked like an elk Luke had probably handcrafted as a toddler struck twelve times. Noah yawned and stretched out his legs. He was on second shift while Jen took a nap. She'd wrapped herself in a blanket and gone straight to sleep on Luke's recliner in the window recess. He supposed that in her profession, as with his, the ability to take a nap when things went quiet was essential.

From his position on the other side of the bed he could barely see the top of her head, but she was still a solid, comforting presence. Max had come in for an hour earlier while Jen put Sky to bed and was now sleeping with the baby monitor on his nightstand in case Sky woke up. He'd been quiet, helpful, and very un-Max-like. He'd even apologized several times to Jen for putting her to so much trouble, even as he avoided having the same conversation with Noah.

Watching Jen take charge in her natural environment had made Noah respect her even more. She might be soft-spoken, but there'd been no doubt who was the boss, and that he and Max had better knuckle down and do as they were told. If she hadn't been there and Luke had arrived in the same state, Noah would've done his best. He was haunted by the notion that he might have missed something, like Luke's broken arm, and done more harm than good.

Luke was resting quietly, his face contorting into the occasional grimace as he dreamed or the pain in his arm bothered him. Jen said he'd warmed up nicely and was no longer in any danger. She'd asked Noah to wake Luke up around midnight because of the possibility of concussion.

After a glance over to make sure Jen was still asleep, Noah leaned over Luke and gently shook his right shoulder.

"Luke? You asleep?"

His boss opened one bleary eye. "I was." He winced at the light. "My head hurts."

"That's what happens if you land on it," Noah reminded him as he repositioned the lamp.

"Is Sunset okay?" Luke sounded croaky, and Noah helped him raise his head to sip some water.

"Yes, according to Max. He's doing great."

"If he hadn't stayed put you would never have found me."

"He's a good horse." Noah didn't address the rest of Luke's remark. It was too close to the bone.

"Apart from the bit when he spooked at nothing, stopped dead, and I catapulted over his head."

Noah shrugged as he set the water glass back on the bedside table. "Not his fault you're not as good a rider as I am."

Luke's faint smile made the anxious knot in Noah's gut loosen up a little.

"Where's Jen?"

"Sleeping over there." Noah angled his head in the direction of the window. "Main power's gone out, but the generator is holding up well. We've also lost cell phone and internet."

"Shit," Luke murmured as his eyes started to close again. "I need to get up."

"No, you don't, bro," Noah said firmly. "Max and I can handle this."

"How's Max doing?"

"Who knows? He's here and that's all that matters right now."

"Cool." Luke frowned, "Don't call my mom, okay?"

"I can't. Cell phones are down."

"Awesome." Luke let out a long breath and went quiet.

Noah resumed his seat and checked his cell just to make sure everything was still out. There was no signal. He was supposed to wake Jen up in two hours. The wind was still prowling around the house, huffing and puffing like the wolf in that stupid fairytale Sky loved. He and Luke had spent a lot of time last summer weatherproofing the old house, and it looked as if all their hard work had paid off.

He glanced over at Jen again. She was snoring very quietly, and her head had fallen back to reveal the long line of her throat. For a stupid moment Noah wished he had the right to walk over, pick her up, set her on his lap, and hold her close while she slept.

"Dammit," Noah muttered. "Stop torturing yourself."

When she'd started talking about what had happened between her and Dave, he'd been torn between really wanting to hear her reasons and not wanting to think about her having sex with another man. How typical that he couldn't even work out how he felt about that. He was the kind of guy who hated indecision, and yet he was waffling around like a pile of jelly. He couldn't blame Jen for that. It was all on him.

Everything she'd told him indicated there was nothing between her and Dave. But was he deluding himself? She might say that she was through with her ex, but they'd had Sky together . . . Despite professing to hate each other, his parents had gotten back together long enough to produce three more kids, and his dad had paid them no more attention than he'd given Noah.

He sighed and rubbed his hands over his face. When the weather cleared up and Jen was able to leave, maybe Noah could keep in touch with her. Then he could find out whether she was amenable to seeing him again when everything was more settled.

Because he did want to see her again and having a plan—even a sketchy one—made him feel more in control. Right now, all he had to do was focus on getting Luke on his feet, stop Max from doing anything stupid, and never ever kiss the living daylights out of Jennifer Rossi.

"I'm fine," Jen reassured Noah for what felt like the fiftieth time. "I'm used to sleeping in shifts. You can go back to your own room. There's no need for you to stay here."

He frowned. "You stayed here."

"Because I didn't want to wake Sky," Jen explained. "Go on, you must be exhausted."

Noah shoved a hand through his disordered hair. He'd been up all night and out in the snow to find Luke and bring him home. The strain was showing in his brown eyes.

"You might need my help."

She smiled at him. "Then I'll come and find you."

"That would take too long, and you'd have to leave Luke alone." He gestured at the recliner she'd only recently abandoned. "I can sleep there."

"Fine." Jen concealed a yawn. She must look an absolute fright with her day-old clothes and wispy, ratty hair. Normally in the delivery room no one was looking at her, but she felt Noah's gaze quite acutely. He'd been a rock throughout the whole process of getting Luke fixed up. She now understood why Luke valued him so highly and had asked him to come and work at the ranch. She knew she only had to ask and he'd be right there for her, too. Colleagues like that were invaluable.

"Colleagues," Jen muttered to herself.

"What's that?" Noah, who had walked over to the recliner looked back over his shoulder at her.

"Nothing!" Jen said brightly. "Just thinking aloud that you would be great to work with on the ship."

He grimaced. "I get terribly seasick."

"Really?" She pretended to sigh. "Then there's no hope for you because no one on the ship ever suffers like that." She tried not to remember some of the more gut-heaving days and the thirty-foot waves crashing over the bow of the ship while they bobbed around like a cork. "You're a certified landlubber."

"And I'm happy to keep it that way." He settled into the recliner and wrapped the blankets she'd only recently vacated around his large torso. "Still warm. Thanks."

"You're welcome." Jen watched as he buried his nose in the wool and slowly inhaled.

"Smells like you," Noah added.

She didn't know what to say to that. "Can you stay awake for five more minutes while I run and get some more coffee and check on Sky?"

"Sure."

"Do you need anything?" she paused at the door to ask.

He took his time to answer her. "Nothing I can have."

She hurried off wondering what he'd meant by his last remark. Was he still interested in her? It sure sounded like it, or maybe he was just tired, not thinking straight, and was just babbling. The thing was—in any other circumstances she'd be all over Noah Harding because he was everything she wanted in a man.

"Our timing sucks," Jen whispered. "Like, big time." She filled up her mug with the coffee Max had left warming and peered in on Sky, who was sleeping like an angel.

When she let herself back into Luke's bedroom Noah had already fallen asleep—or if he hadn't, he was doing a good job pretending. Maybe he wasn't keen on having another low-voiced confidential chat over Luke's bed. She wasn't sure if she was either. His reaction to her attempt to talk about Dave hadn't been encouraging. But what did she expect? He was an honorable man, and he'd already pointed out that he wouldn't take advantage of her when she was a guest in Luke's house.

Why did he have to be honorable? Jen sighed at her own contrariness and took out her cell phone. For some reason, her network had come back while the guys' was still down. Luke was sleeping peacefully, Sky was in good hands with Max, and Noah was already out for the count. She would wake Luke in a couple of hours, but until then her time was her own. The reassuring rumble of the generator cut through the howl of the storm, making her feel a lot safer than she probably should. But she'd been in dangerous and difficult situations before, and she wasn't a panicker by nature.

She found Heather's number and started to text.

Hey you. ☺ Got a minute to listen to me emoting?

Always. Go ahead. I hope it's juicy.

Jen let out her breath. I'm kind of interested in one of the guys here but it's not great timing.

Why not?

1. He's Dave's friend. 2. He's not the kind of guy to take advantage of me when I'm stuck at the ranch, and 3. Sky.

He hates kids?

No! He's been great. It's just not something he's ever wanted. I guess he's leery about getting in the middle of me and Dave.

There is no middle, tho. You and Dave were over before you started.

I tried to tell him that, but he didn't want to talk about it.

He's a man.

Jen made a face. Retired Marine. ☹

Waste of time then. How about you just jump his bones?

Wouldn't that be counterproductive?

How?

Jen considered how to reply, her gaze moving over to Noah's oblivious face.

I don't want to blow it.

You don't need to do that on a first date, ha. Jen tried not to roll her eyes as Heather kept typing. Maybe just go with the flow and if something happens between you then don't try and stop it?

He's way too controlled to ever let anything happen.

Then wait until you're in a better place and try then.

I think that's the best advice. Jen sighed. I really like this one.

YAY!!! FINALLY, JEN WANTS SOME ACTION!! Go get him, babe. Gotta go. Keep me updated, okay? Xx

Will do. Xx.

Jen closed down her phone and set it on the bedside table beside Luke's pain medication. Having Sally's medical kit was such a bonus. She wished she'd gotten to meet Luke's mom. She sounded like an amazing woman. Practicing in such a remote location was a bit like working on the ship—

you had a schedule, but you never knew what might come up to derail your plans.

Jen settled back in her chair and stared at the brown-checked drapes that covered Luke's window. She had to work out what to do with the rest of her life. . . .

She had six months left to run on her current contract, which she would spend at the hospital in San Diego rather than at sea. She could re-up with the navy for another four years or leave and find a job where she could be with Sky full time. At some level she'd been hoping Dave would become such a responsible parent that he'd be willing to spend a minimum of six months every other year looking after Sky while she fulfilled her commitments to the ship because she loved her current job.

The latest debacle showed why that was a terrible idea. Jen couldn't expect Martha to pick up the slack again. It just wasn't fair. Which meant that in six months' time she had to find somewhere affordable to live and a job that paid the bills. Martha had offered Jen her San Jose condo rent free for six months while she remained in Florida, which was super helpful, but did she want to live in such a bustling city? And her current job was in San Diego, which was hardly commutable.

"You'll do what you have to do," Jen reminded herself firmly. "For Sky and for the rest of our lives."

She couldn't help looking over at where Noah was sleeping, his face relaxed, which was not his usual state. He was a lot taller and stronger than she was. He could probably sweep her off her feet, an unknown experience for someone who was five feet ten in her socks and big-boned, as her mother had dismissively called her. Dave was an inch taller than she was but always claimed he was six feet, which was *so* Dave.

She picked up her cell again and searched for his number. There was a text from him dated the previous day she'd somehow missed, or that had just come through since the storm?

Things getting too hot here. Back soon. Where are you?

She debated answering him but decided it would be far more interesting to send him on a wild goose chase to see how he liked it, and she deleted the text. She'd have to see him eventually to discuss Sky, but until then, she'd enjoy lusting over what she couldn't have until cold, hard, reality intruded, and she had to make some life changing decisions.

Noah woke up to the siren smell of freshly brewed coffee and opened his eyes to find Jen holding a mug under his nose.

"Max told me that this was the best way to wake you up."

"Works for me." His voice was gravelly with disuse and his throat was sore. "Hang on a sec."

He eased his arm free of the cocoon of blankets and noticed that someone had placed an extra pillow against his shoulder. He took the mug and sipped gratefully.

"Thanks."

Jen regarded him critically. "Are you feeling okay?"

"I'm fine."

She placed her hand on his forehead. "You're very warm."

"I'm wrapped in blankets." He cleared his throat, which still hurt, and took another glug of the scalding hot coffee. "Once I get up and start moving, I'll feel great. How's Luke doing?"

"About as well as you are." Jen continued to look concerned. "Slight temperature, but no permanent damage from being stuck outside in a snowstorm."

"Marines are tough." Noah finished the coffee and stood

up. Every bone in his body immediately protested him sleeping in a recliner instead of a proper bed.

"Tell me about it," Jen muttered as she got out of his way. "And stubborn as mules."

Noah sauntered off toward the bathroom as if he hadn't a care in the world. He was glad she didn't follow him because he was hacking like a dog. If he was honest, he felt like shit. He washed up and went into the kitchen, where Max was feeding Sky his breakfast.

"Nono!" Sky beamed at him and held out his arms.

"Buddy." Noah patted him on the head as he went past to get more coffee and something to eat that wouldn't exacerbate the scratchiness in his throat. "How's Max doing in the parenting department?"

"Not as good as you and Jen," Max said. "He's so disappointed when I turn up."

"He looks great." Noah turned to study Sky from his position by the microwave. "He's clean and still smiling."

"Not for long." Max sighed. "He cries every time Jen leaves him."

"Understandable." Noah got his oatmeal and sat opposite Max at the table. He tried a spoonful. It felt like he was swallowing gravel, but he persevered. "What needs doing today?"

"That depends on what Jen needs." Max scraped Sky's bowl clean and placed it on the tray so Sky could practice with his spoon. "We can just about get to the barn to see to the horses right now, but no farther."

Noah grimaced. "Let's hope we don't lose too many cattle."

"It's not looking good. But don't tell Luke, okay? I want him on his feet before we knock him straight back on his ass with all the bad news."

"He's not going to be doing much for a while," Noah said. "His left arm is fractured."

"Not sure how we're going to get things done, then." Max made a face. "None of the hands are going to make it up from town, either."

"We'll manage," Noah said. "We always do."

Jen came into the kitchen and looked over at the table. She was way more awake and perky than Noah and Max. She was probably one of those morning people he'd heard about.

"What's wrong?"

"The weather sucks, we're a man down, and we've still got to keep this ranch running," Max said bluntly.

"I can help," Jen offered as she took Sky's bowl away and picked up the spoon from the floor just before Winky licked it.

"You've got Luke to worry about," Noah pointed out.

"But I can take Sky into Luke's room leaving you two free to get on with whatever needs doing, or one of you can sit with Luke and I can help out in the barn." Jen looked between the two of them. "I'm really quite capable you know."

"No one doubts that," Noah said. "I could set up the playpen in Luke's room so you'd have a way of containing Sky if you needed it."

"That would be great," Jen smiled at him. "And, when he's napping, I can take care of the cooking and chores so you guys don't have to worry about anything."

"Sounds like a plan." Max sat back. "How's Luke this morning?"

"Sleeping in right now, but he had a relatively good night."

Some of the tension in Max's face disappeared as he nodded and went to get a washcloth for Sky. He still hadn't had a proper conversation with Noah about what had gone down the previous day. Noah knew that if he didn't push it, Max wouldn't bring it up because that was just how he was right now. If Noah felt better, he'd probably be all over him, but he didn't, and as he didn't want Jen to know how bad he was feeling, he was keeping his mouth shut.

Even as he thought that a piece of oatmeal stuck in his throat, and he started to cough. Jen handed him a glass of water, and he sucked most of it down.

"You look like crap," Max said.

"Thanks." Noah pushed his bowl of oatmeal away and made sure not to look at Jen. "As I keep telling everyone, I'm fine."

Jen stood and picked up Sky. "Come and find me when you're ready to admit you're not."

Max grinned as she went past him and down the hallway. "She told you, big guy."

"Two painkillers and I'll be good for the rest of the day," Noah insisted as he found the container and swallowed some down. "It's not like I haven't had a cold before."

Max didn't bother to reply as he went into the mudroom and pulled on his work boots, fleece-lined jacket, and a knitted hat. "I'll see you in the barn."

"Yup. I'll just move Sky's stuff into Luke's room, and I'll be right with you."

Jen smiled at Luke as she removed the thermometer and checked his temperature.

"You've definitely got a fever."

"Great, from freezing my nuts off to burning in hell," Luke murmured as he closed his eyes. "My arm hurts."

"I bet." Jen kept her voice calm as she gently uncovered his lower left arm.

When she'd checked yesterday there'd been no sign that

his skin had been perforated anywhere. Today the bandages still looked clean, which was reassuring. She wished she had some antibiotics to give him but hadn't discovered any in Sally's magic box. At least she had professional-grade painkillers, which were really useful.

"My cell's working," Jen said. "Would you like to call your mom?"

Luke's brow crinkled. "Why would I do that?"

"In case she's worried about you? I bet she keeps an eye on the weather out here even when she's away."

"She does, but I still don't want to give her anything else to worry about."

Jen tried to sound casual. "Would you mind if I called her? It might be helpful to get her perspective."

"On me?"

"On what to do if there's an emergency." Jen decided to be frank. "I'm a midwife. I'm not a primary-care physician, and I don't want to mess up."

"Then go ahead. Mom used to be the local emergency coordinator for this part of the national park, so she'll know exactly who to call if there's a problem. Take her number from my phone."

"Thanks, Luke."

"No problem." He half smiled. "Can I go back to sleep now?"

"Be my guest." She smiled back. "I'll make sure Sky keeps it down."

"Don't think I'm going to hear him over my happy-pills buzz."

Jen glanced over at her son, who was energetically chewing his plastic bone and watching them from his playpen. She'd felt carefully along his gums earlier and discovered the sharp points of a couple of emerging teeth, which explained why he was a little out of sorts. She hoped he'd wait until she'd dealt with Luke before going into full-blown teething mode, but knew the odds weren't in her favor.

She'd taken the precaution of freezing a couple of knotted washcloths for the inevitable grizzling stage and had a good supply of infant painkiller if needed. Sky wouldn't be the first baby she'd helped through teething, and she'd learned a few tricks along the way, which should help him. Multitasking wasn't a problem, in fact she thrived on it, but she was used to having a whole support team behind her. A quick chat with Sally would certainly help.

She waited until Luke was fast asleep and she'd put Sky down for his nap before she called Sally's number. She'd settled on the family room as in between the two spaces she was currently monitoring.

Luke's mom picked up immediately.

"Hello?"

"Hi, this is Jennifer Rossi. I'm currently staying with—"

That was as far as she got before Sally gave a delighted squeal.

"Hi, Jen! I've heard so much about you."

Jen found herself smiling even though Sally couldn't see her. "Luke's phone isn't working so I wanted to check in with you."

"How's the weather?"

"Terrible," Jen admitted. "The guys can't get beyond the barn to check on the cattle."

"Darn it," Sally muttered. "I guess that means no one can get out there from town either."

"Correct," Jen said. "And there's been another complication. Luke fell off his horse yesterday and fractured his left arm."

"He's left-handed so he probably tried to use his hand to break his fall."

"I guess. He's also suffering from hypothermia and a mild concussion."

"Poor Luke." Sally sighed. "I assume you weren't able to get him to an ER?"

"Nope. I set the bones and splinted his arm, and everything looks good this morning, but his temperature is up. Obviously, I'm concerned about infection or any repercussions from the hypothermia. If you have any advice for me, I'm all ears."

"To be honest, I'm just glad you were there. Luke always threw high fevers when he was a kid, so I'm not surprised he's still doing so." Sally paused. "It's probably just the beginnings of a cold, but you're wise to keep an eye on him."

"I don't suppose you have a secret stash of antibiotics anywhere at the ranch?"

"I wish. But if you do need them, call my partner, Dr. Carlo Rodriguez. He'll get them to you somehow."

"Unless he's Superman, I'm not sure he can. We're completely cut off right now." Jen tried not to let her growing uneasiness creep into her voice.

"Luke's a strong man, he'll probably be fine, and it sounds like he's in very capable hands."

"Just remember, I'm a midwife not a physician."

"From what I've heard, you're pretty handy," Sally said. "I've met a couple of people from hospital ships, and they were multitalented due to the necessity of their work."

"I'll do my best," Jen promised.

"And I'll be here if you need me," Sally said. "I'll call Carlo, give him your number, and ask him to get right back to you, okay?"

"Thanks," Jen said, her gaze on the huge banks of snow. "I appreciate that."

"Take care now, sweetie. You've got this."

Jen ended the call, and her smile faded as she talked to

herself. "I'm not so sure about that, but I guess I'll just have to do my best to keep this particular ship afloat."

Two minutes later her cell buzzed again with a text from Dr. Carlo introducing himself and offering his help if things went pear-shaped. She asked him about the possibility of getting hold of some antibiotics. He suggested that if she really needed them, he might be able to get the county services to leave them by the main ranch gate off the road.

Jen texted back a thank you and left it at that. How she'd get from the ranch up to the county road was something she didn't want to have to worry about until it became a necessity. There was no way she would send one of the guys or herself out into the blinding whiteness of the snow, where visibility was almost zero and the chances of getting lost about one hundred percent.

She went back into the bedroom and glanced over at a sleeping Luke. She prayed his mother was right and that he had a strong enough constitution to fight off any infection by himself. She also hoped Noah wouldn't get sick too—although, he'd probably never admit it anyway.

After another check on Luke, she went into the kitchen and started prepping for dinner. They'd started to run out of Sally's prepared meals, but there was enough frozen meat and vegetables in the chest freezer to feed them until the end of the year. She found some ready-chopped pork, put it in the slow cooker with vegetables, potatoes, and stock, and set it on low to cook. She'd adjust the seasoning later in the day.

As she stirred in the stock she listened to the sounds around her—the ticking of the kitchen clock, the reassuring rumble of the generator, and the silence emanating from Sky and Luke's rooms. She knew the calm wouldn't last, but in her line of work, she'd learned to appreciate the peaceful moments between the chaos. She glanced out toward the barn, where she knew Max and Noah were working their asses off and brewed a fresh pot of coffee.

It was lunchtime, and she'd already prepared soup and sandwiches for when they came in. She made herself a tray of food and took it back into Luke's bedroom. When he woke up, she'd help him eat and take some more painkillers and hope that his fever didn't climb any higher. Despite Sally's reassurances and knowing Dr. Carlo was nearby, her gut was telling her that things might be getting worse before they got better.

"Here." Jen set a glass in front of Noah who was sitting at the table. "It'll help your throat."

"There's nothing wrong with—"

Jen was already walking back to the stove, so he couldn't see her expression, but he guessed she was either biting her tongue or rolling her eyes at his stubborn insistence about being fine.

The enticing smell of lemon and honey cut through the hoarseness in his throat, and he surreptitiously inhaled before raising the glass to his mouth. Man, that tasted good. He and Max had barely made it back to the house as they'd worked with the horses and made attempts to get out to the fields that hadn't gone well. They'd ended the day cold, wet, exhausted, and barely on speaking terms.

Noah fished in his pocket for the painkillers he needed to swallow down with his drink and took a quick look around to make sure Jen wasn't watching.

"How many did you just take?" Max asked from the other side of the table. "You've been guzzling those things like candy all day."

Noah glared at Max as Jen came back to the table. "Thanks, snitch."

"I hope you're not exceeding the recommended dose, Noah," Jen said. "Even over-the-counter products can cause stomach problems, liver and kidney issues, and nausea if taken to excess."

"I know that thanks." Noah finished up his lemon drink. "Any dessert?"

"There's ice cream," Max suggested. "It's the only thing left because for some reason we're just not into it right now."

Noah actually shuddered at the thought of putting anything cold down his gullet. He might be burning up, but there were limits.

Max rose to his feet. "I'll clean Sky up and get him ready for bed, Jen."

"Thanks," Jen smiled at Max. "I'd appreciate that."

"Having looked after him twenty-four seven, I know you'll need a break." Max picked Sky up. "I'll take him into the family room when I'm done, and you can join us after you've dealt with Luke."

Jen was still smiling fondly after Max left with Sky.

"I could've done that," Noah said.

"Max offered." Jen picked up the used plates.

"Only because he wants you to like him."

Jen raised her eyebrows. "How old are you again?"

Noah shrugged. "I'm just stating a fact. Max doesn't like being out of favor."

"Who does?" Jen opened the dishwasher, stacked the plates inside, and shut the door with some force.

"Why are you being so salty to me?"

She swung around to face him, her hands on her hips. "Because you refuse to admit you're ill?"

"I've got a fricking cold," Noah protested. "Why would I bother you about that when you've got far more serious things to worry about?"

"Because I don't want you keeling over as well?"

"I won't do that." Noah brought his own glass and plate over to the dishwasher, where Jen was standing. She didn't budge, and he found himself staring down at her. He got a kick out of the way she wouldn't back down with him. "I can take care of myself."

"What if you share your cold with the rest of us?" Jen wasn't giving up.

He considered her slightly flushed cheeks and oh-so-kissable mouth. "I'd have to get pretty close to do that to anyone."

"You're pretty close to me now."

"Yeah, I am."

He leaned in and her breathing hitched as his lips met hers. "Damn it, Jen."

He kissed her very carefully until she kind of melted against him, and then all bets were off. Her hand stole around his neck and her nails dug into his skin in a way that made him shudder with need. She kissed him back, and he wrapped one arm around her waist to keep her exactly where he wanted her.

She ripped her mouth away from his. "I thought we weren't doing this."

"We're not. That was just a little experiment." Noah made no effort to hold on to her.

"About how infections spread between people?" Jen asked.

He shrugged. "Maybe."

She made a huffing noise, retreated to the far end of the kitchen, and busied herself cleaning the stove, and emptying the rest of the pork into a bowl. He leaned against the counter-top and watched her as he waited for his unruly body to calm down. If kissing her had been an experiment, then he'd fallen even harder for her than before. She tasted like heaven, and he wanted more.

Except nothing had changed, and if he didn't start to feel better soon, he'd be proving her right and collapsing into bed like a wuss. But then maybe she'd look after him. . . .

He cleared his throat, which made him wince, and she looked over at him.

"I might take an early night—unless you need me to do anything?"

She folded her arms across her chest. "I'm good, thanks. I'm sure Max will help if I need him."

"I'm sure he will." He pushed away from the counter. "Night, then."

"Don't forget to drink lots of fluids."

"I won't." He paused at the doorway. "Do you want to come and tuck me in?"

"Hell, no."

He found himself smiling at her. "You sure?"

She sighed. "Go to bed, Noah."

He blew her a kiss and turned to find Max in the hallway behind him with Sky on his hip.

"Nice, bro." Max moved past him. "Absolutely showing you don't have the hots for her at all."

"Shut it," Noah said as he headed toward his room wondering exactly how much Max had seen and heard. "Call me if you need anything."

There was no reply. Alone in his room, Noah let his shoulders sag and coughed his heart out as he used the bathroom, drank a load of water, and collapsed into bed. He felt like he had the worst hangover of his life, and he hadn't even been drinking. He wanted to think about that kiss, but the moment his eyes closed he was a goner.

Chapter Twelve

Okay, so Noah had kissed her, and she'd let him.

Jen stared off into space. It was almost ten, and Luke was sleeping peacefully. Her main concern was that his temperature remained high, and that there was still a threat of an underlying infection that she couldn't test for. If he didn't feel better by the morning, she might have to consult with Dr. Carlo about how to get hold of some antibiotics.

Actually, she'd not only let Noah kiss her, but she'd been an active and willing participant. . . .

If she hadn't been standing in the middle of Luke's kitchen, with her son and Max about to come back in, she would've had a hard time letting Noah go. One thing about being a mother was the ability to multitask, and that included being more aware of her surroundings and knowing exactly where her baby was at all times. Being selfish was no longer an option, and her personal needs had to come after those of her child.

Max had winked at her when he'd come in with Sky. She wondered whether he'd overheard her and Noah talking—or even worse—witnessed the kiss, which would mean Sky had seen it, too.

If no one else had been there, would Noah have picked her up, sat her on the countertop and—given her his cold?

Jen sighed. Having now kissed Noah, she was even more sure he was just right for her. But nothing had changed, and until she could move out and establish herself somewhere new, she had to be careful. Heather might tell her to have fun and accept the consequences, but having a child made things way more complicated. Jen had screwed up once with Dave and had no intention of rushing into anything ever again.

"You okay?" Luke asked.

She turned to see him studying her from his bed. He'd developed a black eye from his fall and had purple shadows under his eyes.

"I'm great!" Jen said brightly. "How about you?"

"The same." He frowned and pressed his hand to his chest. "Although, I hate to mention it, but my breathing is getting a little tight."

Jen found a stethoscope and listened intently to Luke's chest. There was a definite rattle that hadn't been there earlier.

"I think we need to get you some antibiotics," Jen said. "Seeing as this place is cut off, what's the best way to get something like that delivered out here?"

"Carrier pigeon?" Luke grimaced. "We've never had this much snow in my lifetime, so I'm out of ideas."

"Dr. Carlo said he could probably get something delivered to the top of the county road."

"Makes sense." Luke considered his next words. "One of us could take a snowmobile and try and make it out to there."

"You have those?"

"We have a couple in the barn just up the road. We use them for the cattle when we have weather like this and the horses and trucks can't get out there." Luke took a sip of the water she offered him. "Both Noah and Max know how to operate them."

"Okay, then I'll text Dr. Carlo and ask him if he can make

that happen by the morning." She held Luke's gaze. "I just want to make sure I'm not missing anything."

"You sound like my mom." Luke smiled. "I appreciate that."

"Can I get you anything more to eat?" Jen asked. "You hardly touched your dinner."

"I can't taste anything." Luke made a face. "I'll keep hydrated though. I promise."

"Good man." Jen put the stethoscope away and rose to her feet. "I'm going to make some more lemon drink and check in on Sky. I'll be back in ten."

"You do that." Luke was already closing his eyes. "I'm not going anywhere."

Jen slipped out and walked toward the kitchen. The soft glow and murmur of the TV caught her attention, and she paused to look at Max, who was stretched out on the couch watching an old baseball game.

"How's Luke?" he asked without taking his eyes off the game.

Jen took the seat opposite him. "I might need you or Noah to try and get to the main gate tomorrow morning to pick up some antibiotics."

"Noah's sick, so it will have to be me." Max frowned. "That's not going to be easy, even with the snowmobile, but I guess if you're asking it must be important."

"I'm concerned about Luke," Jen said. "I think he has an infection."

"Makes sense," Max nodded. "Let me know when you want me to go."

Like all the military folk she knew, Max made the impossible seem straightforward and easy. It was something she'd learned to appreciate during her years in the service. If it was possible to get through to the gate, Max would do it.

"I guess I owe Luke one since he was out looking for me," Max added.

Jen definitely wasn't getting into that. The tension between Noah and Max was still palpable. Without Luke in the middle to glue things together, Jen didn't want to be the one keeping the peace.

"Noah really likes you," Max said as he settled back against the cushions.

Jen stood up. "I'm going to check on Sky. I'll let you know what Dr. Carlo says tomorrow, okay?"

"Fine, I'll keep my nose out of your business." Max sighed. "He won't tell you because he's trying to be respectful of you being stuck here with us."

"And I appreciate that," Jen said firmly. "There's a lot going on right now without worrying about hurting someone's feelings."

"You're not interested?"

Jen gazed heavenward. "That's none of your business, is it?"

"Because if you aren't, just remember that even though *I* respect you, I don't have any scruples about hitting on you when we're all trapped in the same place."

"Thanks for the heads-up, but I'm definitely not interested in you." Jen looked back over her shoulder and kept her tone light. "I regularly ship out with a boatload of men who flirt with me all the time, and I'm not so easily swayed."

"Good to know." Max grinned at her. "Noah's a lucky guy."

"And you're a pain in the ass," Jen retorted.

"Yes, sir!" Max was still chuckling as she walked away.

She checked on Sky, who was sleeping with a smile on his face, checked the baby monitor was on, and went back into the hallway. Her gaze moved to Noah's door at the end of the hallway. Should she go and see if he was okay? He hadn't looked too well at dinner and, as the closest thing to a resident physician the ranch had right now, she did feel responsible for all the occupants.

"And you just want to see him," Jen murmured to herself. "Because you're an idiot who can't keep away."

She knocked softly on his door and there was no response. She considered leaving, but couldn't seem to make herself stop from turning the handle and going in. She paused with her back to the door and surveyed his domain, which was illuminated by the bedside-table lamp he'd left on. There was nothing very personal about his space except for a photo of four smiling women on the desk who must be his family, and a battered military-issue kit bag hung on the side of a chair.

The man himself lay sprawled on his back in his bed, arms spread wide and the covers pulled down to his waist to highlight an impressive display of heavy muscle, tight abs, multiple tats, and dark chest hair that made everything female in Jen howl with appreciation. She gave herself a moment to enjoy the sight of such hot masculinity before reminding herself that she wasn't there to drool but to offer a medical opinion on his current health.

He still looked flushed, and he'd thrown off the covers even in the current freezing climate, confirming that he probably had a fever. He was also quite restless, his expression changing as he turned from side to side as if seeking a better position. Jen checked if she had her thermometer in the pocket of her shirt and slowly advanced toward the bed.

One thing she already knew about veterans who had been engaged in active combat was not to startle them awake. She'd learned that valuable lesson on the ship; she tried to turn a patient on his side and ended up with a black eye when he'd treated her like an enemy. He'd been mortified when he'd regained consciousness, but Jen hadn't blamed him one bit.

She sat on the side of the bed and regarded Noah carefully. Even at this distance, she could feel the heat rising from his skin, which wasn't reassuring,

"Noah?" She pitched her voice low. "It's Jen. How are you doing?"

He furrowed his brow but didn't respond.

"Noah? It's Jen." She leaned a little bit closer and raised her voice a touch. "Can you open your eyes?"

"Don't tell me I'm in a fricking hospital again," Noah rasped. His voice was like sandpaper, and his eyes remained closed.

"No, you're still at the ranch. I'm just checking in on you," Jen hastened to reassure him. There was nothing big, strong men like Noah disliked more than being stuck in a hospital bed. "You're very hot."

"Thanks." He flexed his biceps. "You, too."

"You know what I mean." Jen touched his arm. "May I take your temperature?"

"Sure."

She eased closer and stuck the thermometer in his ear. "Stay still."

She checked the time as she lightly clasped his wrist and took his pulse. He'd opened his brown eyes and she was subjected to his supercritical gaze, which should've been unnerving, but somehow wasn't. His pulse was fast, and his temperature was way above normal.

"One hundred and two," Jen informed him. "You're going to need to stay put for a while and get some antibiotics into your system."

"You know I can't do that." Noah objected as he struggled to sit up against his pillows. "With Luke out we need everyone to step up."

"You can't step up if you are sick," Jen said, too aware that his covers had slipped down even further to pool just over his groin. "You're a trained medic, you know that."

"I'm not a quitter, either."

She reached out and cupped his bearded jaw, her thumb smoothing over his lower lip. "Please stop talking. I've heard this one too many times—usually just before some big macho man gets out of bed and face-plants on the floor."

"My throat's not so sore, and I've stopped coughing."

Jen sighed. "That's because you've been asleep and you're currently horizontal. The moment you start to move around, I bet you'll start coughing again."

"Then maybe I'd better stay here," he murmured as he turned his head to graze his mouth over her thumb. "It's kind of cool having you fussing over me."

Jen tried to lighten the mood as her body shivered from his touch. "At least you didn't say mothering."

"I can honestly say that the last thing I would ever think about you is that you're like my mother."

She went to move her hand away, and he caught her wrist. "Stay."

"I'm not getting in there with you—you're way too hot—and you're infectious."

"In a good way?"

"How many of those painkillers did you take?" Jen asked suspiciously. "You're all loopy, and we agreed—"

"We didn't agree. We avoided."

"Nothing wrong with that when talking things through wouldn't change anything," Jen reminded him.

He kissed his way down her wrist. "I took a few pills along with my nighttime meds. I'm obviously delirious, so don't blame me for anything right now, okay?"

"I think you know exactly what you're doing. You always do."

"A man with a plan." He paused to gently suck one of her fingers into his mouth, "You taste good."

"If disinfectant does it for you, knock yourself out." Jen was very aware of the warmth of his mouth and the delicate way he was using the tip of his tongue against her finger. "At least I won't catch anything if I wash my hands."

She desperately tried to change the subject. "Luke's not doing too good. I've talked to Max. He's going to coordinate with the local doctor and pick up some antibiotics at the main gate tomorrow."

Noah abruptly let go of her hand. "You talked to *Max*?"

"Yes. It's not a competition, Noah. He's the only one capable of doing anything physical right now."

Jen jumped as Noah suddenly sat up, swung his legs over the side of the bed, and rose to his feet. He jabbed a finger at his chest.

"*I'll* go."

Jen resisted the desire to jab him right back in the chest to emphasize each word. "You're not well."

"I'm—"

Even as he spoke, his knees buckled. It took all Jen's expertise to direct his fall back onto the bed and not on top of her. The downside was that she was now lying on top of him, and he was very, very naked.

"Idiot." She braced both hands on his muscular chest and glared down at him. "You could've flattened me."

He was breathing hard, his gaze fixed on hers as his hand came to rest on the jut of her hip.

"I got what I wanted, though."

"Which was what, exactly?"

"You on top of me in bed." He glanced down at himself. "Although, in my dreams you definitely had less clothes on."

Jen climbed off him, and he winced as her knee almost connected with his nuts.

"Careful."

"Man of steel, my foot," Jen muttered as she smoothed down her shirt.

"It wasn't my foot I was worried about," Noah said and started to cough.

"See? I told you." Jen shook her head. "I'll get you some hot lemon and honey to ease your throat. If you'd asked me nicely earlier, I could've given you some of Sally's super painkillers, but I don't think that would be advisable now."

Noah was too busy coughing to offer much of a comeback, which gave Jen immense satisfaction. She went through to the kitchen and heated up a mug of the lemon mixture she'd made earlier. The wind was still howling and battering at the house. For the first time she understood how people could go mad listening to that constant sound, knowing it was destroying everything they prized.

"Here you go."

Jen set the mug next to Noah. Considering his condition, he still looked good enough to eat. At some level, Jen wished she could curl up beside him and take care of him while the weather raged around them. She had a sense she'd feel safer with him than with anyone else in her life. She found herself lingering, sitting down, and reaching out to pat his hand.

"How are you feeling?"

He frowned. "Don't get all professional on me because I almost crushed you."

"I've been told I have a very good bedside manner." Jen went to draw her hand back, but he caught it in his larger one.

"You do. I just don't see you as my doctor, my mother, or my superior officer."

Jen sighed. "Sometimes I feel like I'm so busy being all three of those things that the Jen part of me gets left behind."

"She's there."

"I'm not sure I even know who she is anymore. I enlisted in the navy right out of school, and that's where I found my identity." She hesitated. "It sounds stupid, but after being in and out of foster care I *liked* having rules to follow and knowing my role in things. It made me feel more secure."

"I get it." Noah gently rubbed his callused thumb against the side of her hand. "I needed someone to set boundaries and kick my ass if I didn't follow through."

"I can't imagine why."

Noah smiled. "Now, you're just being polite."

"Maybe." She smiled back. "I'd better get back to Luke."

"Yeah. You're all right, Jennifer Rossi." He raised her hand to his mouth and kissed her fingers. "Give Luke my best and tell him if he wants anything done to ask *me*, and not Max."

Jen rolled her eyes as she stood up. "Right, I'll definitely do that."

She headed for the door and looked back at him from a safe distance. "Do me a favor and stay in bed tomorrow morning? I'll come and check you over."

"Not happening." He folded his arms over his chest and closed his eyes. "I'll be up at my usual time."

"Of course, you will," Jen muttered as she closed the door and walked down the hallway. "Why should I expect anything less?"

Her steps slowed as she reached the kitchen. She couldn't believe she'd confided in Noah again. There was just something about his rock-solid presence that encouraged her to sing like a canary. Maybe it was because he got it? That shared sense that the military had given them both something important. From what he'd let slip about his childhood, he'd been given the responsibilities of a parent far too young. It wasn't surprising his views on having his own kids were so negative. But he was so good and patient with Sky. . . .

Jen let out her breath. She liked him, and not only because he was tall, dark, and sexy, but because at his core, he had similar values to her own. That didn't change anything about their current situation, but at the very least she had a feeling she had found a new friend.

Jen put the jug of lemon away in the refrigerator and made sure all the outside doors were locked. Winky and Blinky slept quietly in their baskets in front of the range, and Max had gone to bed.

She hoped they'd get the antibiotics for Luke the next day, and that Noah would shake off his cold. If she and Max could stay well, then they'd get through this. She stared out at the unending, swirling whiteness beyond the frosted glass. They had to, because from the look of it, no one would be saving them anytime soon.

Chapter Thirteen

"I've got this, Arkie," Max repeated for at least the third time as he buttoned his ski jacket over his thermal sweater. "You look like shit. Go back to bed before Jen catches you."

"I just want to make sure you know what you're up against," Noah croaked. His voice was almost gone, and he felt like hell, but he wasn't going to let Max leave until they'd hammered out every detail.

"I've got my radio. If I run into any trouble, I'll let you know." Max found his gloves and walked over to the kitchen door. He was trussed up like an astronaut going off to space. "I'll stick to the track and come straight back, I promise."

"You'd better." Noah wheezed as he almost coughed up a lung.

Max stepped back from him. "Dude, I hope Jen ordered up some medication for you."

"I did." Jen appeared behind them carrying Sky.

Noah noticed she was keeping her distance, which made sense. She was pissed with him right now, and he didn't think it was just because he'd got out of bed without waiting for her okay, He tried not to remember the feel of her landing on top of him and the sensation that she belonged there. He'd wanted to wrap his arms around her and keep her there forever. Thank God she had more sense than he did and had remained sane enough to gracefully push him away and get out. Hopefully, she'd blame his meds and not think he'd gone soft on her.

From the way she was avoiding eye contact with him, he wasn't her favorite person in the world right now.

"If you *insist* on staying up, Noah, why don't you set up on the couch in the family room? I'll put Sky in his playpen as far away from you as possible while I tend to Luke. Please don't attempt to pick him up."

"I won't." Noah tried to speak more clearly, but his throat felt like it was full of rocks.

The look she gave him before she turned her attention to Max was enough to make him retreat to the family room, where she'd made him a comfortable spot on the couch, complete with extra pillows and blankets. He sank gratefully into his new space and immediately noticed the steaming mug of lemon beside him, a new box of tissues, and a small working humidifier.

Man, he hadn't been looked after like this since . . . he frowned. Scratch that. He'd *never* been looked after like this. His mother had worked three jobs and he'd been the one doing the coddling for his little sisters. It was kind of nice.

Jen came in and set Sky in the playpen. The little guy had very red cheeks and was grizzling, which wasn't like him.

"Teething?" Noah asked as Jen gave Sky his plastic bone. He immediately jammed it into his mouth and started drooling.

"Yup." Jen smoothed Sky's curls. "Poor little guy."

"I'll keep an eye on him," Noah said.

"I appreciate that." She cast an eye over Noah's setup. "Do you need anything else?"

"I'm good."

"Sally's painkillers should help with your fever, and when the antibiotics arrive, we'll be able to stop any secondary infection getting out of hand."

She was all business today, which was okay by him, as he was focusing all his energy on staying upright and pretending everything was fine.

"How's Luke?"

"Not great." Her smile dimmed. "I really hope Max makes it back."

"Don't we all," Noah agreed as he set the radio on his knee. "I'll shout if I hear anything."

"No, you won't."

"Okay, I'll croak loudly," Noah conceded. "It's going to take him a while."

"So, I should imagine." Jen shivered. "I'll make sure Luke's comfortable and be right back for Sky, okay?"

Noah nodded, his attention on making sure the radio was functioning correctly. He hated being the man left behind, but someone had to do it. He might not admit it to Jen, but he wasn't fit enough to venture out to the barn, let alone to the top gate. He settled in to wait, one eye on Sky, who looked remarkably glum, while the rest of his mind was busy calculating all the things that could go wrong for Max.

To his relief, as the morning wore on his temperature came down and his throat felt marginally better. He'd always been a fast healer. He'd never had the luxury of lying around while someone looked after him. Without appearing stressed in any way, Jen was in constant motion between him, Sky, and Luke, her smile always present, and her ability to know what each of them needed from her almost magical.

"How do you do that?" Noah asked as she refilled his coffee and set a fresh glass of water at his elbow. "It's as if you know what I need before I do."

"Practice?" She raised her eyebrows. "Witchcraft? Who knows?"

"I was thinking more of the tooth fairy," Noah said. "You'd look good in pink."

"I love pink." Jen removed his old glass just as the radio crackled to life.

Noah clicked twice to tell Max he was clear to go ahead.

"Got the stuff. I'm on my way back." Max sounded out of breath. "Should be easier now I've cleared a path, but the snow's still falling and filling in the tracks."

"Copy," Noah said. "Take your time and stay on the road. We'll keep an eye out for you coming in."

"Got it. Over and out."

Noah put the radio down and turned to Jen. "You heard all that?"

"Yes. I hope he's okay. He sounds exhausted." Jen wasn't smiling anymore.

"He'll make it back." Noah tried to sound reassuring, which wasn't his strong point. "As he said, he's already carved out a path. You should go and tell Luke."

"Luke's sleeping. I'll wake him as soon as I can get some of those antibiotics down his throat." Jen patted Noah's shoulder as she turned toward Sky. "It's almost lunchtime. I'll settle Sky in his high chair and bring you something on a tray."

For the first time Noah caught a hint of tiredness in her voice. He waited until she left the room with Sky, set his feet on the floor, and cautiously stood up. For the first time in a while, not only would his legs hold him, but he wasn't coughing like he smoked sixty a day. He cleared his throat experimentally, and even though it was still sore, it wasn't like it was crammed full of rocks.

He could make it as far as the table. After that, he wasn't so sure. He grabbed hold of the radio and made his way slowly through to the kitchen. He sat down, feeling like he'd climbed a mountain. Jen came in carrying Sky, looked at him, opened her mouth, and then gave a little shake of her head.

"Fine. Keep an eye on Sky while I get us all something to eat."

"Luke?" Jen sat on the side of the bed and considered her patient. "It's Jen. I need you to wake up so I can give you these antibiotics."

Max had arrived back frozen to the marrow but still grinning like he'd won some kind of tough-guy competition. Dr. Carlo had placed the medications in an insulated box, which meant everything had survived the journey in usable condition. Jen had taken a moment to text him a thank you before she dosed Noah and was now ready to deal with Luke.

Luke's eyelids fluttered, and he stared at her like he had no idea who she was.

"It's Jen," she repeated patiently. "Remember me?"

"Yeah." He licked his lips; his forehead was hot to the touch. "What do you need?"

"You, slightly more vertical so I can give you this pill." She expertly helped him sit up. "Hang in there."

A minute later, he'd swallowed the antibiotic and finished the glass of water. He leaned back against his pillows and sighed. "I feel like crap."

"I can see that." Jen checked his pulse and then his breathing, which was still worrying her. "Hopefully, you'll start to feel better very soon. Any pain or warmth in your fingers?" She touched his left hand.

"Nothing new."

"Good."

"I need to speak to Max."

"Sure." Jen stood up. "I'll go and get him."

Max was still in the kitchen eating his lunch, while Noah had retreated to the family room. Sky was taking his nap, so things were relatively quiet. It wasn't until she'd escorted

Max into Luke's room with a stern reminder not to tire him out that she realized she hadn't eaten anything herself.

"Sit down."

Noah appeared behind her as she entered the kitchen, his voice still gravelly.

"I'm fine. I just need to—" She waved vaguely at the pot of soup simmering on the stove.

"I'll get it for you."

Unlike him, she didn't need to be told twice. She took a seat and let him ladle out a bowl of soup, find her some bread rolls, and make her a fresh cup of coffee. He didn't fuss as he worked, his movements as precise and thorough as everything else he did. While his back was turned, she surreptitiously rubbed her eyes and fought a yawn. Two nights in a row without much sleep wasn't unusual for her, but she was out of practice.

"Why don't you take a nap while Sky's asleep?" Noah asked as he set the food in front of her. "Max and I are here if Luke needs anything."

Jen gazed longingly at the door that led to all the bedrooms.

"I guess I could do that."

"Then eat your lunch and go," Noah said firmly. "I promise I'll wake you up if all hell breaks loose."

"Thanks." She started on the soup and realized she was starving.

It didn't take her more than ten minutes to eat everything Noah had prepared for her. Mindful of his infectious state, he'd retreated to the family room, but the moment she put down her spoon he appeared again,

"Do you want more?"

"I'm good, thanks."

"You look worn out." He put her bowl in the dishwasher and her mug in the sink.

"It was a busy morning," Jen admitted.

"For you, sure." He grimaced. "While I sat around letting you do all the work."

"Hardly," Jen objected. "It's not your fault you were sick."

"True, but . . ." He held her gaze. "I'm glad you were here to hold things together."

"Hey." She shrugged. "Thank Dave."

His slow smile was a revelation. "That's funny."

She rose from the table and tried not to yawn. "It's hysterical."

Noah went over and opened the door for her. "You've got at least an hour before Sky wakes up."

"Does it say so on your spreadsheet?" Jen inquired as she paused to look up at him.

He raised an eyebrow. "Nah, I usually have this slot filled in as afternoon sex with Jen."

"In your filthy mind, maybe."

This time his smile was hot and dangerous. "Oh, yeah."

She gave him a gentle shove in the chest. "Move out, Marine."

"Yes, ma'am." He stepped smartly out of her way. "Enjoy your nap."

"Cell phone network is back up," Noah informed Max and Luke as he went into Luke's bedroom.

While Jen and Sky were napping, Max had called Noah to come and see Luke. Noah was shocked how worn-out his boss looked. It was as if the fever had burned him from the inside out. But Jen said Luke was on the mend, and Noah hoped she was right. If this was progress, he didn't want to know what state Luke had been in before.

"How's your arm?"

"It's healing." Luke turned to look at him. "I wanted to check in how things are going."

Max caught Noah's eye and gave a minute shake of his head.

"Hard to tell right now." Noah had never been a good liar, and despite what Max thought, Noah believed Luke should know the truth. "We've been pretty much limited to the barn and paddock for the last couple of days."

Luke briefly closed his eyes. "Shit."

"The majority of the cattle are close to the house so they're in the most protected area of the ranch," Max added. "They stand a better chance of surviving this, with the added advantage that we can get to them quicker as soon as the weather clears."

"That was the plan," Noah agreed. "We couldn't have done much more."

"Other than invite them in through the front door, no," Max agreed. "And I didn't want any scenes when they realized we were serving up Great Aunt Daisy medium rare."

Luke rolled his eyes, but even Noah acknowledged that Max's joke had broken the tension.

"We can't control the weather," Noah said. "All we can do is be ready to deal with the aftermath as quickly and efficiently as possible." He glanced toward the window. "This storm can't go on much longer."

"Sky will be off to college before this one stops," Max groused. "And Noah's never going to get it on with Jen because she's going to be stuck here with us forever, and he's too much of a gentleman to tell her how he feels."

"Jen's been amazing," Luke said.

Noah nodded along with Max. "I don't know how we'd have coped if she hadn't been here."

"Well, to be fair, if she and Sky hadn't arrived, I doubt we would've ended up in this mess anyway." Max held up his hand before Noah could speak. "Hear me out. Luke wouldn't have gone out looking for me if I hadn't been salty with him for getting in my face about Jen."

"You're trying to say this is all her fault?" Noah asked. "*You're* the problem, Max. You always are."

Max gave him the finger, turned on his heel, and stormed out, leaving Luke staring at Noah. So much for defusing the tension.

"Harsh."

"But true. He has no right to bring Jen into this. His behavior's been deteriorating for months, and we've both been too busy or too scared to deal with it."

Luke leaned back against his pillows. "I know this is a lot to ask, Noah, but can you hang in there until I'm on my feet and not start World War III with Max? I need him here."

Noah stared at the closed door. "I'll do my best, but if he keeps snipping at Jen after everything she's done for us . . ."

"Jen's quite capable of taking care of herself," Luke commented, his voice now thin and raspy.

"I know that, but in this case, she shouldn't have to. We're responsible for Max's behavior. I'm not having him making her feel uncomfortable in the only home she's got right now."

"We're not responsible for Max."

Noah grimaced. "I know that in my head, but I still think of him as part of the team."

Even though his eyes were closed, Luke smiled. "You really like Jen, don't you?"

"Maybe, but nothing's changed," Noah said firmly as he headed for the door. "She's got enough on her plate without having to worry about me."

Luke didn't reply, and Noah guessed he'd run out of energy. There was nothing he could do to make his boss feel better about the cattle, but he could at least attempt to keep the peace with Max.

He went into the kitchen, where Max was making coffee. "Hey."

Max swung around and regarded him. "Come to take another dig at me?"

"I was out of bounds. I apologize."

"Right . . ." Max leaned back against the countertop. "I think I prefer it when you're honest. At least we both know where we stand."

Noah frowned, "I am being honest."

"That I'm the problem, or that Luke told you to keep the peace by apologizing?"

"I was going to apologize anyway," Noah countered. "None of this is Jen's fault. I don't see why she should get dragged into it."

"Fair enough." Max nodded. "I'll keep her sainted name out of my mouth, okay?"

Noah nodded back and took the mug of coffee Max offered him.

"I'm going to take a quick shower to warm up and then I'll be back at it in the barn," Max said as he picked up his coffee.

"You did great today," Noah called out as Max headed for the door.

"You would've done the same." Max didn't bother to turn around. "We both want Luke to be one hundred percent."

Left alone in the warm kitchen, Noah shook his head and stared down at the dogs, who were lurking, hoping for scraps. "Let's go and sit in the family room."

The dogs obediently followed him and jumped on the couch to sit either side of him as he drew the blanket up. Noah yawned, aware of the weird taste at the back of his throat he always got when he took an antibiotic. It meant things were working, and he was grateful for that. Anything that speeded up his recovery and made it more likely they'd survive the storm was good by him.

With everyone else either asleep or otherwise occupied, it was up to him to stay awake for at least another hour. Even as he had the thought, he yawned hard enough to crack his jaw. He was way too comfortable on the couch, but his body was weaker than he wanted, and he didn't have the energy to walk around.

He patted Blinky's head and let his thoughts turn to Jen. He really should stop flirting with her, but he couldn't seem to stop himself—which was a first for him. He got out his phone, glad that the service had been restored, and noticed at least fifteen messages from his various sisters.

He started reading and within two minutes was texting Bailey.

Sorry, the network's been down. What's happened?

It took her less than a minute to respond.

I ditched Will.

Noah blinked at the screen before typing a careful reply.

Okay.

That's all you've got?

Depends what he did. Noah's fingers tightened on the phone.

It was my decision. I didn't want to move. He wanted to take the job, so we agreed to split up.

Are you okay about that?

Not really.

Noah let out a breath. It's okay to have regrets. I usually find my gut decision—the one I make first—is the right one.

I hope so. I wish I could see you right now.

We can facetime if you'd like, Noah offered.

No thanks, I'm all puffy eyed and sad looking and I'm sick of crying. I meant I could do with one of your bear hugs and tough love talks.

We can do that as soon as you want. Noah glanced out of the window. You can come here, or I can come to you.

Thanks, Bro. I love you. xxx I have to get my stuff out of Will's place now. Cameron's coming with me to help. I wish we had your muscle.

Noah grimaced. Not sure you'd want me around Will right now, but you know I'd be there for you.

He's sad, too, Noah. Neither of us wanted this. Gotta go. Love you xx.

Noah was left staring at his phone, his thoughts far away in San Diego where his sister was hurting, and he couldn't get to her. If things couldn't work out for good people like Bailey and Will, what chance did anyone have? What was the point of even trying when the odds were stacked against you?

Maybe he should remember that when he was dealing with Jen. He needed to continue to play it cool and leave the decision as to whether there was anything between them worth pursuing until after she left the ranch. He set his phone beside him on the couch. Now, all he had to do was get his stupid emotions to go along with his intelligence, which was a new thing for him. He never usually had a problem separating business from pleasure, but Jen challenged everything he'd ever thought about himself and what he wanted in a partner.

"And then there's Dave," Noah muttered to himself. "Rule number one: never, ever date a team member's ex."

But Jen had indicated very clearly that things between her and Dave had never really been right, so it wasn't as if he was getting in the middle of anything. Noah groaned and smacked himself on the side of the head. He was making excuses and exceptions for her and that wasn't like him.

What about Sky?

Noah winced at that one. He'd been loud and definite about his aversion to ever having kids. Jen wasn't exactly going to give up Sky. If push came to shove, he'd be the one walking away. What the hell was he doing, and what did he really want?

He had no answers for himself, which he absolutely hated. He reached for the remote and turned on the TV. If he had to stay awake for an hour, he'd better find something to look at, or he'd soon be sleeping as soundly as Sky.

Chapter Fourteen

Well, at least it had stopped snowing . . . Jen sighed as she sat at the kitchen table, her hands wrapped around a mug of hot chocolate. She'd just put a fractious Sky down for his nap and was taking the opportunity for a rare moment of peace and quiet. Luke was on the mend after four days of antibiotics, and Noah was perfectly fine again. She hadn't realized that a side effect of Noah taking the antibiotics would be an aversion to her company, but he'd definitely pulled away. He was still polite and helpful, but the easy banter and not-so-subtle flirting between them had disappeared.

"Maybe I imagined it?" Jen murmured. "I mean, he was delusional."

"Whatever I said, I was heavily medicated, and I deny everything." Luke came into the kitchen to sit opposite her. Even though he looked a lot better and was desperate to get out of the house, Jen had asked him to wait a few more days. "Unless I said anything you liked, which I'll take full credit for."

Jen smiled back at him. "You're good. I'll still keep the recordings though—just in case."

There was something about Luke's quiet confidence that

resonated with her. He was an excellent person to be around in a crisis and would fit in well on the Mercy.

"How's Sky doing?"

"Crabby, hot, and clingy," Jen said. "It's hard to get anything done when he's permanently attached to my leg."

"Sounds like Max on a good day." Luke sipped his coffee. "It'll be interesting to hear what the guys have to say when they come in for lunch. The snow has stopped; they might have been able to get out to the fields."

Luke was trying to sound upbeat. From listening to Noah and Max talk at breakfast, Jen was well aware of what might be at stake for the ranch and the prospects for the rest of the year. Neither of them had looked happy when they'd left this morning,

"If the snow really has stopped, do you think the roads will be passable soon?" Jen asked.

Luke made a sympathetic face. "Because the temperature is still below freezing, the snow compacts into ice, and that tends to make everything even worse."

"Dammit," Jen said.

"I know it sucks to be stuck here, but I'm glad you were around when we needed you."

"You're welcome. It was the least I could do to thank you for putting up with me."

"So, we're good?" Luke grinned at her. "All square?"

"I suppose we are," Jen agreed. "I'll be glad when Dr. Carlo can get here to take a look at your arm."

"Hopefully he won't have to break it again if you screwed up," Luke teased.

"Don't even think that!" Jen shuddered. "I'd be mortified."

"But you'd be miles away by then. Where were you planning on going with Sky before Dave gave you the runaround?"

"I was expecting to stay in San Diego with my boat

bestie, Heather, for a couple of weeks. I gave up the lease on my old apartment because it wouldn't have worked for Sky." She made a face. "I've got to get back to work. I've used up every drop of maternity leave, compassionate leave, and my regular leave."

"That sucks."

"And now I've missed all the appointments I set up in San Diego for childcare for Sky, which means I'll have to start again." She sighed. "I do have an option to work near San Jose, which is where Martha has her apartment. She offered it to me rent free for six months, so I suppose I might even end up heading there."

"You'd better make sure I have both your addresses."

"So, you can sue me?"

Luke laughed. "Hell, yeah! Why else would I want to keep tabs on you?"

"I've no idea."

Luke reached across the table and patted her hand. "Maybe because you feel like family now? I know my mom will love you."

The side door banged, and Noah and Max came in, their expressions grim, which meant they'd either been fighting again or they didn't have good news. Noah's gaze lingered on the table, where Luke was still holding Jen's hand.

"What is this—a séance?" Max had no difficulty butting in. "Or are you getting one over on Noah and asking Jen to marry you?"

"I would if she'd have me," Luke said as he sat back. "We were just discussing her future plans if she ever gets out of here."

Noah's impassive gaze flicked to Jen's. She realized he'd never really asked her what she intended to do next—probably because once she'd left, he'd forget all about her.

She smiled sweetly at Luke. "You'd make a great husband."

"See? She's amazing," Luke said as Max set two mugs of coffee on the table and sat down with Noah.

"She is, but if she's going to marry anyone, it's definitely going to be Noah," Max said. "Not that he believes in any of that crap."

"Good to know. I can't say I'm keen on the idea myself." Jen carefully avoided Noah's gaze as she went to rise to her feet. "I've got a quiche warming in the oven for lunch. I'll go and get it out."

"Hold on a sec." Max touched her shoulder. "You should hear this as well as Luke."

Jen sank back into her seat as Noah cleared his throat.

"We managed to get beyond the barn to the immediate fields behind, and . . . things aren't looking good, Luke."

All the humor drained from Luke's face. "Go on."

"I'd say we've lost at least a third of the herd."

"*Shit*." Luke's hand closed into a fist. "That's . . . bad."

"I could be wrong," Noah hastened to add. "But I just wanted to prepare you for what we might uncover when the thaw sets in."

"Anything we can do right now to help the survivors?" Luke asked.

"We wanted to talk to you about that." Noah exchanged a glance with Max. "You know this ranch and the cattle better than anyone. This must have happened before."

"Yeah, but not like this in the last hundred years." Luke nodded. "I've already talked to Mom about worst-case scenarios and how to handle the aftermath."

"Then we'll work it out," Noah said. "Let's eat and talk it through afterward."

Jen went to take the quiche out of the oven, leaving a heavy silence behind her. She wished there were something more she could do, but nothing obvious came to mind. She cut up the quiche and brought it to the table with the plates and a side of pan-fried potatoes. The guys worked hard and needed to keep up their calorie intake.

They ate in silence, which was unusual. Luke pushed more food around his plate than went in his mouth. He'd already told Jen that the antibiotics made everything taste horrible, but she didn't think that was the only reason he'd lost his appetite. He finished first and pushed his plate away as his cell buzzed.

"Sorry to be that guy, but I need to take this call." Luke stood up. "It's Mom."

"Go ahead," Noah said. "We'll be here when you're done."

Max waited until Luke left the room before he sat back and scowled.

"That felt like kicking a man while he was down."

Noah shrugged. He and Max had already had this argument in the barn. "He deserves the truth. He's the boss."

"We could've waited until we had more accurate information." Max was obviously still in argumentative mode. "It's not like we can do much to make things better right now."

"How about we wait and see what Luke has to say before we rush to any conclusions?" Even as he talked to Max, Noah was aware of what Jen was doing in the background. He'd been avoiding her, which was difficult when they were all trapped in the same space.

She came to sit back at the table, her expression troubled. Her hair was bundled up on top of her head in a messy bun, and she wore at least two layers of clothing, including a sweater she'd borrowed from Luke.

"I know things look bad right now and you need all hands on deck, but if you can persuade Luke to stay inside at least until he's finished the course of antibiotics, I'd be really grateful."

"His mom's a doctor," Max said. "If he gives you any trouble, call Sally, and ask her to set him straight."

"*Is* there anything you can do?" Jen asked.

Noah shrugged. "Not much, but Luke might have some insight because of his familiarity with the land."

"Can you set up shelters for the cattle?"

Noah liked the way Jen looked for solutions rather than just giving up.

"That's something Max and I discussed. The problem is not having the manpower to get any structures built."

"Or person power," Max chipped in.

"I could help." Jen looked at them both. "If Luke stays in with Sky, I can come out with you guys and do my part."

"It's tough work," Noah reminded her.

"I've never been afraid of that." She didn't look away. "Sometimes we literally had to build our own clinic when we arrived in a disaster zone. I know how to construct shelters."

"Let's wait for Luke. He's the boss," Noah said.

"Sure." Jen gathered up the last few plates and took them through to the kitchen. "Whatever he needs."

Two hours later Noah cupped his gloved hands around his mouth, his breath condensing in the freezing cold, and shouted to Max and Jen, who were farther along the field.

"This one's ready to go!"

Jen waved a hand in response as she and Max worked in tandem to lash a tarp over the wooden poles Noah had hammered into the ground with the pole driver. They'd started at the far end of the field and worked their way back toward the ranch house constructing rudimentary shelters from wooden stakes and tarps that had been stashed in the barn.

Some of the cattle had already migrated into the extra

shelters, which pleased Noah greatly because he wouldn't have to attempt to drive them all in. Max had got one of the snowmobiles out to ferry supplies and had been gently persuading the cows to move in front of him.

Noah made sure the last post was secure and decided to start unfolding the tarp. The wind kept trying to catch it and drag it out of his grasp, and his language grew increasingly worse.

"I've got it!" Jen yelled from behind him as she grabbed the flapping corner and expertly tied it to the post. "I'll tie the left side on as well."

"Thanks," Noah shouted back and then went to join her, out of the wind. She was so well wrapped up he could only see a wisp of her curly hair, her bright eyes, and the tip of her nose, which had turned pink.

"Max said that if we're done, we should go in, and he'll finish up with the cattle," Jen said.

"Fine by me." Noah gathered up his tools and turned toward the barn. "I'll lead the way."

When they reached the solid structure of the barn, Noah set the tools down, took off his gloves, and reached behind Jen to shut the door, enclosing them in what felt like tropical heat after the frigid outdoors.

"Oh . . ." She pushed down the hood of her borrowed ski jacket and shuddered dramatically. "It's so warm."

Noah looked down at her, one hand still braced against the door behind her.

"You are fricking amazing."

She raised her head, her amused gaze steady, and that was it. He leaned in and took her mouth with a swiftness and urgency that defied everything logical. She made a soft sound and wrapped her arm around his neck, bringing them even closer. Her lips fused with his as the kiss grew deeper and more frantic with every second.

Her fingers unzipped his jacket and she snuck inside, her

arm now locked around his waist. He reciprocated, drawing her tight against his body, groaning as her breasts pressed against his chest. Without conscious thought he backed her up until they were inside the feedstore. He shut the door and hoisted her up onto the nearest horizontal surface, scattering bowls, scoops, and seed trays to the floor.

He pushed his thigh between her legs, and she let him in, her spread knees gripping his hips as he ground himself against her.

"Jen . . . ," he groaned. "I want—"

"Don't talk!" Jen gasped into his mouth. "Just . . . do."

He continued to kiss her, the rhythm of his tongue mimicking what the rest of his body wanted so desperately to do with her. She grabbed his wrist and placed his hand between her legs. He didn't need any more of an invitation and quickly unzipped her jeans and spread his callused fingers over her already wet panties.

She said his name and rolled her hips against his palm. He forgot about caution, about sense, about the future, and simply thrust two fingers deep into the core of her until she started to come around them, making him curse against the curve of her throat. He pressed his thumb against the swollen bud of her clit, and she came again. He held her tight until she finished shaking. His breathing was ragged and echoed the throb of his hard cock enclosed in the rigidity of his jeans.

She kissed her way gently up his throat and sighed into his mouth, which made him feel like thumping his chest and roaring. Her fingers toyed with the button of his jeans, and he instinctively sucked in his gut so she could slide her hand down lower.

A whistling sound, followed by the outside door banging, made him go still.

"Anyone here?" Max called out.

Jen buried her face in his shoulder as Noah made sure to reach out and quietly lock the feedstore door.

After what seemed like hours, Max left the barn, and Noah allowed himself to relax—except he couldn't, because he was currently pressed up against Jen, whose hand was still inches away from his rock-hard cock. Reality washed over him like a dump of snow down the back of his neck. He eased away so that he could see her face, which didn't help much when her lips were red from his kisses and her eyes held a satisfied, sensual glow.

"Should I apologize?" Noah asked.

Her smile dimmed. "Only if you think you did something wrong."

"I . . . took advantage of you."

She took her hands off him, sat up straight, and busied herself zipping up her jeans. "That's how you're going to play it?"

He frowned. "I'm not playing. I'm trying to make sure you were okay with what just happened and that I didn't overstep."

"What you're trying to do, Noah, is frame this in a way that lines up with all the bullshit you said before and gives you an out."

"Yeah?" He stepped back until they were a few feet away from each other and folded his arms. "Maybe you'd care to explain what that means, because I have no idea what the hell you're talking about."

She pushed a strand of hair behind her ear. "You want me to give you an out for what just happened so that you can go back to pretending there's nothing between us."

"That's not true," Noah said.

Jen raised her eyebrows. "You think you're so strong and in control that you couldn't possibly have done anything as stupid as kissing me again." She slid down off the table and looked up at him. "But, hey, I'll play it your way. You have nothing to worry about, Noah, you totally didn't offend me, and I'll pretend that nothing ever happened until the next time it does, okay?"

She pushed past him, wrestled with the door lock, and walked away, leaving Noah with the taste of her on his tongue, a raging hard-on, and the sense that if anyone had been outplayed, it was definitely him.

After nearly falling on her ass twice on the ice because she was trying to get away from Noah too fast, Jen forced herself to slow down and walk up to the house. Despite the lack of falling snow, the landscape remained uniformly white, with the added glitter of ice in unexpected places. It was like when soft caramel became shards of sugar— impressive but still deadly.

Jen took a deep shuddering breath as she took off her borrowed ski jacket, down-filled vest, thermal pants, and boots. If she could recognize that the chemistry between her and Noah was off the charts, why couldn't he? She already knew the answer; she'd just told him to his face. She didn't fit in with his spreadsheets and future plans, so he'd continue to put her down as an aberration and pretend nothing had happened. Which made her feel like what? A nuisance? She was sick and tired of being seen like that.

"Hey."

She looked up to see Max regarding her intently from the kitchen.

"Hi."

"I thought you were ahead of me."

Jen turned her back to hang up her various borrowed garments. Max had sharp eyes. Would he notice she'd just had two of the quickest and best orgasms in her life? Heather always said Jen's face gave everything away.

"Where's Noah?"

"I don't know." At least she could answer that truthfully.

For all she knew, he could've taken himself back out into the snow to cool off. "Is Luke okay with Sky?"

"I just heard them laughing about something when I went by, so I guess so." Max eyed her curiously as she walked past him. "Are *you* okay? You look a bit flushed."

"It's the heat after all that snow." Jen kept moving. "I need to relieve Luke."

"Give him an update on the shelters, will you?" Max called after her. "Saves me having to do it."

"Sure."

"I'll get the coffee on."

Jen escaped down the hallway and knocked on Luke's door. He was sitting up in bed with Sky on his right side, watching some kids' show on the TV.

"Hey." Luke smiled at her. "He's been great company."

Sky gave her a severe look as she sat next to him on the bed and pointed at the TV as if she was disrupting his viewing.

"We got all the shelters in the first field built, and the cows are moving in."

"That's great news." Luke hesitated. "Did it look bad out there?"

"It's hard for me to tell when everything's covered in snow."

She hadn't wanted to think about what the various lumps and bumps had concealed. She'd faced death in all its horror and didn't flinch from it, but it wasn't something she sought out or cared to speculate about.

"Fair enough. You okay?" Luke asked.

"I'm great, thanks."

"Did you hurt yourself or anything?"

"Nope." Jen found a smile. "Once I started working, I forgot how cold it was and just got on with it. Max and Noah were great."

"Teamwork. Who'd have thought it?"

"I'll take Sky," Jen said. "You must be ready for a nap."

"He was really good, but he does take some watching. If you're not paying attention, he's trying to fall off the bed, stuffing things in his mouth or up his nose, and generally bouncing off the walls."

"That's my boy." There was a protesting yell from Sky as Jen picked him up.

"He might have eaten too many chips," Luke confessed.

"You gave him chips?" Jen sighed and settled her son on her hip. "Better than the sweet stuff."

"Er . . . he might have had some of that, too."

Jen was still smiling as she walked into the kitchen and set Sky in his highchair. Max and Noah were both present, so she tried to pretend everything was fine.

"I told Luke we finished the first field." Jen offered Sky a hard chew that wasn't made for dogs, although if Sky let it fall to the floor, all bets were off. "He's really pleased."

"Thanks." Max brought her a mug of fresh coffee. "I'll get dinner tonight. We've a load of eggs that need using up, so I'm going to make a frittata."

"Awesome." Jen focused on Sky even as she was totally aware of Noah circling the kitchen like a shark. He was frowning, but what else was new? He wouldn't like being called out, and yet she knew in her bones that she was right.

"There's cake to finish up if you're hungry," Max offered.

"I'm good." Jen smiled at him.

Max nodded and looked between her and Noah. "I'm going to take a nap before I start cooking. Dinner will be around six."

"Great."

Max left, and there was an uncomfortable silence broken only by Sky babbling nonsense in Noah's direction.

"If you want to take a nap, I'll take Sky," Noah offered.

"I'm fine, thanks," Jen replied in a determinedly cheerful voice as if she wasn't addressing the man who'd made her come twice in less than two minutes. "You're the one who's been sick."

"You know I'm one hundred percent recovered."

She mopped Sky's chin and refused to look at Noah, who remained leaning up against the countertop, scowling at her. She wanted to ignore him but even now the sexual tension sizzled in the space between them. What would she have done if Max hadn't turned up? She hadn't wanted to stop.

"We should talk about what happened," Noah suggested.

"We did." She picked up Sky. "And we're done now."

"You talked."

"I don't get a say in this, Noah? I just have to accept your definition of everything and move on?" She shook her head. "I'm not that person."

"You didn't give me a chance to explain." He held up his hand as she went to speak. "You're doing the same thing again."

"Fine." Jen turned to face him. "Explain."

He let out his breath. "Nothing's changed. You're still a guest here, and I shouldn't have let myself kiss you."

"*Let* yourself? Like I had no part in it?"

"I started it."

Jen rolled her eyes. "Okay, great, yes you did. So what?"

"That's it. You need to understand my position."

"I understand you perfectly well." She held his gaze. "But I'm not the problem here."

"What exactly are you trying to say?" His brows came together. "Spell it out to me, Jen. I'm just a stupid guy."

"I think that a man who prides himself on being such a smart tactician would've worked out that he was deceiving himself and found an alternate solution." She headed toward the door, Sky on her hip. "Chew on that for a while and let me know what you're going to do about it."

* * *

Noah stood in the barn doorway and stared out over the whitewashed fields, sky, and hills. He couldn't decide if he wanted a thaw to set in immediately or for the current situation to stay exactly as it was.

If Jen could leave, would he want her to?

He grimaced. He could duck out of making any decisions, leave a decent interval, and go see her when she was settled in her new place. From the look of things, he didn't get to take the coward's way out—and when had he ever done that anyway? Having tasted her he wanted it all, her naked skin against his, her arms around him as they had the most incredible sex for hours.

But what did she want? She'd seemed to suggest that she wanted him, and that if he could get over himself, she'd be willing to consider some kind of relationship right now. But how would that even work? She had Sky to take care of, and he had Max and Luke constantly breathing down his neck. They might be on an isolated ranch, but they were still holed up in a house.

He let out a frustrated breath that immediately condensed into the freezing air. He was supposed to be a tactical expert. He'd used those skills to get out of many sticky situations in Afghanistan. Surely he could use them to get laid. His gaze settled on the two outbuildings across from the main barn that housed the snowmobiles and other ranch machinery that needed protecting from the weather. Now that the snowstorm had passed it was possible to move around the ranch if you took care on the ice.

If he focused on the practicalities maybe the rest of it would fall into place, because he sure as hell wasn't ready to deal with the emotional fallout yet. He closed the barn door and went back up to the house. Max was still napping, and Jen and Sky were nowhere to be seen. Noah continued down the hallway, knocked on Luke's door, and went in.

"Hey." Luke jumped a mile, and Noah held up his hand. "Sorry, I didn't realize you were sleeping."

"I'm not now." Luke rubbed his eyes and sat up against his pillows. "Sky wore me out."

"He's like a little tank," Noah said as he sat beside Luke's bed. His friend looked a lot better already. "Unstoppable and highly effective."

"True." Luke searched Noah's face. "What's up?"

Noah smoothed his hand over his bearded chin. "If I asked you to take care of Sky for a couple of hours tomorrow, would you help me out?"

"For what reason?"

Noah shrugged. "I need to talk to Jen alone."

"Talk?" Luke asked. "I didn't know you could talk for more than one minute, tops, Arkie. What are you going to say for the other one hundred and nineteen minutes?"

"That's the million-dollar question."

"I'm guessing talking wouldn't be high on your agenda anyway."

"That's what I'm trying to find out." Noah sighed. "I'm in unknown territory here, boss."

"That's not like you." Luke leaned back against his pillows; his expression amused. "But maybe we all need to be taken out of our comfort zone sometimes."

"I can't say I'm enjoying the experience," Noah grumbled. "I prefer to have everything under control and five additional exit plans on hand just in case."

"What *is* your exit plan?" Luke asked. "I mean, are you looking at a long-term relationship here, or some kind of 'there's only one bed in the snowstorm so of course we have to make out' kind of thing?"

"*What?*"

Luke grinned. "Sorry, I've been reading too many romance novels. Carry on."

"I don't know what I want or what I'm doing," Noah

confessed. "Jen challenged me to come up with some kind of alternate scenario to me lusting after her and then running away and behaving like an ass."

"Clever Jen."

"We already know she's way smarter than me," Noah confessed. "So I need to come up with a plan to present to her. There's no guarantee she'll listen or agree to anything I suggest, so don't get too excited."

"The fact that you're willing to try tells you something, doesn't it?" Luke asked. "If you didn't want her, you'd just stay away."

"I can't." Noah sighed. "She's gotten under my skin."

Luke considered him for a long moment. "Okay, I'll do it."

"That's awesome." Noah hesitated. "I don't want Max to know."

"I'm not lying to him."

"I wouldn't expect you to," Noah reassured his friend. "But if I give you a credible reason for taking Jen somewhere while you're keeping an eye on Sky, will you stick to that if Max asks?"

"Sure, but I'm not tackling him to the ground if he decides to go and find out for himself."

Noah gave a sharp nod. "Works for me. Thanks, boss."

Chapter Fifteen

"Wrap up warm, okay?" Noah advised Jen as he went past her toward Luke's room carrying the baby monitor. "I'll let Luke know we're leaving. He said he'd keep an ear out in case Sky wakes up before we're back."

Jen struggled into her borrowed coat. With this many layers she felt like a walking, talking sleeping bag. Although she and Sally were a similar size, Jen was much taller, which meant everything felt a little short. She wasn't quite sure why she'd agreed to Noah's request to talk to her, but she supposed she was stupid enough to still be hopeful that he'd worked something out.

She'd never been the kind of person who could jump in and out of bed with various people and enjoy the experience. Some of her friends were good at it because they knew what they wanted going in and didn't expect anything afterward. She always had *expectations*. Her short but spectacularly messy relationship with Dave had dented her confidence in her ability to choose wisely. Her attraction to Noah was way outside her comfort zone.

One thing she'd learned during her navy career was that sometimes you had to live in the moment and enjoy the *now* because things could come to an end far too quickly. She'd been so caught up in her visions for her future with Dave she'd forgotten to be aware in the present and had missed some huge red flags. Noah wasn't Dave, but she was determined not to allow him to take control of everything. She was hugely attracted to him, and when he wasn't being a pompous ass, she liked him as a person. She'd texted Heather the previous night, and her friend had urged her to take any opportunity Noah offered her and run with it. Despite the slow growth of her attraction for Noah, he was no Dave. He planned, he prepared, and if he really did want a relationship with her, she was confident he'd know how to handle the details.

"You ready to go?" Noah came back into the mudroom. He wore a thick red-flannel shirt and a down filled-vest and was pulling on a long western-style slicker that made him look like a gunslinger.

"Where are we going?" Jen asked warily.

"Out."

"Where exactly?"

He looked down at her. She remembered the last time he'd been that close—she'd been coming around his fingers—and her knees went weak with lust.

"I'm not planning on murdering you or anything." There was an answering glint of lust in his brown eyes as he nodded at her. "You'll work it out when we get there."

"Does Luke know?"

"Yeah, it's never good to wander off without telling someone where you're going, especially in weather like this." He opened the back door and peered outside. "It's not snowing, so take it slow on the ice and follow me."

"Yes, sir," Jen muttered as she followed him out into the cold, snapping breeze.

Unfortunately he had sharp ears. "Glad we've established the proper chain of command, Lieutenant."

When they cleared the barn, the wind whipped up, and she lowered her chin into the neck of her jacket. Noah reached back, took her gloved hand, and moderated his longer stride so they were walking together. He squeezed her fingers.

"Not far now."

There was a slight incline. Someone had already been out and salted a path up to a structure at the top of the rise. Jen allowed Noah to tow her up the hill and secretly enjoyed the experience, although she'd never admit that to his face. They reached the structure and he pushed open the wooden door and ushered her inside.

"Oh," Jen said. "This wasn't what I was expecting."

Her gaze swept over the four neatly parked snowmobiles and the rows of shelving filled with fuel, spare parts, and emergency supplies.

"Am I here to admire your organizational abilities? That wasn't quite what I was expecting but it's all very nice."

He was busy switching on lights and adjusting the heating before he turned to look at her.

"I thought you should learn how to operate one of these babies."

Jen raised her eyebrows. "You think I don't know how to do that?"

He stared at her for a long moment and then smiled. "You're amazing."

"You've mentioned that before." Jen took off her gloves and stuffed them in her pockets before wandering over to inspect the snowmobiles. "They're not up to military spec, but I suppose they'll do."

He followed her over, unzipping his coat as he walked. "When we get back to the house maybe you'd consider sparing my blushes and tell Luke and Max that I taught you everything you needed to know about how to drive a snowmobile."

"Why would I do that?"

He reached for her hand. "Because you're all about protecting my manly pride?"

Jen snorted. "You'll have to be far more persuasive than that."

He cupped her chin. "I guess I can give it a try."

Jen held up her finger as he attempted to close in. "Back off, dude."

He sighed and dropped a kiss on her forehead. "This place does have other things to explore."

"The place, or are we talking about you again?"

"Both maybe?" He raised his gaze upward. "There's a loft. We can get coffee."

"Okay, now you've got my interest."

She let him lead the way up the narrow, wooden staircase to a surprisingly large loft space. There was a basic kitchen setup, a couch, a small table, and, most importantly, a coffee machine stocked with pods.

"Luke's dad used to call this his man cave." Noah looked out of the window. "Sometimes if the house gets full, it's used as a spare room. That's a sofa bed."

"Nice." Jen tried the faucet and was pleased when water came out. "Is this good to drink?"

"It's from the well that feeds the main house, so, go for it."

"Do you want something?" Jen asked as she fiddled with the coffee machine.

"Maybe in a while." He turned to face her, his features cast in shadows and dark against the whiteness of snow outside the window behind him "I guess I have a few things to say first."

Jen retrieved her coffee, threw away the used pod, and took a seat at the small table under the window. Noah came to sit opposite her. For some reason she wasn't willing to make things easy for him, so she sipped her coffee and waited him out.

"I thought a lot about what you said to me the other day." Noah looked down at the table and traced an intricate pattern on the worn surface. "I guess the first thing we need to do is establish the parameters of our relationship."

"As in?"

"What's the goal here? Are we both on the same page? How do we logistically make it happen?"

Jen nodded. She was both impressed by his all-business attitude and finding it incredibly hot. "All good points."

He looked up at her. "So, tell me what you want."

"After you." She smiled sweetly, and he groaned.

"I knew you were going to say that." He sat back and slowly rubbed his hand over his mouth as he observed her. "Okay, this is how I see it: We're physically compatible, and I want to explore that option."

Jen noticed that he started with the least complicated part, which suited her fine.

"Agreed."

"Good. Now, let's move on to how we could make that happen without inconveniencing Sky or anyone else."

Jen shuddered. "We certainly can't do anything in the house. It would feel really icky on so many levels."

It was Noah's turn to nod. "With this place being so close, we could plan to get away occasionally when Sky is taking a nap or is down for the night."

"Only if someone is listening in on the baby monitor," Jen added.

"Sure. We can even bring one with us. It's a five-minute run downhill to the house. Or Luke might be willing to help out while he's stuck indoors."

Jen considered him. "You told Luke?"

"I asked for his help. He's the one listening out for Sky right now."

"What did he think of all this?" Jen made a vague gesture

at the loft space. She liked and respected Luke. If he wasn't okay about anything, she wouldn't feel comfortable.

"About us getting together? Let's just say he wasn't surprised."

"What about Max?"

For the first time, Noah looked away from her. "I'll handle Max."

"He's not stupid, Noah. He'll work out what's going on in a nanosecond. You need to make sure he's onboard. Remember, I'll be leaving at some point, and you'll still have to live with Max. And he's one of your best friends."

"Noted," Noah said. "Now we get to the tricky part. What are we doing here, Jen? Is it just sex, or—"

"Maybe it should just be about sex for now," Jen hastily interrupted him. She didn't want to get onto the topic of Dave, or her expectations, or anything complicated, or she might lose her nerve. "I doubt either of us are in a position to want more."

"But is that okay with you?" He sat back again and looked at her.

"You don't think I do this all the time?" Jen countered.

"No." He hesitated. "I've had all kinds of relationships in my life, Jen. Some of them were one-night stands where both parties knew exactly what they wanted. We waved goodbye with no regrets the next morning, or sometimes even the same night."

"Okay." She didn't really like to think about him with other women.

"It's okay if you're not hurting anyone." He locked gazes with her. "But I guess I'd hate to hurt you."

"Because you think I'm too stupid or naïve to understand what you're offering me?"

He grimaced. "No, because I like you as a friend. I've been practically living with you for a month. This is uncharted territory for me. Maybe I'm afraid we'd hurt each other."

Something inside Jen turned slowly to mush at his thoughtful tone. She took a deep breath. "I like you, too."

"Then we go into this not expecting any explanations or relationship stuff from the other person. We keep it about sex. And we need to agree that if either of us wants out for whatever reason, we let them go, no questions asked and no recriminations. Okay?"

"I can do that," Jen agreed. Even if the weather continued to be bad for another week, she'd be gone before there was any chance of her developing serious feelings for Noah. For the first time in her life, she really wanted to just have sex with someone without any repercussions. "I mean the snow isn't going to last forever."

"Yeah, there's a natural separation point coming up, which gives us both an out."

He looked very serious, which she appreciated.

"Okay, then."

"You're in? he asked.

She held out her hand and he shook it. "As long as you square things with Max, I'm good."

Noah slowly let out his breath and stared at Jen, who had gone back to sipping her coffee as if she didn't have a care in the world. He surreptitiously checked the time, but she caught him looking.

"You were thinking of starting right now?" Jen blinked at him.

He shrugged. "I'm the kind of man who likes to make the best of his opportunities." He patted his shirt pocket. "I've got protection right here, Sky's still asleep, and Luke's okay to keep him for another hour or so regardless."

"Can I finish my coffee first?"

"You can finish your coffee and tell me to take a hike if that works better for you. This is supposed to be mutual."

He waited for things to feel awkward, but Jen started chuckling, and the next minute he was smiling back at her like a fool.

"This is so stupid." She took off her coat and hung it over the back of her chair. "But can we start with some kissing and see how we feel?"

Noah stood and offered her his hand. "You wanna make out on the couch? I can go for that."

He didn't care what she asked for. He was willing to give her anything she desired. He drew her down beside him on the upholstered couch and waited for her to get comfortable, which involved kicking off her boots and removing her thermal vest. As far as he was concerned, the more clothes she shed the better.

"Okay?" He put his arm around her, and she curled up against his side.

"This is . . . nice."

He kissed the top of her head. "Nice wasn't quite what I was aiming for, but I guess it's a start."

Her fingers moved along his bearded jawline, and he shuddered under her touch. Two minutes in and he was hard and ready for anything. She made a purring sound and he looked down at her. Her thumb teased at his lower lip, and he growled and lowered his mouth to meet hers. She tasted like coffee and mint as his tongue parted her lips, and he groaned. Man, he'd never been so turned on in his life.

She kissed with a straightforwardness and strength that made him want to meet her halfway and prove worthy of her. She was strong, too, her hands gripping his shoulders, her nails digging into the back of his neck while he nuzzled and bit at her throat. She arched against him and drew one knee up over his lap so that she was almost sitting on top of him.

He wrapped his arm around her hips and anchored her firmly against his body, the seam of her jeans right over his bulging zipper.

"Oh, God," she breathed into his mouth. "You feel . . . amazing."

"I thought we were taking this slow?"

"Oh—" She eased back, her hands on his shoulders, her brown eyes contrite. "You're right. Should I—?"

"Hell, no." He shoved his fingers into her hair and hauled her back against him, rocking his hips into the rhythm of his thrusting tongue until she was moving with him.

"I need to see you." She attacked the buttons of his down-filled vest and shirt.

"You've seen it all before," he reminded her as he helped. "When I was sick."

"You've no idea how much I wanted to touch you back then," she confessed as she planted a kiss on his exposed collarbone.

"Not half as much as I wanted to touch you." He decided to help her remove her fleece sweater and was immediately confronted by a long-sleeved T-shirt. "This is exhausting. We should try for less clothes next time."

"And freeze to death?"

"I'll warm you up, don't worry about that." He finally got to skin level and stared at her sports bra, which looked tricky. He pressed his lips against the hollow above her collarbone, and she shivered. She tasted like lavender soap and his shower gel, which made sense as they currently shared a bathroom. He slid his fingers around to her back looking for the fastening and found nothing to get hold of.

"Noah . . ."

"Mmm?" He cupped her breast, his mind already focused on the sight of her pebbled nipple.

"It goes over my head. I didn't dress for seduction today."

"You didn't need to. Haven't you worked that out yet?" He leaned in, gently set his teeth over the stretchy cotton, and sucked her nipple into his mouth. The way she bucked against him set his cock throbbing even more as he fondled her other breast.

"Let me . . ." She struggled against him until he realized she was trying to get out of her bra. "It's not easy."

She'd barely removed the garment and thrown it onto the pile on the floor before he was on her like a starving man, his hands, fingers, and mouth all plundering her rounded breasts. She writhed against him, and he flipped her onto her back and crouched over her, his knees now on the floor, his hands busy with her jeans and panties, his patience gone as her flesh called out to him.

"Jeez . . ." He pushed his shoulders between her thighs and kissed her stomach and the dark curls surrounding her sex. "You're soaking wet for me."

"Duh," she gasped. "Then stop talking and do something about it."

"Maybe I'll take my time," he murmured as he lightly licked the already swollen bud of her clit. "Play with you a little, make you beg for it."

"Oh God."

He smiled as he slid one finger inside her and launched a dual assault, tonguing her clit as he thrust in and out. She came almost immediately, her fingers twisting in his hair to hold him exactly where she wanted him. Not that he planned on going anywhere for a considerable amount of time. Learning what she liked, tasting her pleasure, was like a drug, and he just wanted to give her more.

He added another finger and eased back so he could watch her face as he pleasured her. Her eyes were closed, and she was frowning, which made him want to smile.

"Hey."

She opened one eye.

"What?"

"Look at me."

"It's too much." She gave a shaky breath. "I need to concentrate."

He grazed his thumb nail over her clit and pressed a third finger inside her. "Does that help?"

She grabbed hold of his wrist and climaxed again with a shuddering moan that almost made Noah come in his jeans. Her eyes flew open.

"Take off your pants."

He raised an eyebrow as he continued to finger her. "Why would I want to do that when I'm enjoying this so much?"

She scowled at him. "You don't want me to touch you back?"

"One touch from you right now and I'd go off like a teenager."

"Good." She tried to sit up. "Get them off. I want to see that."

He shrugged and set his hand on the top button of his jeans. It was a fight to take down his zipper when his cock was so hard, but he managed it somehow. He pushed down his black boxers along with his jeans and tossed everything to the floor. Jen sat up, her face flushed as he slicked the hand he'd used on her over his shaft.

Even at that light contact, he swallowed hard, "I wasn't kidding about coming."

She folded her arms under her breasts and stared at him. "Then do it."

"You want me to come for you?"

"Oh, yes."

"I might need some encouragement." He nodded at her breasts. "Touch yourself while you watch me."

"Sounds fair." She cupped her breasts and rubbed her nipples between her fingers and thumbs. "Like this?"

"Hell, yeah," Noah breathed as he wrapped one hand around his cock. "That's inspiring."

It didn't take more than a couple of hard yanks before he

was coming, his gaze fixed on Jen's breasts as he groaned and bucked his hips. He was still recovering as she leapt off the couch and brought him over a wad of tissues.

"That was glorious."

"Yeah?" He slid his hand around the back of her neck and kissed her. "You wait until we get onto the main course." He paused. "If that's what you want."

Was that what she wanted?

Jen kissed Noah back, her body aligning itself with his muscled torso, her breasts squished up against his chest, obscuring the large tattoo of some majestic bird. His cock was already stirring to life again against her stomach, and she rocked into him. She was so turned on she wanted him, like, that second.

"Do we have time?"

Noah glanced down at his watch. "Not for everything I want to do with you, but we could make a start."

"I'm good for that, as long as I get to be on top."

He bit her neck. "You think that will put me off? Watching you ride me, your breasts right there for my hands and mouth, and your clit waiting to be rubbed as hard as you want it?"

Jen sighed. God, he was an excellent filthy talker and had the biggest physical attributes she'd ever gotten close to. He was tall and strong enough to match her, and yet made her feel soft and feminine at the same time.

He also took direction really well. She pushed gently on his chest until he got the message and lay back against the couch.

"My turn," she said firmly. "Stay there, don't move, and do not touch."

He sighed, placed one hand on the back of his neck and bent his left knee at an angle so she could kneel between his thighs. She kissed him for long magical minutes, drowning in his taste and textures as she grasped his broad shoulders.

He hummed his appreciation against her mouth, making her body throb with anticipation.

She sat back to trace the lines of his tattoo, noting the nicks and scars of warfare along the way, and stopping to kiss each one. He muttered something under his breath as she circled his nipples and licked them with the tip of her tongue.

"Something you wanted?" she asked sweetly even as his cock prodded her stomach.

He shook his head and she smiled into his eyes as she kissed her way down over his spectacular abs. His hips rocked forward. She stuck out her tongue to lick the wetness away from the crown of his cock as her hands pressed his thighs wide.

He gave a guttural groan when she carefully sucked the first two inches of his impressively thick and long cock into her mouth. She took a moment to look up and hold his gaze as she cupped his balls.

"Please . . ." he said hoarsely.

If she hadn't wanted to see if she really could take his whole length into her mouth, she might have played with him for longer, but she was on a deadline. She humored him allowing her jaw and throat to relax as he filled her mouth and beyond. The thought of what he could do with his impressive length inside her made her shake with need. She sucked gently on him, aware that he was trying not to rock into her and cram himself right down her throat. She appreciated that caution, but the thought of him doing it was hot as hell.

She released his shaft, her teeth grazing his skin, making his breath hitch, and looked into his eyes.

"You have a condom?" He pointed at his shirt and went to move. Jen pushed him back. "I'll get it."

She extracted one of the foil packets from the box, carefully opened it, trying not to think of the Dave fiasco, and rolled the condom over Noah's shaft. He reached a hand down as if checking she'd done it right and slightly readjusted his position.

"Permission to board when you're ready, princess. I'm good to go."

"Princess?" Jen looked at him.

"You prefer, sir?"

"Goddess will do." She straddled his hips, her breathing fast as she contemplated his oh-so-willing flesh. He helped by easing his cock away from his stomach and offering it up to her like a willing and pleasurable sacrifice. "Noah . . ."

"Yeah?" his voice sounded strained. "You wanna stop? That's okay, we—"

He stopped speaking as she slid down over him, her body adjusting to his size with a willingness she appreciated, and the sharp sudden shock of a climax before she'd even finished.

"Shit . . ." Noah grabbed for her hips. "That's . . ."

She paused to enjoy the immense wave of clenching pleasure his cock had just given her, her breathing uneven, her breasts hanging so close to his face that he almost had no alternative but to kiss and suck them into his mouth, which set off another climax. He pressed down on her hips, seating her right over him, and thumbed her clit, making the already spectacular climax go on forever.

When she finally stopped shuddering, she raised her head to see that Noah had his head back against the couch. His eyes were closed, and he was breathing through his nose. She tried a small experimental pulse of her inner muscles and he groaned.

"You're killing me here."

"You want to come again already?"

He met her challenging gaze. "Not until you give me the okay."

"I think," Jen said, "that if this gets any better, I might explode with lust, and I'd like to live long enough to try again."

He reached out and ran his finger along her lips. "Yeah, you beneath me, your heels on my shoulders while I screw you hard into the bed and you scream my name."

Her body liked that idea. "Or behind me."

He groaned as she started moving on him again. "Or up against a wall, or . . ."

She climaxed and with a ragged cry he joined her, his hands like iron bars at her waist as he held her over his pulsing cock, and she milked every drop of come out of him. She fell forward and was met by the comfort of his arms and a soft place on his shoulder to settle into.

Eventually, he smoothed a hand over her hair. "You okay?"

She nodded. "It was just more . . . everything than I expected."

Dammit, she'd promised not to get emotional. She moved off him, suddenly clumsy. It was just about the sex, which had been spectacular, so there was no point in talking it through or getting all mushy with him. They'd already agreed they wouldn't go there. "I don't suppose this place has a shower? I should have asked that upfront."

"It does, through there." Noah pointed to a door at the rear of the room, his voice careful "Water should be hot, so go ahead. It's a one-person bathroom."

"I'll be as quick as I can." She gathered up her clothes and made a run for it.

"Jen . . ."

She barely made it through the door and turned the shower on before she started bawling in earnest. There was a small mirror above the sink. She stared at her well-kissed lips, bed hair, and satiated expression. Noah Harding was one hell of a lover.

But they'd agreed it was just about the sex. She couldn't let him see it had been an emotional experience for her too, let alone expect him to listen while she tried to explain. She took a deep, steadying breath. All she had to do was deal with the unexpected "feels," concentrate on the physical, and show him her best smiling face when she emerged from the bathroom.

Noah stared at the closed bathroom door and then slowly got off the couch and gathered his clothes together. One of Jen's socks was caught up with one of his, and he set it carefully to one side. His body was purring like a fine-tuned engine, and he kept wanting to smile, which wasn't like him at all. He and Jen just fitted together. It was as simple and as complicated as that.

His emerging smile died a sudden death. Was that why Jen had rushed off so fast? She'd said something about it being more than she'd expected. Was it too much? He didn't want to complicate things either. Maybe his initial instinct to wait and follow up with her when she was stateside and settled had been the better idea all along. Except he didn't want it to go that long before he got to touch her again.

"Man, you're screwed," he muttered to himself. "Make up your goddamn mind."

Jen emerged from the bathroom just as he was checking the time again. If he was a betting man, he'd say she'd been crying. His stomach plummeted.

"Was I that bad?"

"No! Not at all, it was all wonderful!" She smiled like she didn't have a care in the world. "Did you start to worry because I was so long in the bathroom?"

"Nah, we're good." He smiled back like they'd just been

drinking coffee together rather than having amazing sex. They'd agreed to keep things simple. "I'll take the quickest shower of my life and we can get back to the house, okay?"

"No worries." She pointed at the couch. "Oh, there's my sock! I was wondering where it had gotten to."

Noah headed for the bathroom. If she wanted to talk about what had happened between them, he was surprisingly willing to have that conversation. But if she didn't? He was good with that as well. After all, wasn't that what he'd said he wanted? Sex and no complications?

Chapter Sixteen

"What's going on with you and Jen?" Max asked as Noah joined him in the barn after dinner the next day to settle the horses for the night.

Noah set down his rake. "I was just going to talk to you about that."

"You obviously overcame your scruples and decided to get it on with her." Max went into one of the stalls with a bucket of water. "It's hardly surprising. You've been panting after her for weeks."

"She's only here until the thaw sets in, and then she'll be leaving."

"So, you decided to get in there while you could?"

"It's not like that." Noah scowled. "You make it sound as if—"

"You calculated the odds, did one of your spreadsheets, and figured she couldn't get close to you in such a short length of time, so everything was good to go?" Max shook his head. "I hope Jen knows what she's dealing with here."

"You think we didn't talk it out first?"

"Oh, I bet you talked. But did Jen?"

"Hell, yeah. She was the one who made me lay it all out."

"And she agreed she was happy to be dumped when she moves out?"

"She *agreed* that we like each other, and that we're adults who can make informed decisions about what we need," Noah said evenly. "The rest of what we discussed is private. Stop trying to make me out to be some kind of asshole."

"I don't need to make you look like anything, Arkie. You manage that all by yourself." Max slammed the stall door shut and pushed past Noah. "I just hope Jen's okay after you dump her."

"I'm not planning"—Noah realized he was talking to himself as Max disappeared out of the barn, leaving all the chores behind—"on dumping anyone."

Just sitting across the table at dinner watching Jen deal with Sky, applaud Luke for making it to the kitchen, and joking with Max had made him realize something important: It wasn't just about the sex. There was a real possibility he'd found something special with Jen Rossi. But the last thing he wanted was to blow up their current agreement and scare her off. He was too terrified to verbalize his revelation to anyone, in case he screwed up or, worse, completely misunderstood what Jen wanted and overreached.

He was a planner and rushing into stuff wasn't his thing. He needed time to consider his options. But being honest with himself was also important. He'd learned young that if you pretended shit like your dad would suddenly come home, you'd be bound for disappointment when he turned up with a new wife in tow. Facing the tough stuff had saved him and his whole teams' lives in combat, and he wouldn't lie to himself.

Jen had agreed that their relationship was just about sex, and unless she changed her mind, Noah had no business trying to change it for her. Once she was settled, he'd have plenty of time to revisit their agreement and see if she'd be willing for more.

He finished his chores and walked slowly back to the house. The sky was a clear black, dotted with stars, and the wind had finally died down. The severe frost was still holding, but the weekly forecast indicated that the temperatures might be on their way up.

In a week or so Jen and Sky would probably be gone. He could wait that long.

He went into the house and took off his boots and heavy coat before heading to the kitchen. Luke was still sitting at the table, but there was no sign of Jen and Sky.

"I made a fresh pot of coffee," Luke said. "And then I had to sit down again because I'm as weak as a pint of skimmed milk. Don't tell Jen."

"I won't." Noah helped himself to coffee and came to sit opposite Luke. "At least you're vertical."

"Not for long." Luke sighed. "I want my warm bed right now."

"Do you need a hand getting back there?" Noah offered. "I'd like a word with you and I'd rather it be in private."

"Sure." Luke rose to his feet and kept one hand on the back of his chair. "How about you bring the coffee, and if I end up on my ass you help me back up?"

"As long as you're okay if I save the coffee first, I'm good with that." Noah picked up Luke's mug along with his own and followed his friend's slow progress back to his bedroom. "Where is Jen by the way?"

"Giving Sky a bath."

"Lucky kid." Noah held open the door for Luke, set the coffee mugs down, and went to close the drapes. "Do you need tucking in?"

"I can manage that part myself." Luke climbed into bed and flopped back on the pillows with a groan. "That's better."

"How's your arm doing?"

"It's getting there. Dr. Carlo says he'll come and check me over if it thaws and Mom's not yet back."

"Good to know." Noah sipped his coffee and considered what to say.

"Is this about you and Jen?" Luke asked. "Because it's pretty obvious from your goofy expression that you're getting laid."

"We came to an agreement about some stuff," Noah agreed. "But I wanted to touch base with you about something else."

"Okay."

"Has Jen said anything to you about her future plans?"

Luke frowned. "Why are you asking me and not the source?"

"Because we agreed not to get into specifics right now."

"But being a forward planner, you still want to know." Luke picked up his coffee mug. "Dave's mom offered her apartment in San Jose rent free for six months while Jen works out what she's going to do next."

"San Jose?" Noah nodded. "That's . . . doable."

Luke hesitated. "I got the impression Jen loves her current job and that she was hoping to stay in San Diego, but Dave's lack of interest in parenting full time during the months she's away means she'll have to let it go."

"That sucks."

"Yeah. Dave's never going to be reliable, and she wants to do what's best for Sky."

"She would." Noah contemplated Luke's words. "Thanks for telling me. It helps."

"That's all I know." Luke shrugged and then winced. "You'll have to ask Jen for the rest of it."

"I think I'll wait until she tells me herself," Noah said. "I'm trying not to frighten her off."

"If you haven't scared her off yet, I think you're good,

Arkie." Luke grinned. "I mean, she forgave you for pointing a gun at her and thinking she was a freeloading loser."

"True," Noah acknowledged. "I haven't exactly covered myself in glory, have I?" He set his mug down. "I don't want to hurt her."

"Damn straight, because you'll have to answer to me, Max, and probably my mom if you do."

"I'll leave you in peace." Noah stood up. "Max didn't take it well, and he's pissed at me, by the way."

"Figures." Luke yawned. "If you could keep your pants on around the house, I'd sure appreciate it."

"Absolutely." Noah gave him a salute. "We'll respect your privacy and your home."

Noah walked back down the hallway to the kitchen and found Jen holding Sky, who was wrapped in a huge bath towel. She was humming something as she expertly prepared his bedtime milk with one hand. He stopped before she noticed him and just appreciated the sight of mother and child like the dork he was obviously becoming.

She did a little twirl to make Sky squeal and caught sight of him, her smile so warm he wanted to wrap himself up in it.

"Hey! Want some warm milk?"

"I think I'll sleep just fine tonight." He advanced toward them. "Can I hold the little scamp?"

"Be my guest."

Noah inhaled the sweet smell of cherry bubbles coming off Sky's hair. "I wish he smelled like this all the time."

"Me, too." Jen made herself some hot chocolate. "Usually, he reminds me of the dogs."

Noah winked at Sky, who was patting his beard. "Makes sense when they chew the same bones, and he licks their faces back."

Jen shuddered. "Did I tell you I caught him eating their kibble the other day?"

"I hear pet food is made to higher standards than people food so I'm sure he's okay." Noah walked Sky through to the family room, where Jen had laid the baby clothes out to warm in front of the fire. "I'll keep an eye out for him barking and cocking his leg though."

Jen was still laughing as she joined him on the rug in front of the fire, where he'd started on Sky's diaper. He was pleased to see she was her usual self, which meant that his decision not to get into anything with her had been a good one.

"It's his birthday on Friday."

"The big number one, buddy." Noah tickled Sky's tummy. "What do you want on your cake?"

"Probably a horse," Jen said. "He likes nothing better than being taken down to the barn to pet them." She handed Noah a onesie, which he put on Sky, who was already trying to wriggle away. "Do you reckon we'll be able to travel by then?"

Noah thought fast. "Even if you're good to go, would you consider staying here to celebrate with us? It would be a great way to end your stay. I know Max and Luke would agree with me."

For the first time she looked uncertain. "Can I think about it?"

"Sure." Noah kept his tone light. "Just give us time to get started on frosting that cake."

As Sky tried to make a run for it, Noah scooped him up, making sure all the fastenings on his clothing were aligned before handing him over to Jen.

"Bedtime?"

She glanced over at the old clock above the fire. "Yup. Although, he doesn't look very sleepy." She rose to her feet. "I'll be back in a minute, okay?"

"Cool."

He went to sit on the couch and found the remote. There

wasn't anything he particularly wanted to watch, but at least the service had been resumed. Jen came back in carrying the baby monitor, which she set on the coffee table beside her seat.

"Sky's definitely teething. Max gave him some kind of leather strap to chew this morning, and he's almost gnawed his way through it already."

"Max did?" Noah risked putting his arm along the back of the couch as Jen sat next to him.

"Max hasn't been near me since then." Jen hesitated. "Did you talk to him?"

"Yeah. He's fine with it." Noah chose his words carefully. "And when I say fine, I mean he bawled me out, but that's just Max."

"What was he worried about?"

"Me being as ass."

"Understandable." She nodded, her expression serious. "I mean, you are really good at that."

He frowned down at her until she was finally betrayed into a smile.

"Just kidding."

He leaned in until his nose was touching hers. "I'm going to enjoy making you pay for that."

"Such a big man with his big threats." Jen rolled her eyes. "When we both know you'll be begging like a baby next time I'm—"

He kissed her and she kissed him back, and this time it was like welcoming an old friend, which somehow made it even better. He was really getting into it when the baby monitor came to life and Sky started wailing.

Jen gently disengaged herself from his arms. "Duty calls."

"We both know all about that."

He watched her leave and settled back on the couch, his

attention on his phone where his sister Bailey had left him a text message.

CALL ME

He sighed and made the call.

"Hey, what's up?"

"I'm moving in with Maya and Cameron."

"The triple threat," Noah muttered. "That's good, right?"

"We've found this great new apartment."

"And?" Noah knew what was coming.

"We need a character reference, so we thought of you."

"You don't need me to cosign the lease?"

"No! Gosh, Noah we are fully capable adults who earn enough and have good credit histories these days."

"Glad to hear it." Secretly Noah was hella proud of them, but he wasn't going to let on just yet. Having all three of them gainfully employed was amazing enough. He almost felt like a proud parent. "I'd be happy to do that for you."

"Good, because we already gave them your name and number. You should hear from them fairly soon."

"You guys okay with the deposit?"

"Yes, we've got this. If all goes well, we'll be in by the end of the month."

"If the snow clears, I'll come down and help you move."

"That would be awesome, especially if you can bring Max and Luke for extra hot muscle."

"Someone's got to stay here and run the place."

Bailey sighed. "True. Maybe you could stay and send them?"

"Not happening. How are you doing otherwise?" Noah asked. "Has Will left for New York yet?"

"Yeah, he left yesterday. He came to say goodbye and said that if I change my mind to let him know."

"That was . . . nice of him."

"He really meant it. We're trying to be mature, but it's still hard."

Noah hated the hint of tears in her voice. "I bet, but you're a strong woman, Sis. You've got this."

"We'll see how it goes. How are things with you?"

"Good. Still stuck in the snow, but there are signs it might be thawing soon."

"You've still got Jen and that baby there?"

"Yup. She's been great. Luke took a tumble off his horse, and she fixed his broken arm right here in the house."

"Sounds like a good person to have around if Sally's not there."

"True." Noah glanced up to see Jen coming back into the room. "Anything else I need to know about right now, because otherwise, I have to go."

"No, we're good. Love you, Bro."

"Right back at you. Don't forget to send me your new address."

He ended the call and looked up at Jen, who was hovering in the doorway.

"Is Sky okay?"

"I managed to settle him back down again." She pointed at his cell phone. "I didn't mean to interrupt your call."

"That was my sister Bailey, checking in. She's moving into a new place with the twins and used me as a character reference. No idea why."

"Because you're a good man?" Jen came to sit on the couch beside him.

"To be honest, I thought they'd need help with the finances, but she assured me they were all square—which is a first."

"What do they all do?" She leaned against his side, and he put his arm around her.

"Bailey works as a paralegal, and she's studying for her

law degree on the side; Cameron's a veterinary technician; and Maya does some kind of software coding."

"Does your mom live there, too?"

"No, she stayed in LA and married a nice guy named Sid. They spend the majority of their lives traveling the world on cruise ships." He smiled. "The girls turned up in San Diego after I enlisted, and I made a home for us all there."

"How nice to have that to come back to," Jen said.

Noah thought about that for the first time in a while. "It was."

"I never really had a home base," Jen continued. "My family wasn't together, and I didn't really build the kind of relationships with my foster families that meant I was welcome to visit after I turned eighteen." She paused. "Except for Auntie Brenda, who was awesome."

"The one who brought you up here for summer camp?"

"Yes," she smiled. "It's a small world, isn't it? If I hadn't mentioned her to Dave, I'd probably never have ended up here again."

"I guess we should thank Dave's weird logic then." Noah said as he dropped a kiss on the top of Jen's head and risked another question. "Have you heard from him recently?"

"Nope, complete radio silence, but that's Dave for you." She sighed. "I'm already trying to think of ways to prepare Sky to be let down by his father. I know how it feels."

"You and me both," Noah agreed. "My dad walked out on us, rarely paid child support so my mom had to work three jobs, and turned up two years later with a new twenty-year-old wife who 'didn't like children.' In the end I was glad he didn't want to see us."

"But it still hurts."

He hugged her hard. "Yeah, it does."

The baby monitor came to life again, and Jen groaned.

"It's going to be one of those nights." She got off the couch, picked up the monitor, and looked down at Noah.

"It's probably better if I stay in the room with him, so I'll call it a night."

He blew her a kiss. "Thanks for yesterday."

She blushed. "No, thank *you*."

"We should do that again, soon."

"I'd like that."

"I'll check my schedule and get back to you."

She laughed and walked out of the room, leaving him with a smile on his face and a renewed appreciation for the love his sisters and mother had always surrounded him with. Jen hadn't had that, and Dave seemed ready to repeat that absent parent crap with Sky. He knew that wouldn't sit easily with Jen and that she'd blame herself. One thing he'd learned over the years was to place blame where it was deserved, and that was directly on Dave.

No one was perfect. In a crisis, people behaved in all kinds of unexpected ways. Dave had risked his life to save Luke, but he'd never been interested in long-term issues like having a military career or, apparently, raising a child. Why Jen had been so taken in by Dave remained a mystery to Noah—one he was unwilling to explore. She hadn't said much about her father, and he wasn't going to ask. The closer they got, the more it felt like a real relationship, and that wasn't what they'd negotiated.

Noah checked the time, turned on the TV, and found a military movie to scoff at. It was one of his and Max's favorite ways to unwind. He hadn't seen Max since their discussion in the barn, and he hoped his friend wouldn't go AWOL again. Even as he had the thought, he heard Max come into the mudroom.

"Hey." He gestured at the screen as Max went past the door. "Want to watch a war movie?"

Max paused to look at him and then at the screen.

"What the hell are they doing out in the open like that

during a fire battle" He joined Noah on the couch. "What kind of military do they get to advise them on these movies?"

"Veterans of the war of 1776?" Noah suggested.

"Might as well be." Max pointed at the screen again. "And what kind of weapon setup is that?"

Noah settled in for a good evening, glad that Max was still speaking to him and that everything was okay with Jen. Life could be worse, and for once he was going to allow himself to enjoy the moment and not obsess about all the things that could, and would, go wrong tomorrow

Chapter Seventeen

"Noah?"

Jen peered through the gloom at the entrance to the barn. It was late by her standards, but when Max had come in, he'd said Noah needed her help. He'd offered to keep an ear out for Sky, who was already in bed, and sent her on her way with a smile.

"Down here."

She sighed. She still couldn't see him. Using her cell as a flashlight, she made her way down the center of the barn, avoiding the drainage channels and the flattened mounds of horse manure. There was the occasional whinny or movement from the stalls, and the cheep of birds up in the rafters, but the overwhelming sound was the nothingness of the middle of nowhere, which she appreciated. How she was going to deal with San Jose after this much needed solitude was something she tried not to think about.

"Hey," Noah whispered from somewhere around knee height. "I'm in the feedstore to your left."

"Why are we in the dark?" Jen whispered back. "And what are you doing on the floor?"

His hand appeared out of the gloom, and she grabbed hold of it and allowed him to gently maneuver her into the space, where she joined him crouched on the floor.

"What?" Jen slowly closed her mouth as she realized what she was looking at. "Oh."

"I found them when I came in to lock up." Noah spoke so close to her ear his beard brushed against her skin. "There are four of them so far, plus the momma cat. I thought you might offer a professional opinion as to whether there are any more babies to come."

Jen leaned in to scrutinize the small, female tabby cat who was energetically washing her new offspring.

"She doesn't look like she's preparing to have any more, but I'm happy to keep an eye on her." She sat down properly on the floor, her back to the shelving, and turned off her phone. Now that her eyes had adjusted there was enough moonlight streaming through the window and the open door to see relatively clearly. "It's not the first time I've done this, you know."

"Really?" Noah sat beside her, his broad shoulder wedged against hers.

"Guinea pigs, goats, dogs, calves, pigs . . ." Jen counted them off on her fingers. "I think I'd be okay to birth a cow if you need any help with that."

"Not at this time of year." He nodded at the kitty. "Not a great time for her to be producing young, either, but we can always do with more barn cats. At least we can keep an eye on them for her."

"Just don't let Sky near them," Jen advised. "He'd love them *way* too much."

"Or he'd end up with a scratched face."

"I don't want either of those things to happen," Jen said firmly.

"Fair enough."

With the warmth emanating from Noah's large body, Jen almost forgot how cold it was. He put one arm around her shoulders while he used his phone with his other hand.

"Who are you texting?" Jen asked.

"Max, to tell him we're on kitten watch for the next hour or so."

"He already said he'd listen out for Sky."

"Good man." Noah finished texting and put his cell away in his pocket. "This floor is hard. You'd be way more comfortable in my lap."

Jen looked up at him. "What about you?"

His quick smile was way too sensual. "I'll survive if I've got your sweet little ass snuggled up against my favorite parts."

"You wouldn't find it . . . constricting?"

He shrugged. "I'm kind of getting used to feeling like that these days."

She climbed into his lap so that she was facing him and unbuttoned her jacket and then his. "I make you . . . hot?"

"You know what you do to me."

She pretended to pout, which was so not like her. "I'm not sure I understand."

He took hold of her hand and placed it right over the zipper of his jeans. "Feel that?"

"Hmm . . . there's definitely *something* there." She stroked him through the harsh fabric until he cursed under his breath. "Something hard."

"And wet." He covered her mouth with his own and thrust his tongue deep. "And ready and willing if you want to ride me again."

Jen gave an experimental roll of her hips and realized she was not only willing, but ready herself.

"I spent way too long in the shower this morning getting myself off because the moment I smelled the shower gel I thought of you and got hard." Noah kissed her throat, her neck, and unbuttoned her shirt so he could get his hands on her. "I remembered what it felt like when you watched me come."

Jen sighed against his beard. He really was excellent at talking dirty.

"It was something worth seeing," she agreed. "But this time I guess we're going to have to go by feel, as I'm not taking any more clothes off than absolutely necessary."

"I hear ya." His teeth grazed her throat. "I'd rather be balls deep in you than freezing my nuts off."

"How sweet." She nipped his lip. "You're such a romantic."

He growled as he palmed her ass and slid his hand beneath the waistband of her fleece-lined pants. His long fingers caressed her flesh and curved around to finger her already swollen clit.

"Man, I love the way you feel."

She rocked forward against the pressure of his fingers. "Tell me you have a condom."

"Always, when I'm around you." He used his other hand to extract it from the pocket of his jeans.

"You planned this?"

His smile was crooked. "Let's just say that I did want you to check out the kittens, but I was definitely open to other possibilities."

"A planner's gonna plan." Jen attacked the zipper of his jeans with great enthusiasm. "Give that to me."

"Yes, ma'am."

She shoved down his jeans and boxers as far as they needed to go and sheathed his straining shaft with the condom. She considered her own garments and shimmied out of one leg of her pants and panties before grinning up at him.

"I think this will work."

He frowned. "Don't you need more—"

"Nope." She straddled his lap and settled herself over his cock. "I'm good to go."

At some point during their frantic encounter, Noah locked one arm around her hips and one behind her knees, stood up, and turned her so that she was sitting on the workbench. He continued thrusting as if he hadn't just lifted her like a feather.

She wrapped her arms around his neck and raised her heels until they were on the edge of the bench.

"Jeez . . ." Noah groaned as he slammed even harder into her. "That's . . ."

She didn't need his fingers or her own to climax now, the force of his thrusts was powerful enough to shake the bench and her soul. She gasped for air as he pounded into her, holding on for dear life as he came with a stifled roar, his face buried in the curve of her shoulder.

She slid her fingers into his hair and held him until his breathing returned to normal, and he raised his head to look at her. The rawness and need in his eyes were achingly familiar to how she felt herself. Could he see that? Would he want to? The vulnerability of the moment threatened to overwhelm her, and she pressed her face against his shoulder.

His grip on her relaxed, and he eased back. "I need to deal with the condom."

"Yes, of course."

She let go of him, suddenly aware of the chill of the night air and how desperately she wanted to pull him back into her arms and just breathe him in for a little while. But that wasn't what he wanted, and she'd agreed that all she wanted was sex.

"I'll be back in a minute," Noah said.

"Okay."

Jen suddenly felt ridiculous sitting there with one leg of her pants swinging free. She eased down to the floor, aware of several muscle twinges that would remind her tomorrow that she wasn't a teenager anymore. As she hurriedly got dressed, she used her tissues to wipe up and promised herself a shower before she went to bed.

Noah returned with a bowl and a washcloth and stopped short in front of her.

"I brought you warm water."

"You're so thoughtful." Jen patted his cheek. "I think I'll get back to the house and take a shower, if that's okay with you."

"You're leaving?"

She shrugged like it was no big deal. "I don't think the kitty needs my help, and we're done here, right?"

He looked down at her. "If you say so."

"Great!" She offered him a bright smile. "Are you coming?"

His mouth turned up at one corner, "Not anymore apparently."

Jen blinked at him. "You're not done? I thought—"

"It was a joke, Jen." He half turned away from her. "We're good, okay? I've got a few things to do here before I come back to the house, so the bathroom's all yours."

He walked away again leaving her feeling like she'd screwed up—and yet wasn't she doing exactly what they'd agreed? No hanging around exchanging gushy love talk? No shared confidences in the safety of her lover's arms? The fact that she wanted those things should be warning enough. If she couldn't abide by the terms of their agreement after only two days, she might as well give it up entirely.

But how could she leave him when he'd looked like that?

She followed him to the other end of the barn where the tack room was situated. There was a light on, and Noah stood with his head down and his hands braced on either side of the sink. Something about his defeated stance stirred her soul.

"Noah?" she said.

He immediately straightened and turned to look at her. "What's up?"

"I feel like I messed up somehow," she blurted out.

"You didn't." He smiled, his expression guarded.

"I can stay and talk if you want me to," Jen offered.

"No point when I'll be on the move." He set a bucket in the sink. "Why don't you head back to the house and make sure Max hasn't fallen asleep on baby monitor duty?"

"If you're sure we're okay."

"We totally are." He turned on the faucet and directed his attention to the rapidly filling bucket.

Jen waited a moment, but he didn't look back at her, so she turned around and walked out of the barn. He wasn't happy, she wasn't happy, and yet they'd still had the best sex of her life. What did that mean? And how on earth was she going to deal with wanting him all the time and coping with the weird aftermath?

She sighed as she zipped up her jacket. There were no good answers, and maybe that was what she deserved for being stupid enough to get involved with a man who lived by spreadsheet. He'd already checked her off his to-do list for the evening. Perhaps she had better do the same.

"I'll stay until Sky's birthday," Jen announced at dinner the next day.

"Awesome!" Luke said. "I'll get on that cake."

"You can bake?" Max looked skeptical.

"I've watched my fair share of cooking shows, it can't be that difficult." Luke shrugged. "I hear Sky wants a pony cake? He goes nuts when he sees them in the barn."

"If you can manage one."

Max grinned. "Luke's got a better chance of turning up with a real live pony than a cake one."

"I can multitask," Luke said loftily. "My mom taught me how to bake a cake using her secret family recipe."

"You've never bothered to make a cake for me or Max." Noah joined the conversation.

He'd deliberately kept out of Jen's way all day because

for once in his life he didn't know how to solve the issues between them without creating a whole new mountain of issues. He couldn't think straight—he couldn't plan a forward trajectory, and he didn't know what to do with that information. His heart was telling him Jen was in as deep as he was and that she was abiding by the rules because she was that kind of woman, whereas his head said the opposite.

She'd been way too eager to agree with him about everything, and after having to deal with Dave, who could blame her for protecting herself? If he could just get through the next few days, let her leave, and then instigate a new plan . . .

"Why the sad sack-face, Noah?" Max asked. "You don't like chocolate cake?"

"I love it," Noah answered automatically. "I was thinking about something else."

"The forecast is a lot more positive for the end of the week," Luke said. "If things go as planned, Jen and Sky could be on their way just after the birthday party."

"Sounds good," Jen said with a smile.

Max reached out and put his arm around her. "I'll miss you a lot."

"Thanks." She turned to smile at him. "You've all been amazing."

It dawned on Noah that Jen wasn't making much effort to engage with him either. His little display of petulance in the barn, when he'd wondered aloud why she was intent on leaving, had obviously scared her off.

"When's your mom due back, Luke?" Jen asked.

"As soon as the thaw sets in. She's already on her way. She's visiting family in several states."

"She's driving from Texas?"

"Yeah, she's not a big fan of planes."

"I love planes. I just can't afford them." Jen sighed. "I've been paying Sky's upkeep and trying to put some money away for a deposit on a place of our own."

"Doesn't Dave pay half?" Max asked.

"He's . . . not great at that. I decided I'd rather be certain Martha wasn't out of pocket while I was away."

"Fricking Dave," Max muttered. "Father of the fricking century." He stabbed his chicken with unnecessary force. "If he ever shows up here again, I'm going to pick him up and shake him down for every cent he owes you."

"It won't make any difference," Luke said. "Dave never had any money."

"Which is why it's on me," Jen smiled at them all. "I'm okay with that because it means I don't have to deal with Dave and get stressed about him not paying up."

"But doesn't that let him get away with it?" Noah couldn't help himself. "From what I've seen, no one ever holds Dave accountable for anything—not you, not Luke, or even his mom. He just sails through life using other people and never suffers any consequences."

Silence fell around the table as everyone stared at him. Noah shrugged.

"Sorry, I'm just telling it how it is."

"I thought that was my job," Max commented.

"What exactly do you think I should do, Noah?" Jen looked directly at him for the first time. "Take him to court? That costs money, and from my experience with the legal system, I'd probably end up owing more money and Dave would get full custody of Sky."

"Doubtful," Noah said. "I mean—"

Jen talked over him. "I'm the one who left Sky for months and didn't get back in time. *I'm* the one who reneged on my agreement with Dave. Do you think once Dave's lawyer shares that info with the court I'd stand a chance? Mothers are always penalized way more harshly than men for leaving their children."

She shot to her feet, her voice trembling. "Can someone get Sky a drink? I'll be back in a minute."

Luke looked at Noah as Jen shut the door behind her. "Nice."

"I was just trying . . ."

"To help, sure." Luke sighed. "But she's right you know. We were all ready to condemn her on Dave's say-so when he turned up."

Noah rose, too. "I'll go and apologize."

"I would." Max spoke from the kitchen, where he'd gone to get Sky's sippy cup. "Or no more sex for you."

"Don't you fricking *dare*—" Noah swung back toward the kitchen, but Luke got in his way.

"Both of you shut the hell up. This is about Jen, not you two fools." Luke gave Noah a shove in the direction of the door. "Go grovel and leave Sky and Max to me."

Noah took a moment to control his temper before he walked down to Jen's closed door and knocked.

"Jen? Can I come in?"

He was relieved when she opened the door. She immediately walked away and looked out of the window, her back to him and her arms crossed over her chest. She'd tied her hair in its usual ponytail and added a red ribbon. There was a slight bruise on her throat, which he guessed had something to do with him.

"I was out of line. I'm sorry."

She didn't turn around, and he took a couple of steps toward her.

"I wasn't thinking about the impact on you, just the implications of the law."

"And I just set you straight about how messed up that sometimes can be." She finally looked at him. "How do you think Dave ended up sharing custody with me in the first place? He didn't want to, but Martha hired a lawyer who was dazzled by Dave and determined to get him rights he didn't even want because she felt sorry for him and despised me for 'duping' him."

"No one who sees you with Sky could ever doubt that you love him."

"Dave loves Sky, too." She shrugged. "In his own way, of course, but enough to convince the judge—except he decided that because I had a full-time job and Dave didn't, that I should be paying the majority costs of care."

"That's . . . shit."

"That's life." She blew out a breath. "I guess I'm a little bit touchy about it."

"I can see why." Noah's hands fisted, and his desire to murder Dave increased tenfold. "You know my sister works in a family law firm. I could ask her—"

"It's okay." She tried to smile. "It's done now, and I've learned to live with it. It's kind of ironic, really. My mom was constantly at odds with the court system. Whenever she decided to go off with my dad, we would end up in care. Eventually, they stopped letting her have us back and we were separated into different foster homes."

Noah tried to reconcile Jen's uncertain existence with his own childhood, which had included an absent father but had given him a mother who'd done everything in her power to keep her family together.

"You have siblings?"

"A younger brother and a sister, but I have no real relationship with either of them. They were both formally adopted by loving new families, whereas I was kicked out of the foster care system at eighteen. We are in contact, but those bonds between us were stretched too thin when we were young to ever mend properly."

"Jen . . ."

He reached for her and wrapped his arms around her. He often complained about the burdens put upon him by his parents' decisions, but they seemed minor compared to what had been done to Jen and her family.

For a moment she remained stiff, and then she leaned against him and pressed her cheek to his chest. Noah shut his mouth and just held her. Luke would deal with Sky, which meant that neither of them needed to rush back before they were ready.

Eventually he kissed her neck just over the bruise and cleared his throat.

"You know that if it came down to it Luke, Max, and I would all vouch for you and not Dave?"

"That's very sweet of you."

"You're a great mom, Jen." He kissed her mouth. "You're patient, kind, loving, and everything Sky could ever need."

"Thank you." She offered him a wobbly smile that almost broke his heart. "Now, I'd better get back before Luke gets fed up babysitting."

He forced himself to step away when he wanted to hold on to her forever.

"Then I'll get out of your way. I promised Luke I'd make a start on cutting some paths through the snowbanks to the outer fields."

"It's dark out there, doofus."

He grinned, relieved that she'd somehow found the courage to lighten things up between them—but wasn't that just like her? Always stepping in to defuse a crisis or smooth over a problem. "I'm not doing it now. I just need to check some of my equipment is ready for the morning."

"Gotcha."

She nodded and walked toward the door, her expression calm. She concealed a lot behind her quiet, competent exterior, but he'd still trust her to have his back in a firestorm. And wasn't that the true measure of a person? That they kept going even when they were scared as shit, like he'd often been, and yet still managed to come through? He respected

her, he liked her, and sometimes, like now, he began to think
he really understood her.

He followed her along the hallway to the warmth and
light of the kitchen, where Luke was entertaining Sky by
making silly faces. Sky's giggles made both him and Jen
smile. There was no sign of Max, but as Noah had no intention of either hunting him down or apologizing, that was fine
by him.

He stayed by the doorway and watched Jen interact with
her son. If there was anything he could do to make sure Dave
couldn't disrupt Jen's life again he would do it. With that
thought in mind, he took out his cell, put on his jacket, and
stepped out on the porch.

Bailey didn't pick up, and he waited for her voicemail.

"Hey Sis? No rush on this but if you get a moment can
you give me your thoughts on this custody situation of
Jen's? It goes something like this . . ."

Chapter Eighteen

Luke came over to where Jen was sitting on the couch reading and cleared his throat. He'd recovered so well that Jen felt a certain amount of pride.

"I've got something for you."

Jen raised her eyebrows and looked around. "Why are you whispering?"

"Because it's for Sky's birthday tomorrow."

"He's in bed." Jen pretended to look under the couch. "Unless he's become quite the escape artist."

"I wouldn't put it past him." Luke sat beside her and handed over a brown paper bag. "I know you were worried about not having anything to give Sky, so I talked to Mom, and she directed me to her secret closet full of useful gifts for her grandchildren, present and future."

"She really has a closet for that?"

Luke grinned. "Actually, she calls it Grandma's hoarding cave. She told me to pick out some stuff for you to give Sky."

Jen opened the bag and began to lay the items on the couch. There were a couple of baby outfits in just the right size, a squeaky stuffed giraffe, and three different kinds of age-appropriate games.

"That's . . . way too much." Jen looked up at Luke.

"Nah, you'll be doing her a favor. She said it's getting too packed in there because I have failed in the grandchildren department. And she wants to thank you for taking care of me."

Jen held up a cute three-piece outfit consisting of green pants, a tiny white shirt with a duck pattern, and a vest covered in rabbits. "Sky could wear this for his party tomorrow."

"Totally."

Jen swallowed hard. "I . . . don't know how to thank you, Luke. You've all been so kind."

He shrugged. "Kind makes the world go around, in my opinion, and you've been an awesome addition to our bunkhouse during the shut-in."

"I still appreciate everything you've done for us."

Luke rose to his feet. "Hey, you've even made Noah smile occasionally. That has to be a win for everyone, right?"

"I guess." She looked toward the outside door. "Are he and Max still working?"

She'd hardly seen either of them over the last two days.

"They had something to finish up in the barn."

Jen swung her feet off the couch. "I could go and help now that Sky's asleep."

Luke started typing furiously on his cell. "No need, I think they're on their way in right now." He consulted his phone and glanced up at her. "Yup. They're on their way. If you want to wrap anything, I left the gift bags and tags on Mom's bed."

"Then I'll do that right now." She paused beside Luke and kissed him on the cheek. "You're the best."

He winked at her. "You're welcome."

She made her way to the end of the hallway, where Sally had the largest of the four bedrooms. It had its own bathroom, which Sally probably appreciated since she shared the house with three men. The high, four-poster bed was covered in an intricate patchwork quilt and adorned with several pillows. The room smelled like lavender and some vaguely familiar brand-name perfume. Jen strolled over to the dressing table and immediately spotted the square glass Chanel bottle. Her mom had loved that scent.

She turned back to the bed and set about wrapping the presents. It would be easier to stick them in gift bags, but once Sky got the idea, he would have more fun ripping the paper apart. She kept the little rabbit outfit out on the bed. If she hand-washed it tonight it would be dry enough for Sky to wear in the afternoon.

After she'd finished, she took a moment to sit on the bed and consider how lucky she was. Despite her terrible start with Luke, Max, and Noah, she'd found not only security but genuine friendship. With Noah, she'd found even more. The thought of walking away from him was increasingly hard to imagine, but as Auntie Brenda liked to say, she'd made her bed and now she'd have to lie on it.

Noah hadn't even bothered to ask what her plans were after she left the ranch. Was he waiting for her to share that information, or was he not even interested in acquiring it? The problem was that she couldn't even start the conversation because they'd agreed not to do that kind of thing. Which meant she'd wave goodbye at the end of the week and walk away with her head held high and some fantastic memories.

She slid off the bed and spoke into the silence. "And there's nothing wrong with that."

She'd learned early on to enjoy the good things because they'd been few and far between in her life. Her job had only confirmed that to her. Helping people who'd lost everything in a hurricane or volcanic eruption put her minor worries into perspective. She cherished each happy moment like a jewel strung on a necklace and Noah—she sighed—would be right up there, shining away like a diamond in the rough.

A tap on the door made her straighten up as Noah looked in. He'd obviously taken a quick shower, as his black hair was damp and threatening to curl.

"You okay?"

"Yes." Jen held up the bag. "Luke found some presents I can give Sky."

"Yeah, so he said." He waited until she reached him. "Luke said you were asking after me."

"Only because I haven't seen you or Max all day."

"We had a lot to do." He propped his forearm on the doorframe over her head trapping her, and looked down, his expression hard to read. "Did you miss me?"

"It was certainly a lot quieter around here." Jen wasn't falling for that.

"The thaw is setting in."

"Awesome."

"You'll probably be able to leave soon."

"Luke already told me." God, she wanted to kiss him so badly right now. . . . She frowned as he continued to gaze at her. What else was she supposed to say? "You've been great." Jen held his gaze. "I can't thank you enough."

"My pleasure." He leaned in and kissed her. "I know you've probably got a lot to do tonight, but can you spare an hour for me?"

"To do what, exactly?"

He brushed his mouth over her throat as his hand caressed her hip. "You know."

Her knees threatened to give way. "I think I can manage that. What time do you want me?"

"All the time," he murmured. "We already had this conversation, but I promised Luke I wouldn't get busy with you in the house."

"Okay." She locked her hands together behind her back to stop herself from touching him in return. "I'll be ready to go in half an hour."

"Good." His mouth returned to hers and he kissed her more deeply. "Man, that bed behind us looks so damn inviting right now."

"I am not doing anything in Sally's bed," Jen said firmly. "She'd *know*."

He groaned and slowly eased away from her. "Okay, see you over at the snowmobile shed at nine. I'll salt the path and get the heating on."

She was already smiling as he strode off down the hallway. That was Noah all over—the planner who'd never ever let you get cold or injured, and the lover who'd never leave you unsatisfied.

What a man.

As he waited for Jen, Noah made sure clean sheets were on the foldout bed and the fire was good to go. He hadn't meant to ask her to meet him here, but their last encounter hadn't ended as well as he would've liked. If this was the final time he got to be with Jen, he wanted to set that right.

She'd given no indication that she minded leaving the ranch, but why should she? The snowstorm had disrupted her life for weeks, something that would have driven him crazy, and she'd dealt with everything with calm, good sense, grace, and determination. She hadn't even bothered to tell him where she was heading next, which said a lot about her confidence that he'd want to follow up with her. He only knew because he'd asked Luke.

"Hi!"

He heard her call up the stairs and went to greet her. He'd warmed up the place sufficiently to strip down to his long-sleeved Henley, and he'd already taken off his boots.

"Hey, you." He started unwinding the knitted scarf around her neck and bent to kiss her cold lips. "I've got it nice and toasty in here so you can strip down at will."

"How romantic," Jen commented as he unzipped her coat.

"I can make you hot chocolate?"

"Lovely, but I'd rather you focused on my other needs right now." She glanced down the stairs. "I have to get back in an hour."

"Also romantic."

Jen cupped his bearded chin. "Maybe that's why this is working."

He helped her remove her coat as she stepped out of her boots to reveal soft sweatpants and her usual combination of two long-sleeved T-shirts. He'd never seen anything sexier in his life.

"You look good enough to eat," Noah murmured as he buried his face in her neck. "And just for your information, that's stage one of my plan for tonight."

"You have a plan?"

He lifted his head long enough to give her a lustful stare and to pick her up. She squeaked like a damsel in distress, which made him feel like a fire-breathing dragon. He laid her gently on the bed and followed her down, his hands braced on either side of her head as he straddled her. She was already flushed and breathing hard, and she wasn't the only one responding so fast. His cock was ready and willing, but he wanted to savor every moment—just in case it was the last time.

He leaned in and kissed her gently on the mouth, and she let him in, her tongue tangling with his in a lazy erotic dance that enthralled him. Eventually she pushed at his chest, and he reluctantly drew back, only to have her take both her shirts and her bra off in one sweep.

"Man . . . you're so beautiful." He cupped her breast in one hand and bent his head to suck her already tight nipple into his mouth. He took his time, his thumb caressing her other breast, making it ready for him. She sighed and half closed her eyes as he continued to arouse her. He already knew she loved the feel of his beard against her skin, so he slowed right down.

"Noah . . ." She tried to grab his wrist and direct his hand downward.

"So impatient." He took both her hands in one of his and brought them over her head, which made her arch her back in a very satisfying way. He returned his attention to her breasts and stomach, his callused fingers brushing her hip bones as he gently kissed his way down her body.

She lifted her hips so he could remove her sweatpants, but he left her in her panties, which were black cotton with a narrow band of lace along the top.

"Mmm . . ." Noah tugged at the lace with his teeth, inhaling the intoxicating scent of her arousal and the damp state of her panties. "You want me?"

"God, yes, Noah." She breathed his name like a prayer. "I want all of you."

He eased back onto his knees and cupped her mound, his thumb working the slight swell of her clit as he watched her writhe against the sheets.

"Look at me." She opened her eyes and he locked gazes with her. "Watch me make you come."

He increased the speed of his thumb, alternating between the slight rasp of his fingernail and the pad against the soaked cotton cloth. Without taking his eyes off her, he used his other hand to rip open his own jeans so he could cup himself while he watched her come apart. The pulse of his cock matched her climax, and he wanted to fit himself inside her so badly, he shook with it.

"Noah . . ." She almost arched off the mattress as she came, her hips rolling forward, her heels digging into the bed.

He caught her around the waist and brought his mouth to the pulse of her clit, stripping her out of her soaked panties. He let the short tremors subside against his tongue and then

licked her hard again and again until she climaxed again.
She was so wet and open now that he could get two fingers
inside her. He thrust back and forth, still watching her, mem-
orizing every expression on her face for the lonely nights
ahead.

"Please . . ."

God, she was begging now, and it was the biggest turn-
on of his life. He hurriedly stripped off his clothes and put
on protection. He needed to slow things down again or he
was going to come too fast. He sat cross-legged on the bed
and drew her up to sit opposite him. Her hair was a mass of
curls, her face flushed, and her mouth was swollen from his
kisses.

"What?"

"I want to take this slow."

"Why?"

"Because it might be . . ." he almost blurted it out, ". . . fun
to make you beg."

She made a feral noise as he picked her up. "Humor me,
okay?"

He settled her over his spread knees, breast to chest, his
cock between their bellies.

"I'm going to gently lower you over me, but don't move
after I do."

"Fine." She tried to push her hair out of her eyes, but it
wasn't cooperating. "I'll pretend I'm a statue."

He kissed her nipple, and she squeaked. "Some statue."

Once she'd finished complaining, he carefully lifted her
over his cock, holding his breath the whole time that he
wouldn't come. He shuddered as she settled against his groin
and appreciated the pulsing warmth around the hard, slick
length of his shaft.

"Now what?" she whispered.

"We stay like this for as long as we want," Noah said.

Her frown made him want to smile.

"Not moving?"

"How about we call it experiencing?" He stroked a line along her jaw and up the side of her face. "Just being in the moment."

She regarded him gravely and then used her fingertip to shape his eyebrows. "Like a moment frozen in time?"

"Exactly."

She settled more deeply over him, and he fought a groan that turned into a sigh when she framed his head with her hands and gently kissed him. Being there like that, so close and not so caught up in the lovemaking, was something new entirely. But with Jen it felt right. His dick pulsed so hard inside her that she responded with a squeeze of her internal muscles.

"Sorry," she gasped. "This is harder than it looks." She hesitated. "It's nice to see you like this, though. I'll . . . never forget it."

"Me neither." There was so much he wanted to say, but it wasn't the right time or the right place. "I want you."

"With my heels on your shoulders as you drill me into the bed?" Jen asked innocently. "I think that was what you said."

"Okay." He expertly maneuvered her onto her back. "I'm done talking."

She wrapped her arms around his neck and her feet climbed up his thighs to his already thrusting hips. She came almost immediately, but Noah rode through it, his attention on raising her even higher off the bed so that he was driving almost directly down into her. He grabbed one of her flailing hands and pressed it to her clit and everything went wild. He roared like a fool as he finally came and collapsed over her like a newb.

It took him quite a long while to raise himself up on one elbow and look down at her. He was almost afraid of what she'd see on his face.

"Thank you," Jen said softly. "I'll never forget this."

"Me neither." He rolled away from her, frustrated that he had to deal with the condom rather than gather her in his arms and maybe get a few things straightened out while she was in a receptive mood. "Stay right there."

When he got back from the bathroom she was already up and dealing with the bedsheets, not lying naked on her back expecting him to join her. He'd never been a cuddler but getting up and leaving hadn't appealed to him in the slightest. He wanted to hold her until she slept, wake her up later with his dick hard and ready to slide into her glorious wet heat. . . .

Man, he was so gone on her it was ridiculous.

"Are you okay?" Jen asked.

"I'm good." He nodded at the sheets in her arms. "Stick them in the washer. I'll deal with them tomorrow."

They walked back together over the rapidly melting ice, her arm tucked into the crook of his elbow and her face pressed against his shoulder. Neither of them said a word. Noah hoped it was because she felt the same way he did, but he wasn't willing to spoil the moment and ask for details. She'd leave, he'd follow up with her in San Jose, where she'd welcome him with open arms, and they'd take it from there.

She paused at the mudroom door to look up into his face.

"You look happy."

"I am." He risked a kiss on her cold nose. "That's how you make me feel."

She snorted. "That's the sex talking."

"That helped, but it has to be with the right person." He held her gaze. "I wish we could spend a whole night together."

"Not in this house."

"Yeah, I get that." He paused. "But a man can dream, right?"

"Sure." She reached for the door handle and walked past him into the mudroom. "Let me know how that goes for you."

"Jen . . ." He caught hold of her hand and drew her back

toward him. "I know we said we wouldn't talk about what comes next, but—"

"Hey," Max spoke from behind Jen. "Sorry to interrupt, but I need to borrow Noah."

Jen turned to smile at Max. "He's all yours. I'm going to have an early night." She blew Noah a kiss. "'Night Noah, and thanks for showing me how that snowmobile works."

"You're welcome."

She disappeared down the hallway. Noah turned to Max and braced himself for some kind of sarcastic comment.

"Wasn't that the same excuse you used last time?" Max asked.

Noah shrugged. "What can I do for you, Max?"

"I need you to help with that thing in the barn."

"Sure." Noah put his gloves back on. "I'll text Luke when we're down there to make sure the coast is clear."

Chapter Nineteen

"Happy birthday, kiddo!"

Luke came into the kitchen and grinned at Sky, who was sitting in his high chair banging his spoon against his bowl. He looked over at Jen, who was finishing up the bowl of chicken soup she'd had for lunch. Outside, the sun had broken through the sullen clouds and droplets of melting ice were running down the windowpanes in a constant stream.

There wasn't any mail service so the birthday card Martha had sent Sky languished somewhere in the main post office until someone could get out to the ranch. Heather had also bought Sky a present, but she'd already told Jen she'd hand it over next time they saw each other, which, from the look of the weather, might not be that long.

"Okay if I give him his present, Jen?" Luke asked.

"Would you mind waiting until I've gotten him cleaned up and in the family room?" Jen glanced toward the outside door. "Max asked me to hang on until he and Noah got back from the barn. He said they'll be here in five."

"Sure, no problem." Luke left the brightly wrapped gift on the table and helped himself to coffee and a huge bowl of soup. "Do you think Sky knows what's going on?"

"Not really," Jen confessed. "But once he starts opening a few presents, I suspect he'll totally get into it."

* * *

Jen heard voices outside and tried not to smile like a fool as Noah came in followed by Max. Why she'd ever thought Max was the hottest of the cowboys was a mystery when Noah was right there. He was big, tall, strong, and kind, and he made her feel like a delicate flower when he picked her up, and . . .

"Hi." He smiled at her. "You look flushed."

"That's because I'm looking at you."

He raised an eyebrow. "Right back at ya."

She touched his arm. "How's the weather doing?"

"Roads are technically open." His smile died as he looked down at her. "You and Sky can leave by the end of the week." He cleared his throat. "I'm more than happy to take you wherever you need to go."

"The nearest bus station would be good." She held her breath as he considered her. Would he finally ask where she was going?

He nodded. "If that's what you want."

"What else would I want?" She couldn't stop herself adding. "And it's no bother for me to call a cab if you guys are too busy."

"You know that's not what I meant at all—" He sighed. "Dammit—" He looked past her as Luke came toward him with a mug of coffee. "Is that for me? Thanks."

"Jen thought we'd do Sky's presents in the family room," Luke said. "Come on through, and we'll wait for Jen to get organized."

Jen brought Sky back into the kitchen dressed in his new outfit and the guys all cheered, which made Sky clap his hands and bounce up and down until he fell onto his well-padded rear.

"Me first," Luke said. "Here you go, little buddy." He

offered Sky a parcel. "Rip away the paper like this and see what Uncle Luke got you."

He showed Sky what to do and, with a little help from Jen, Sky opened the present to reveal a stuffed toy horse complete with a red velvet saddle, yellow mane, and a matching red bridle.

"Oss, Oss!" Sky squeezed the toy so hard Jen was deeply thankful he'd never gotten near the kittens, who were thriving in the barn.

"You're welcome." Luke ruffled Sky's blond curls. "One day you'll have to come back, and I'll teach you how to ride a real one."

Jen glanced up at Luke's heartfelt tone. "We'd like that."

"We all would," Max said.

She couldn't help but look at Noah, who was nodding in agreement, his dark gaze fixed on Sky's head.

"San Jose's not that far away." Noah handed Jen the bag of presents she'd hidden behind the couch.

She stared at him. "How did you know I was going to San Jose?"

He frowned. "Luke told me. Was it a secret or something?"

"No, I just . . ." Aware that the other two were trying to pretend they couldn't hear the muted conversation, Jen closed her mouth. "I didn't think you were interested in where I was going."

She turned back to Sky. "Right! More presents for the birthday boy!"

While she helped Sky unwrap the last of his gifts from her, Max and Noah disappeared. Luke grinned at her.

"Don't worry, they'll be back." He lowered his voice. "I'm sorry if I wasn't supposed to tell Noah about you potentially going to live at Martha's place. He was worried about you."

"It's all good," Jen reassured him, even though it absolutely was not.

How long had Noah known her future plans? And what did it mean that he hadn't told her he knew or tried to ask her about it?

"One last present," Luke called out as Max and Noah came in carrying something large draped in a cloth. "We'll do the cake after dinner tonight."

Jen held onto Sky as Max slowly removed the saddle blanket to reveal a beautifully carved rocking horse on runners.

"Did you make this?" Jen asked incredulously.

"Yup. I'm surprised you didn't hear me cursing all the way from the barn every time I banged my thumb or shaved an inch off my skin." Max shrugged. "Noah helped."

"And by helped, he means I did half the work." Noah held out his arms to Sky. "Do you want to try it out, kiddo? I won't let you fall."

He sat Sky on the leather saddle and handed him the reins. The horse's mane and tail were made of real horsehair. Holding Sky safely in place, Noah rocked the horse backward and forward.

"Ride 'em, cowboy!" Max whooped. "You're a natural!"

Jen slowly stood up, her hand pressed to her mouth, and looked at the three men, who were all smiling at her.

"Thank you." She burst into tears.

"Hey." Luke reached her first and awkwardly patted her shoulder. "Don't cry."

"Too late," Jen wheezed as everything suddenly seemed too much. "I just don't know what to say."

"Then we're good," Luke reassured her as he handed her his handkerchief.

"Not sure how you're going to get that horse on the bus," Max observed. "I think you should take Noah up on his offer to drive you to San Jose."

Jen blew her nose and accidentally met Noah's level gaze. "We'll work something out." She went over to where Sky was still sitting on the horse and smiled at him. "Isn't this an awesome present, buddy?"

"Oss!" He grinned at her and grabbed hold of the horse's mane.

"What are you going to call him?" Noah, who was holding tight to Sky, asked.

"Oss, I guess," Luke joked. "You guys did a great job."

"It's exquisite." Jen ran her fingers along the smoothly planed wood. "I had no idea."

"I'll keep good hold of him if you want to get rid of the wrapping paper," Noah offered. "I don't think he's ready to come off yet."

"Thanks." Jen crouched on the floor and gathered up all the trash, getting some satisfaction from screwing each piece up into a tight ball. She hated crying in front of anyone, it never did any good. People either ignored you or thought you were weak. She took the paper through to the mudroom, where the large trash cans were situated, and dumped everything in.

She also took a moment to take some deep, calming breaths.

When she returned to the family room, Max and Luke had retreated to the kitchen to finish their lunch, and Noah was persuading a reluctant Sky to let go of the reins. He looked up as she approached.

"He's getting tired, which means he's being extra stubborn and cranky."

"Definitely time for a nap, then." Jen scooped Sky up despite his protests and marched out.

She changed Sky and put him into bed, where he immediately fell asleep. She smoothed his curls away from his cheek and celebrated the fact that she was not only with him, but that he was safe, well, and happy. There was no way she could leave him to the vagaries of Dave's care. She'd have to transfer to a more local hospital and separate from the navy at the first opportunity. Nothing else was as important as Sky's future happiness.

She was still smiling when she exited the bedroom and found Noah leaning up against the wall opposite her door, his expression brooding.

"What?" She faced him.

"We seem to have a misunderstanding here."

"Do we?" She met his gaze.

"I asked Luke about your plans a while ago."

"Before or after we got together?"

"Does that matter?"

"It might."

He frowned. "I'm not following."

"I assumed you didn't ask about my plans because you didn't need to know them," Jen said stiffly.

"I didn't ask because I already *knew*."

"Okay, let's just say that for future reference, I'd rather you ask me to my face than go behind my back."

"Got it." He gave a sharp nod.

"Good. Anything else?"

He stared at her for a long time, as if deliberating whether to push her further. In some weird way, she almost wished he would.

"Nope."

Jen gave him a bright smile, and he looked away.

"You don't have to do that."

"What?"

"Pretend everything's fine," Noah said.

"I've always found it works very well for me."

"Because it's easier than dealing with all the crap?"

She studied him closely. "Because it's easier than ending up in the middle of someone *else's* crap."

He rubbed his hand slowly over his bearded jaw as he considered her. "Nah, that's not it."

"I beg your pardon?"

"You're not willing to take a risk, Jen."

She raised her chin. "And somehow you think you know me well enough to say that?"

"Yeah, I do." There was a definite challenge in his words and his stance.

She almost wanted to get into it with him but was also aware that Luke and Max were just around the corner, and that it was Sky's birthday.

"I have to go," Jen said firmly. "Luke needs my help with frosting the cake."

He straightened and got out of her way. "Sure, just keep on pretending."

She whirled around and poked him hard in the chest. "Do not judge me."

"Hey." He held up both his hands. "Just tell me what you want. Put it out there."

"We agreed to keep things simple, okay? I'm trying to do that."

His smile was both unexpected and infuriating. "Our agreement ends when you step out that door for the last time. Maybe it's time to think about what you want next."

She turned and walked away until she reached the kitchen, where Max and Luke both stared at her. Was Noah trying to tell her that he wanted more, or was he just being his usual infuriating self?

"Is everything okay?" Luke asked.

"Just peachy. Now, how can I help with the cake?"

Noah sat at the kitchen table, where Jen had laid out a party spread of all Sky's favorite foods, which suited him just fine, as he liked most of them, too. The cake was covered in thick vanilla frosting with darker accents for the mane and chocolate buttons for the eyes and nose. There was also one candle taking pride of place in the center.

"Where's the birthday boy?" Max asked as he came into the kitchen and washed his hands.

"Just getting spruced up," Noah reported.

"So he can smear cake all over himself?" Max shook his head. "Might as well sit him there in his diaper and hose him and the chair down afterward."

"Thank God you don't have kids," Noah muttered.

"Don't want them, don't need them." Max joined him at the table. "Way too much of a commitment."

Up until quite recently, Noah would've agreed with him, but Jen had thrown all his certainties up in the air and now everything was crashing down around his head. She was pissed at him, but he'd laid down his marker. What she did with the information was on her. If he could persuade her to let him drive her to San Jose, he'd have a good opportunity to spell things out along the way.

Unless she decided to bail out halfway there because she didn't want to listen to him. He stifled a smile as he pictured her doing just that. But she wouldn't abandon Sky, that was one thing he did know.

Jen came in with Sky, who immediately pointed toward the family room. "Oss."

"Cake first." Jen settled him into his seat and clicked the safety strap in place. "Can someone light the candle?"

Luke obliged, and Sky gazed in wonder at the flickering flame. Jen cleared her throat and glanced expectantly around the table as she began to sing, and they all reluctantly joined in.

As he was closest to the door, Noah was the first to hear footsteps mounting the porch and to turn his head as the door to the mudroom burst open and Dave appeared with a box full of presents in his arms.

"Hey, beautiful!" He grinned at Jen, who was staring at him with her mouth open, and then turned to Sky. "Hi, little bud."

"Da!" Sky squealed enthusiastically.

He kissed Sky's head. "You didn't think I'd miss your first birthday, did you?"

"Er, yeah, actually," Max wasn't playing along. "If I'd ratted out my friends, I wouldn't be waltzing back in with a smile on my face unless I had a very good explanation. And the thing is, Dave, we all know you're a complete asshole, so don't even try it."

"Hey, harsh," Dave made a sad face. His gaze focused on Jen, who was regarding him calmly. "Maybe you'll change your mind when I get to the next reason I'm here."

He walked around the table until he was standing in front of Jen and went down on one knee.

"Jennifer Rossi, will you marry me?"

Noah started to speak, but Max put a hand on his shoulder and held him in place.

"Dave . . ." Jen sighed. "Don't—"

"I've had a lot of time to think about what I want and what I need. And you and Sky are the only good things in my life, Jen."

Luke cleared his throat. "Maybe we should give you two some privacy?" He looked over at Noah. "Why don't we take the cake and go to the family room?"

"Hell, no." Max shook his head. "I'm staying right here for the show."

Jen turned to Luke. "If you can keep an eye on Sky, I'll take Dave into your office and we can finish this conversation."

"Why do you want to hide away?" Dave asked. "I mean, these guys already know what you mean to me."

"You said she was a loser who'd abandoned her kid and left you with nothing," Max interjected.

"I didn't exactly say that," Dave objected with a wary glance at Jen. "I was just so hurt and devastated that she'd left us."

"Bull crap," Max added. "You don't even know the meaning of those words. All you think about is yourself—period." He glanced over at Jen. "She's worth a million of you."

"Max . . . ," Jen said softly. "I appreciate your input, but this really is between me and Dave."

"She's right." Noah rose to his feet. "Let's leave the lovebirds alone."

The hurt look Jen gave him wasn't entirely surprising, but what the hell had he been expecting? For her to leap up and tell Dave she was with him now? Like, to acknowledge him in some way? That wasn't what Jen was about. That wasn't what their relationship was about.

Max rose too. "Noah's only salty because he's got a thing for Jen, Dave."

"What?" Dave's gaze swiveled to Noah. "You've been hitting on my woman?"

Noah stayed where he was as Dave advanced toward him. He looked down from his considerable height advantage.

"She's not your anything, buddy," Noah said softly.

"Who asked you?"

"Don't you dare talk about me like I'm a piece of property," Jen said in a dangerously low voice. "I don't belong to anyone but myself."

She turned on Dave, who visibly flinched. "And I'm done talking to you right now. If Luke chooses to let you stay, you're not welcome in with me and Sky. If and when I get my temper back, I'll consider talking to you in the morning."

She took Sky out of his chair without even looking at Noah. "Good evening, everyone. We'll be taking an early night." As she went past the table, she cut herself a large slice of cake and took it with her.

Dave waited until she'd closed the door to whistle.

"Man, she's cranky today! And she didn't even give me an answer to my proposal!"

Noah took one step forward, delivered the perfect right hook, and Dave crumpled to the floor.

Max crouched beside Dave, who was groaning and clutching his jaw, and looked up at Noah. "Not what I was expecting, big guy, but totally appropriate. Get up, Dave. You'll live."

Luke and Max helped Dave to his feet while Noah stared at him, his hands still fisted as he fought to get the civilized part of his brain to work again.

"That's for walking out on your kid." He faced Dave. "And just FYI, if you say one more thing about Jen, I'm happy to do it again."

"She doesn't approve of fighting." Dave took the bag of ice Luke gave him and pressed it to his jaw as he glared at Noah.

"What? You're going to tell tales?" Noah raised his eyebrows.

"She's hardly going to miss the massive bruise on my face," Dave pointed out. "And I'm not going to lie to the woman I love."

Noah barely managed not to snort, but Dave did have a point. Jen would be furious if she found out he'd been fighting over her.

"You can stay in one of the bunkhouses for the night," Luke said. "There's no room in the house."

"What about your mom's room?" Dave asked. "She's not back, is she?"

"You are not sleeping in my mom's bed," Luke said very definitely. "I have limits."

"Okay, I know you're all mad at me, but I had to do something, and I knew you'd take good care of Sky," Dave said. "I needed the job to make some money to pay back my mom and start building a future for my family."

"Sure, you did." Max rolled his eyes. "Like you ever think about anyone except yourself."

"I've changed, Max," Dave said earnestly. "I came to terms with a lot of stuff when I was away. And Sky and Jen were always on my mind."

"Absence makes the heart grow fonder?" Luke stood up. "How about we get you settled over at your new billet? I'll help with your bags and show you how the heating works."

"I'll do it," Max said. "You're not supposed to be carrying anything right now, Luke."

"Why's that?" Dave asked as he picked up his backpack.

"I fractured my arm." Luke touched Max's shoulder as Dave went to the door. "Promise me he'll still be alive in the morning?"

"I'll do my best." Max looked grim. "But only because I respect Jen too much to implicate her in a murder."

"I guess that will have to do," Luke said as the back door swung shut behind Dave and Max.

"I'm sorry I took a pop at him." Noah grimaced. "It wasn't planned."

"If it hadn't been you, it would've been Max, and you're more likely to let him live."

"Dave's right, though—Jen's going to kill me anyway when she finds out. And what's with Max dropping me in it like that?"

"It certainly wasn't helpful," Luke agreed. "I don't think poor Jen was expecting any of this."

"Typical Dave," Noah said. "He turns up and causes chaos." He glanced at the box of presents Dave had left on the floor. It had just occurred to him that Jen hadn't exactly turned Dave's proposal down. "I'm not touching that stuff. Let's leave it to Jen."

"Agreed." Luke looked back toward the kitchen. "I think we should follow her example and eat all the cake before Max gets back."

Chapter Twenty

The next morning, Jen emerged from her room carrying Sky and looked cautiously around the hallway. There was no sign of Dave or any of the guys, so she tiptoed down to the kitchen. For some reason, possibly involving large quantities of cake, she and Sky had slept in. She settled him in his high chair and started making them both some plain oatmeal that she hoped would settle their stomachs.

Dave's appearance and dramatic proposal had kept her up half the night, reliving each terrible moment frame by frame, like some kind of horror movie. She didn't believe for a second that he wanted to marry her, and she'd make sure he realized that when they talked. He was all about the dramatic gesture and never followed through. She sighed. She didn't want to talk to him, but it had to be done. And as for Noah, and Max's unhelpful comments . . .

"Ugh." She pressed her hands to her cheeks as she blushed like a teenager. She hated drama and never ever wanted to be at the center of it.

"Hey."

She looked up as Luke came into the kitchen. He was still mainly confined to the house because of his arm.

"Hi! Where is everyone?"

"They're all in the fields checking out what's left of the herd." His expression was uncharacteristically grim. "We persuaded Dave to help, so there's no chance of you bumping into any of those idiots until lunchtime."

"I'm so sorry."

Luke shrugged. "Sometimes owning a ranch sucks. But that's what we have insurance for. My guess is we've lost half the herd."

"You're very calm," Jen said. "I think I'd be bawling."

"No you wouldn't." He smiled. "You're like me. You'd make the best of it and stop everyone else panicking as well."

"I can see why you were a good officer."

"I did my best." He poured her some fresh coffee and sat opposite her at the table. "If Dave managed to get up here, I'd say the roads were good enough to travel on."

"Is that your subtle way of asking me to leave?"

"Hell no. I just wanted to make sure you knew it was an option." He paused. "If I were you, I'd wait a couple of days and then get Noah to drive you to San Jose."

"Unless I take Dave up on his fabulous offer of marriage," Jen murmured. "I mean, does he think I'm stupid or something?"

"Well, you did have sex with him."

Jen reached across the table and flicked Luke's nose. "Ha. The sex wasn't the problem. He's damn good at it with all the practice he gets. The *problem* was a failure of contraception."

Luke grinned. "Thanks for spelling it out so graphically."

"You started it."

He met her gaze. "I'm going to miss you. In a totally platonic 'we could be good friends' kind of way."

"Right back at you."

"Do you think you'll continue to see Noah?"

Jen groaned. "I don't know. I think he's already checked me off his to-do list and is ready to move on."

"And I think you're one hundred percent wrong on that."

She wished she had Luke's confidence. "We'll just have to wait and see, won't we?"

She'd just put Sky down for a nap when the guys came in for a late lunch. She'd baked a huge tray of mac and cheese and set it on the table with a pile of garlic bread. Max and Noah went on through to Luke's office, leaving Dave smiling at Jen.

He came over and tried to kiss her on the cheek. "I forgot you like to cook."

"That's probably because I never cooked a single thing for you," Jen said sweetly. "Go and sit down and I'll bring you some coffee."

"Where's Sky?"

"He's taking a nap."

"He's so cool, Jen."

She smiled. "He definitely is."

"I'm sorry for everything." He touched her arm, his expression contrite. "Can we talk after lunch?"

"If we must." She pointed at the table. "But let's eat first."

Noah and Max reappeared with Luke behind them. They all looked somber, which probably meant Luke's estimate of the damage done to the herd was low. Jen's heart went out to all of them. She knew how hard they'd worked to save as many of the cattle as possible during one of the worst storms of the century.

Max nodded to her as he sat down, but Noah remained silent. She handed Luke a spoon.

"Why don't you serve? There's plenty for everyone."

"Thanks for cooking, Jen." Luke set about dumping massive helpings of mac and cheese on the plates while the other guys added the garlic bread. "We need the fuel. I have to go out there myself this afternoon. Don't worry, I'll be careful."

She'd assumed that as a good leader he'd want to survey the damage for himself and just nodded. As far as she could tell, his arm was healing nicely, and she had complete confidence that unlike the other guys, he wouldn't do anything stupid and aggravate the injury.

"Max said you fixed Luke's arm?" Dave asked.

At Jen's nod, he whistled. "You're fricking amazing."

"Thanks." She took the spoon from Luke and helped herself to a small portion of food. For some reason her appetite had deserted her. She wasn't sure if it was Dave's breezy confidence or Noah's withdrawal that bothered her most.

"I had a text from Dr. Carlo," Luke said. "He's hoping to get out here in a couple of days."

"Why not today?" Dave asked. "I mean, I got out here okay."

"Maybe because he's a busy man and you're not?" Max offered between bites of garlic bread. "This is really good, Jen. Thanks." He turned back to Dave. "Do you actually have a job now, or did you run out on that one, too?"

"I had to leave. The local military didn't like us being there."

"Surprise, surprise," Max said. "How are you planning on supporting your family now?"

"Max . . . ," Luke intervened. "That's none of your business."

"When he's leaving Jen to pay all the bills, I think it is."

"I've been offered a new job," Dave said. "By a large private security company. I just need to fill out the paperwork and I'm all set." He glanced over at Jen. "I wanted to offer my son and partner financial security."

Max rolled his eyes but returned to his food, and silence fell around the table. For once, Jen was reluctant to start clearing up because then she'd have to listen to Dave. But she had no intention of getting back with him, so why was she panicking?

She abruptly stood up. "I'll put some fresh coffee on. Are you done, Dave? We can talk in Luke's study."

"Sure!" He grinned at her as he picked up his plate. "Can't wait!"

He followed her through to the farm office and shut the door behind him. His first move was to try to take her in his arms, but she sidestepped that with ease.

"Nope." She pointed at one of the chairs in front of the desk. "Sit down and talk to me."

He sighed and sat in the chair, his fingers linked together in his lap, his blond head down.

"I know I've messed up, Jen, but I still think you should give me a second chance."

"Why?"

"Because as I told you, I did a lot of thinking while I was away. I realized I've been behaving like a kid with no responsibilities—leaving Mom to bring up my son, making it hard for you to do your job. . . ." He raised his gaze to look at her. "I'm disappointed in myself, and you definitely deserve better."

Jen just looked at him, and he sighed.

"Okay, I also realized that Sky needs a stable family around him. Neither of us had fathers around, so we know what it's like to feel unwanted and unloved. We could give Sky that if we stay together and work at our relationship."

"Dave, this is all great, but you aren't the kind of guy who *does* stick around. It's not who you are." Jen tried to be gentle. "And that's okay. We can still coparent Sky. I'd never stop you seeing him whenever you want, but it's my turn to stay with him full time."

"You don't want me as part of your everyday life?" Dave looked genuinely surprised.

"If you are really honest with yourself, Dave, I don't think you want that either."

He sat back. "You'd rather pin your hopes on that bastard Noah Harding?"

Jen frowned. "This has nothing to do with him."

"If he hadn't gotten involved with you, I bet you'd be thrilled that I'd have you back."

There were a lot of things Jen wanted to say to that, but she also needed to remain friends with Dave because of Sky.

"We'd already decided we didn't suit way before Sky was even born."

"But I've changed my mind!"

"And I haven't." She held his gaze. "I'm sorry Dave, but that's my final word on the matter. I respect you as Sky's father, and I will allow you as much access to him as you want, but—"

"*Allow* me?" Dave wasn't smiling anymore. "I am one hundred percent capable of parenting my own child. I did it for months when you were absent. You don't get to 'allow' me anything."

"We both know your mom did most of the looking after Sky."

"That's not true." Dave stood up. "If this is the way you want to play it, I'll talk to Mom and to my lawyer."

Dread rose in Jen's stomach. "Please don't do that. Neither of us can afford a lengthy legal battle over something we can decide amicably between ourselves."

He pointed his finger at her. "If you think my mom would allow you to take Sky away from her . . ."

"I'm not intending to do that—please listen to what I'm saying . . ."

Dave left the room, slamming the door behind him, and Jen abruptly sat down again, her knees shaking. Someone knocked on the door, and she looked up.

"You okay?" Luke asked.

"Not really. Dave doesn't take rejection well." She groaned and buried her face in her hands. "He's threatening to take me back to court."

"That . . . sucks." Luke patted her shoulder. "Would you like me to have a word with him? Sometimes he listens to me."

"I don't want you to put yourself out on my account," Jen said hastily. "You've done enough."

"I'll try anyway." He gave her a determined nod. "You just focus on taking care of Sky and leave Dave to me."

"Why did you drop me in it in front of Dave?" Noah asked Max as they headed down to the barn.

Max shrugged. "I thought he should know what was going down."

"Why? It just made everything awkward and gave Dave an excuse to get at Jen."

"I guess I wanted to puncture that infuriating bubble of self-satisfaction that constantly surrounds him."

"At the expense of Jen, a person you call your friend?" Noah shook his head. "I know we're often at odds, Max, but that wasn't fair for her."

Max stopped walking. "Yeah, you're right. I should've just punched him like you did."

"I'm not proud of that, either."

"You should be. It's the most honest reaction I've seen from you in years. But I will apologize to Jen."

"Okay, then."

Ten minutes later, Noah was leaning up against the barn wall, waiting for Luke to turn up while listening to Dave waffling on about something he knew nothing about. They were due to resume their count of the surviving cattle and Luke had insisted on being part of it.

"Sorry about that," Luke said, "I was talking to Mom."

Noah jerked his head in the direction of the paddock. "We're taking the snowmobiles. You and Dave can ride with me and Max."

"Sure." Luke nodded. "We're not going far."

As usual Dave looked like he didn't know which was worse: going with Max, who openly disliked him, or with Noah, period. He reluctantly chose Noah, and they completed the short-but-bumpy journey in silence. Noah let Max head off into the field while he made sure the vehicles were safe.

He was crouched down examining the rear spoiler of one of the snowmobiles when Luke started talking to Dave.

"You upset Jen."

Dave snorted. "She's upset? I offered to marry her and take care of our family, and she turned me down flat because she doesn't think I'm reliable. How the hell am I supposed to show her that I'm a changed man if she won't give me a chance?"

"By not pressuring her into making an instant decision? Come on, Dave. She has a perfect right to be suspicious of you."

"She's the one who broke our agreement, not me."

"She didn't have much choice. You know how the military works better than most people. You can't blame her for something that was out of her control."

"She'll stop me seeing my own son. She thinks I'm not capable of looking after him."

"But you haven't exactly been pulling your weight, have you?" Luke asked.

"I did my part, and that's not the point. She's trying to change our agreement."

"She's trying to make up for missing so much of her son's life. She wants to be there for him."

"And so do I! And I'm sick of everyone thinking I'm incapable."

"Then maybe you need to suck it up, spend some time with Jen actively coparenting Sky, and see if you can change her mind."

Dave sighed as Noah idly considered how long it would take him to stand, pick Dave up by the scruff of his neck, and shake some sense into him.

"It's not fair, Luke." Dave stomped off toward Max.

Noah was just about to stand up when Luke's boots appeared beside him.

"Hear anything good?"

"Nothing that didn't convince me that Dave's not a dick." Noah rose to his feet. "He has more tantrums than Sky."

"It's all hurt pride." Luke gazed across the field. "Dave can't believe Jen didn't accept his offer while sobbing with gratitude. Now, he's looking for ways to justify his behavior and make her pay."

"Which sucks."

"She's a strong woman; I'm sure she's got his number." Luke let out his breath. "Let's get on with this death count, shall we? I promised Mom I'd have some numbers for her when she called back tonight."

Noah nodded and followed Luke. He really wanted to discuss what they could do to help Jen, but this wasn't the time. And he had a terrible feeling there was nothing he could do because he didn't have the right to defend the woman he'd come to care about. His own stupid insistence on setting rules and boundaries to their relationship had come back to bite him in the ass. Maybe he deserved what he got, but Jen certainly didn't.

"Arkie?" Luke looked back at him. "Are you going to stand there and stare into space all day?"

"Sorry, boss. I'm coming." Noah picked up the pace.

The sooner they got the count done, the quicker he could get back to the ranch to see how Jen was handling everything—probably way better than him.

"What does he like to do after his nap?" Dave asked.

He'd returned to the house early and caught Jen going into her room to wake Sky.

"He likes practicing his walking, chewing his bone, and trying to eat the dog food."

"He's walking?" Dave chuckled. "That's my boy." He held out his hands. "Can I hold him?"

"Of course." Jen passed him over. She wasn't sure why Dave was playing nice, but she wasn't going to say anything in front of Sky.

"Dada." Sky beamed at Dave and patted his face. They had very similar coloring and expressions. "Dadada."

"Hey, buddy. Did you miss me?" He turned to Jen. "Okay if I spend some time with him?"

"Be my guest. I've got a load of laundry to do." She pointed to the family room. She had to show Dave that she'd meant what she'd said about letting him have access to his son. If she could stop him from going after her in the courts, it would be worth it. "He's safest in there, but if you want to get more adventurous, he loves visiting the horses in the barn."

"I heard about that." Dave went into the family room, where the rocking horse took pride of place. "That's neat."

"Max and Noah made it."

"Yeah? It's awesome." Dave grinned as Sky leaned precariously out of his arms toward the horse. "I guess the little guy loves it, too." He paused. "I'm sorry I got mad earlier."

"That's okay."

"I guess that just because I've worked out what I want

doesn't mean it wasn't a surprise to you, and I need to give you some time to get used to the idea."

Jen looked at his handsome profile as he set Sky on the horse. Should she instantly disavow him of the idea that she'd ever come around to marrying him, or was it better to leave him to his delusions until they both left the ranch and went their separate ways? If she could avoid oversharing about her private life in front of the other three guys, she'd be incredibly relieved.

"There's no need to stick around, Jen. I've got this," Dave said.

"Okay. If you need to get him a drink or a snack, they're in the kitchen."

"Got it. And diaper changes in the bathroom, correct?"

"Yup." Jen smiled. "I'll leave you to it."

She walked slowly down the hallway to the stairs that led to the small basement where the industrial-sized washer and dryer were located. If she could just string things out for a while, Dave would probably get bored playing house husband. If she consistently refused his proposal and reminded him that he'd much rather be free to roam, eventually he'd get the message. All she had to do was make sure he didn't take her to court and that he knew he and Martha could see Sky whenever they wanted. That was important to him, and she respected that. It also meant she'd have to continue to keep Noah at arm's length, so Dave didn't freak out . . .

She collected her laundry and went down the steps. There were a lot of "ifs" to deal with. She couldn't even think about Noah in the short or long-term. Sky's future had to come first, and then forging a path for her and Dave to exist harmoniously. She was already laughing hysterically when she reached the bottom step. She was good at calming troubled waters, but this spectacular mess might be beyond even her powers.

Twenty minutes later, she bypassed the family room,

where Dave was having a great time with Sky, put on her outdoor clothing, and walked toward the barn. The snow was melting at a rapid pace, and patches of green were reemerging on the surrounding trees. The silence of the storm had been replaced by ominous cracking sounds as some of the structures beneath the banked snow groaned under the weight or gave into it.

She kind of knew how they felt. She'd never been so conflicted and uncertain in her life.

Far off in the distance, the faint rumble of heavy traffic indicated that the highway might be operable. She sighed and turned a slow circle. Civilization was intruding again, and she wasn't sure if she was ready for it. But had the isolation also created a false sense of community and intimacy? That was sometimes the case on board ship, and relationships that had seemed solid fell apart in the harsh glare of reality.

"Hey."

She turned her head to see Noah regarding her. He had his coat buttoned up to the throat, a knitted scarf covering the lower half of his face, and a Stetson jammed low over his ears.

"You look like a bandit."

"Then don't let me hold you up."

"Ha ha." She blew out her breath. "Sorry about the Dave thing."

"Did you ask him to turn up here?" He pushed the scarf down so that she could see the rest of his face.

"Heck no." Jen shuddered.

"Then you're not to blame, are you? Dave's gonna Dave."

"I like that. How's it going with the cattle count?"

"Not great." He changed position slightly to shield her from both the rising wind and the house. "I reckon we've lost sixty percent of our stock. Luke's gutted."

"That's . . . terrible."

He shrugged. "Shit happens."

"I guess we both know that."

"And we've all dealt with far worse than this." He glanced toward the unpaved track that twisted upward through the trees. "Sally's going to be back soon. She just called Luke and told him the roads will be clear by the end of the week."

"He'll be glad to see her."

"We all will. She's the heart of the house."

"I'll probably be gone by then." She offered him a smile. "I hope you don't get stuck with Dave."

"Not happening. If you're not here to keep us civilized, one of us will hog tie him and dump him on the county line to fend for himself. And when I say one of us—me and Max will probably have to flip a coin."

Jen burst out laughing, and Noah smiled back at her.

"That's better." He searched her face. "You'll get through this, Jen."

"I know. It just doesn't feel like it right now, but I appreciate your confidence in me."

"You're worth a million Daves."

She met his gaze and couldn't look away. "Thank you."

He reached out and flicked her nose with his gloved finger. "I'd like to kiss you, but I guess that wouldn't help right now."

The thought of being held in Noah's arms made Jen sway toward him, but she resisted the temptation. If Dave saw her with Noah, he'd use it as ammunition against her in court. She had her priorities and had to stick to them.

"I . . . have to focus on what's good for Sky right now."

"I get that." He hesitated. "I guess you're not planning on going back to your ship?"

"I can't do both." She pressed her lips together hard. "Not without Dave's buy-in."

"That must be tough. I know you love your job."

The understanding in his voice almost made her cry. "I'd

better get back and see to the laundry." She nodded and turned away.

"Jen?"

She looked back over her shoulder. "Yes?"

"I'll be here if you want to talk."

She didn't have anything to say to that and marched away, her vision blurring as she mounted the steps to the porch. Dave needed to be managed, Sky had to be cared for, but at some distant point in the future, she'd think about what Noah had said and maybe even decide what to do about it.

Chapter Twenty-One

"Why are you out here?" Max asked Noah as he came into the feedstore in the barn the following evening.

"Because watching Dave auditioning for Father of the Year makes me want to puke," Noah said savagely.

"Worse when he's only doing it for an audience of one," Max said.

"Jen's not buying it."

"You sure about that? She does like to keep the peace."

"Which isn't the same as falling for Dave's bullshit." Noah slammed the lid of the feed bin shut.

"She's going to do what's best for Sky, Arkie. You know that."

The hint of sympathy in Max's voice made Noah scowl.

"You think they'll get back together?"

"She had a kid with him. That's a powerful bond." Max held his gaze. "Dave seems to think they're moving in together. I don't want you to get hurt."

Noah shook his head. "It's not about me. Jen deserves better."

Max's smile was slow in coming. "Man, you're totally gone on her, aren't you?"

Noah offered his friend a one-fingered salute and headed for the door. He didn't need Max to analyze what he was currently feeling. He already knew he didn't want to give Jen up. He had a goddamn *plan*. It was taking all his resolve not to say anything while Dave pranced around like he owned the place.

Despite the thaw, it was still too cold outside to linger, and he reluctantly made his way back to the house. Dave was sitting at the table with Sky on his knee while Luke and Jen discussed a medical matter. Everyone looked up as he came in, and Sky held up his arms.

"Nono."

"Hey, little bud." Noah instinctively went to pick him up, but Dave got in the way.

"He's fine where he is, thanks."

Noah held up his hands and backed away. Jen got to her feet.

"I've got to grab a new pack of diapers from the basement. Are you okay with Sky while I do that?"

"Don't fuss, Jen. He's fine. Take your time." Dave winked and shook his head when she was out of earshot. "Women . . ."

Even as Dave was smiling, Sky had picked up his knife from the table. Noah leaned over and removed it from his sticky grasp.

"Nope, don't touch that." He looked at Dave. "Maybe you should pay more attention to your kid and less to making fun of his mother."

"Lighten up, Arkie. He's doing great. I don't know why you guys make such a big deal out of looking after him. It's easy."

Luke and Noah exchanged wry glances.

Noah sipped his coffee. "When are you starting your new job, Dave?"

"As soon as I want."

"So you'll be leaving soon?"

"That rather depends on Jen." Dave handed Sky his sippy cup.

"You've got your own transportation," Noah pointed out.

"Yeah, but Jen doesn't, which is why I'm waiting on her."

"Jen's going with you?" Luke asked, which was a good thing because Noah was searching for the right words.

"Seeing as we're headed for the same place, then yeah. We've got to start somewhere, and my mom's place is ideal for us to work on our issues like you suggested Luke." Dave looked all wide-eyed and innocent at Noah. "Didn't she mention that?"

"Nothing to do with me." Noah shrugged even as his heart plummeted. Max had obviously been right for once. "I only offered to give her a ride."

He caught a flash of movement at the door as Jen returned and met her gaze. "You're going with Dave?"

"Yes." She glanced warily at Dave and back at Noah.

"Cool." Noah got up. "Then you obviously don't need me."

"No, she doesn't, Arkie." Dave sounded way too smug. "I can definitely take it from here." He smiled at Jen. "Shall we take our son to the family room? We've still got to work out a way to get that horse in the back of my rental."

Luke followed Noah into the kitchen, where he was loading the dishwasher, and lowered his voice.

"For the record, I think Dave's a victim of wishful thinking rather than actual facts."

"Doesn't matter, does it? They're back together, and Jen being Jen will do everything in her power to make it right for Sky." He shut the dishwasher. "And I'm not getting in the way of that."

"Maybe you should talk to Jen first?" Luke suggested.

"She said she was going with Dave. What else is there to know?"

"Jeez, Arkie, there's a hell of a lot more. You've got sisters. When they stop talking to you and say everything's 'fine' or 'great,' that's when you're in the greatest danger."

Noah considered that angle. "I promised her I wouldn't

talk long-term or make things awkward while she was on the ranch."

"So now she's leaving. Have the conversation." Luke threw a tea towel at him. "Do I have to do everything around here?"

"I guess." Noah sighed. "Okay. Can you ask her to meet me in the laundry room? I'll go and wait there."

Jen stepped carefully down the steep, wooden stairs into the basement. She'd left Luke distracting Dave but wasn't sure how long it would take before he came looking for her.

"Hello?" She peered into the badly lit interior.

"Hey."

Noah was leaning back against the dryer, his arms folded over his chest and his expression somber.

"What's up?" Jen asked even though she thought she knew and was almost ready to be swept away by his declaration of true love. Considering the circumstances, she wasn't quite sure how to react. But somewhere inside her she really needed to hear him say the words out loud, even if she immediately had to beg him to keep them to himself until she'd solved the Dave problem.

"Okay, can I just run this by you before you get to talk?" Noah asked, his tone brisk. "We agreed that we'd sleep together with no strings attached, no long-term plans, and no recriminations."

"That's right." Jen nodded.

"I'm guessing that Dave turning up here—him being Sky's father and all—messed things up." He met her gaze. "We both had shitty childhoods, Jen. I can totally understand why you want to try and make things work with him."

Jen blinked. "That's what you think I'm doing?"

"You're the kind of person who gives people a second chance, and you're willing to do that for Dave."

"That's what you've decided?"

"Yeah." He frowned at her. "I don't want to be the kind of man who gets in the way of a well-intentioned effort to save a relationship. I always wished my parents had tried harder because my dad said, years later, that he'd made a terrible mistake leaving my mom."

"Well, ballyhoo for you."

Jen glared at him. How could any man who claimed to be so smart be so damn stupid? He'd obviously plugged all the information into his spreadsheet and come up with the completely opposite conclusion to the one she'd been hoping for. And the worst thing was, she couldn't even set him straight because she still had to deal with Dave.

"What's wrong?"

"Nothing." She smiled at him. "Thank you for your generous permission for me to get back with Dave."

His brow creased. "That's not what I meant at all, I—"

"Stop talking right now." Jen held up one finger. "I feel like we've been here before. You rushing to conclusions about me. How did that work out last time?"

"Not great." He watched her intently. "Are you saying I'm wrong?"

Jen was just about to tell him what an ass he was being when she remembered her primary goals: Deal with Dave, get Sky settled in a new home, avoid litigation, and find a job. Adding Noah to the mix was not on her bingo card right now.

"I think I'm going to leave it like I did last time," Jen said. "With you going away, thinking things through, and working out where you might have gone wrong."

"But—"

"No, remember the rules?" Jen knew her voice was shaking but there was nothing she could do about that. "No buts, and neither of us has to explain why we're ending our relationship."

His scowl was something to see. "That's a complete cop-out, Jen."

"It's what you wanted."

"Doesn't change the fact that you're walking away from me."

"I don't have a *choice*." She almost stamped her foot.

He frowned. "There's always a choice. There are *always* other options."

"Maybe on your spreadsheet, Noah, but real life is way messier."

"This isn't about my goddamn spreadsheet!" He raised his voice, and she couldn't blame him because for once she wasn't feeling like smoothing things over herself.

"Then how come it feels like it is?" Jen asked. "Like I'm a project you can now check off your list? I've been on way too many lists, Noah, and I don't like feeling like a package being sent on my way to a new foster home, or a new assignment, or . . ." She shook her head as she ran out of words and met his frustrated gaze. "We're done, okay?"

"No, *you're* done, and maybe that's just fine with me."

She turned on her heel, walked up the stairs, and went into her bedroom. Locking the door, she sank down on the bed and cried her heart out. It was all very well being noble and practical, but sometimes a girl had to mourn what she'd just lost—even if the idiot who'd won her heart totally didn't deserve it.

After rushing to the bathroom to bathe her face in cold water, she made her way back to the family room. There was no sign of Noah, Luke, or Max, which was something of a relief.

"Hey." Dave pointed at the TV. He didn't seem to notice she'd been crying. "Sky's definitely going to be into sports."

"Good to know." Jen sat on the couch next to him. "I hear

that the roads are clear, so if you want to leave for your mom's place, I'm ready to pack up and go."

"Really?" Dave grinned at her. "You're okay about sharing the apartment?"

"Seeing as it's your mother's, and I don't have anywhere else to live right now, then yes." She held his gaze. "But this doesn't mean we're back together, okay?"

"Sure, whatever." Dave grinned at her, picked up Sky and tossed him in the air. "We're going to be a family, buddy! Yahoo!"

The next morning, after a sleepless night where he'd run through every possible permutation of Jen's responses a thousand times and only succeeded in giving himself a headache, Noah came up from the barn to find Max staring at the back of Dave's truck.

"It's not going to fit in there."

"What isn't?"

"The rocking horse."

"They're leaving already?" Noah asked as his stomach dropped to his boots.

"Yeah, we already packed up the back of the truck while you were out, and there's no room for the horse inside."

"Jen didn't say they were going so soon."

"Maybe—and work with me here, Arkie—she didn't think it was any of your business."

Noah stared at the truck. The back doors were open to display Sky's car seat, Jen's navy-issued kit, and various other bundles.

"Luke's lending her some stuff until she gets settled." Max continued like nothing was wrong. "It's not like Brina needs it anymore for her kids."

"I guess not," Noah answered automatically.

"I'll go and tell them the horse is a no-go. It's the last thing we were trying to load." Max went into the house.

Noah stayed where he was, which was where Jen found him when she came out to put a huge diaper bag in the truck.

"Hey, I wasn't sure you'd be back in time to say goodbye."

The sun shone down on her dark hair, which she wore down on her shoulders. She was her usual calm, capable self.

"Jen . . ."

"What?"

"I'm sorry I shouted at you."

She shrugged. "I shouted back."

"You said I should think about what you said."

A hint of wariness crossed her face. "And?"

"I'm not sure I get it." He cleared his throat. "I mean, aren't we both just trying to do the right thing here?"

She reached out and cupped his chin, her brown eyes full of understanding. "Yes, we are."

"But it sucks."

"Correct." She went up on tiptoe and kissed his mouth. "Thank you for everything, Noah. I'll never forget you."

Even as he went to hold on to her, to try and find the right words to convince her to stay, that he was a fool, and that she was wrong, Dave appeared with Sky in his arms and the dogs at his heels.

"Everything okay, Jen?"

Jen stepped back. "Just saying goodbye."

Noah met Dave's suspicious stare head-on. "You take good care of Sky, now."

"I will." Dave smiled. "And of Jen."

Noah nodded. "I'll go and make sure you haven't forgotten anything."

"Thanks, Arkie." Dave turned to Jen. "Shall I buckle Sky in or do you want to do it?"

Noah went into the house, passing Luke, who was on his

way out. There was no sign of Max. Noah wandered through the house making sure Jen hadn't forgotten anything. It was unlikely she would, but Noah had needed a reason to get away from Dave. On the rug in the family room he spotted a dog bone with the letter S written on it and picked it up. He walked back to the front porch just in time to see Dave's truck disappearing down the road. He stood there and watched it wind its way up through the trees, the occasional flash of sunlight catching the glass and chrome.

Luke came to join him.

"I guess you didn't make any progress with Jen, then?"

"Nope."

She'd picked her side, and he wasn't on it.

"She told me I had everything wrong and to go away and think about it."

"Okay." Luke gave him major side-eye.

"What?"

"That usually means you screwed up."

"I get that, but this time I think she's wrong." Noah put the stupid bone in his pocket. "I need to get to work. There's a lot to do now that the thaw's setting in."

"I hear ya. Three of the local guys called to say they're coming up to work this morning, which should make things easier."

"Good."

Noah walked over to the barn and mentally reviewed the rest of his day. The thought that there would be no Jen or Sky to come back to was too hard to think about. He'd do what he did best, compartmentalize, get stuff done, and work himself hard enough that he didn't have time to think. It had always worked in the past, and it was all he had to help him get through the worst of days.

To his surprise Max was in the barn.

"Hey." Max jerked his head in the direction of the house. "Has the dickhead gone?"

"Yeah."

"With Jen and the kid?"

"That was the plan." Noah opened the door into the feed-store to check on the kittens.

"Are you okay?" Max leaned against the doorframe and studied him.

"Why wouldn't I be?"

"Because you're in love with Jen?"

Noah shrugged. "Doesn't matter if the other person isn't into you."

"Did you tell her?"

"When she'd already made it obvious she was going to choose Dave? Hell no. I might be stupid, but I don't need an extra smack in the face."

"She didn't choose Dave. She chose Sky."

"Same thing." Noah glared at his friend. "Will you shut up?"

"How are you going to stop me? You just don't like hearing the truth," Max said. "Jen doesn't want Dave. She wants you."

"She told you that?"

"She didn't need to. It was obvious every time she looked at you and, if you don't mind me saying, she's not the kind of woman who has casual affairs."

"Wrong. That's what she wanted this time." Noah approached the doorway. "If you don't move, I'm still coming through."

Max stepped aside but kept talking.

"You bottled it up and didn't tell her you loved her and somehow that's her fault?"

"She didn't need to hear that when her mind was already made up. Hell, you were the person who clued me in to that."

"Don't shoot the messenger." Max held up his hands.

Noah kept walking, and for once Max didn't follow him. His steps slowed as he approached the tack room. Despite what Max was suggesting, he'd done the best thing for everyone—hadn't he?

Chapter Twenty-Two

"Noah!" Bailey jumped out of her truck and threw herself into his arms. "It's so good to see you!"

Noah picked her up, which he knew she hated, and swung her around. She favored their mother and was about a foot shorter and a hundred pounds lighter than he was, so it wasn't hard. It was two months since she'd split up with her boyfriend, and six weeks since Jen had left the ranch, and Noah still wasn't okay about either event.

"Put me down you great big idiot!" Bailey said. "I'm getting dizzy."

He obliged and stared into her laughing face. She had similar dark coloring to his own, but she smiled a lot more, and somehow his features looked way better on her.

"You look great," Noah offered as he took her bag out of the back of her car and walked with her up to the house.

"I feel great." Her smile wasn't quite as convincing as her words. "Will's settled in his new place in New York. We keep in touch."

"That's good," Noah held the mudroom door open for her. "Any regrets?"

"Plenty, but I haven't changed my mind." Bailey's face lit up again. "Luke! How are you?"

She gave Luke a big hug and then turned expectantly toward the kitchen. "Where's Sally?"

"Here!" Sally came around the corner, her arms open wide. The next moment she and Bailey were hugging and squealing at each other like besties. "How *are* you?"

"Much better for seeing all of you." Bailey grinned.

Noah noticed that Luke hadn't moved and that his gaze was fixed on Bailey. He gave his boss a nudge. "Stop staring at my sister."

"Sorry, I haven't seen her for a while, and she looks . . . different."

"And she's still my sister."

"I hear ya," Luke said. "I'll go tell Max that she's arrived. We can sit down for dinner together and get all the gossip."

"I'll be back tomorrow, Dave," Jen said firmly. "It's less than twenty-four hours, and Sky will be sleeping through the majority of it."

They were sitting in the kitchen of Martha's apartment, and Dave was sulking.

"But I had plans."

"I told you a week ago that I had to go down to San Diego to speak to my boss about separating from the navy."

"But why can't you take him with you?"

"Because I'd have to take him on the plane and there's no one to care for him at the other end," Jen said patiently. "Come on, Dave. You said you'd support me on this."

"What about Heather or one of your other friends down there? Couldn't they watch him?"

She frowned. "What's so important that you can't look after your own son?"

"One of my coworkers is having a birthday party. I can't take Sky to that."

"Then you either find a babysitter or you don't go. I can't

miss this meeting—unless you're okay with me signing up for another tour?"

Dave shuddered. "Hell no—and leave me all alone?" He sighed. "I wish my mom was here. She'd look after Sky in a heartbeat."

"If she was here, it'd be very cramped right now. Didn't this whole mess start with you constantly asking your mom to babysit Sky?"

Dave stared at the door as if he were about to bolt. He'd started not coming home straight from his work shifts. Sometimes Jen could smell beer and cigarettes on him even when he claimed he'd just been working late. It was a good thing her heart wasn't involved. His lies exasperated and exhausted her but didn't affect her beyond his lack of dependability for Sky.

"Dave, I have to go. Will you be here for Sky?" She held his gaze.

"Okay, but you really have to stop doing this kind of stuff. I can't be expected to be here twenty-four-seven."

"I've never asked you to be," Jen pointed out. "You work ten-hour shifts, sleep eight to ten hours a night, and spend about an hour a day with Sky."

"It's hard, Jen." The haunted expression returned to his face. "I'm . . . not good at this shit."

Jen held her tongue. As soon as she settled with the navy and was officially home full-time, she could tactfully suggest they go their separate ways. She already had a sense that he'd be relieved. Staying in one place with one woman wasn't his thing. She'd been looking at jobs and apartments in more rural northern California, and although things would be tight financially, she was confident she and Sky would be okay.

Sally had sent her a lovely letter thanking her for looking after Luke and complimenting her handling of his fractured arm. She'd also extended an invitation for them to visit the

ranch whenever they wanted. Jen missed the place more
than she had expected—the all-encompassing silence, the
way the forest rolled and shifted like the ocean. She missed
Noah most of all. He hadn't contacted her, and she hadn't
reached out to him, but oh, she'd wanted to. . . .

"What time tomorrow, then?" Dave sighed. "I'll cancel
my shift."

"Thank you." She shared the details of her flights to his
cell, and he nodded like he was doing her a great favor.
"Next time can you give me more notice, please?"

She didn't bother reminding him that she'd mentioned it
every single day for two weeks because that would set him
off about her nagging him to death.

He rose to his feet and took his plate to the small kitchen.
"Since I can't work tomorrow, I'll pop in and see if they
want me for the next six hours."

"You only just got home," Jen pointed out.

"Yeah, but Michelle, the office manager, kind of *relies* on
me. I don't want to let her down."

"Michelle."

"Yeah, she's so . . . enthusiastic about life you know? Like
because she's young and she's never gone through half the
stuff we have." Dave's expression lightened as he washed out
his glass. "It makes me smile. We have these really deep
conversations."

"How nice."

"It is nice. She kind of looks up to me, I guess?"

"Fancy you being a role model." Jen rose too.

"I know! It's kind of cool." He grinned at her. "Okay, I'd
better get going. Luke called me earlier, so I'll talk to him
on the way."

"Luke called you?"

"Yeah, something about delivering the rocking horse?"
Dave was already on the move. His desire to get back and

role model with Michelle was obviously far more important than talking about Luke. "I'll patch you in with the details later."

"I left a message with Dave about the rocking horse." Luke briefly looked up from his plate. "I hope that was okay."

"What about it?" Max asked as he passed the green beans across the table to Bailey.

"Whether he wants us to drop it down to him."

"Why should we put ourselves out?" Max asked. "He's perfectly capable of coming up here himself."

"Maybe he doesn't want to." Bailey, who was totally up to date with all the gossip courtesy of Sally, suggested. "Or he's too busy."

"He's just lazy," Max said dismissively. "He expects everyone to run around and make stuff easy for him." He looked over at Noah. "You didn't threaten him before he left, did you?"

"Hell no."

"You sure? I mean, he did walk off with your woman."

"Jen's nobody's 'woman'. She belongs to herself." Noah looked over at Luke. "If you want the horse dropped off to Sky, I can do that."

"I guess you want to see Jen," Max said.

Bailey nodded. "He's *so* not over her."

"I'm fine, thanks." Noah scowled at the entire table. "Can you all stop talking about this?"

"You're not fine." Bailey glared back at him, and the resemblance between them intensified. "You're miserable as hell."

"It doesn't matter if I am. Jen and I agreed we were done. She chose to work things out with Dave, and I respect that."

Luke raised his eyebrows. "Where on earth did you get the idea she was getting back with Dave?"

"Because she left with him?" Noah tried not to snap. "Like, to live in the same place?"

"Where else was she supposed to go?" Luke asked. "Dave's Mom offered her the place while she got her life sorted out. She could hardly tell Dave he couldn't live there, too."

"It doesn't mean they're sleeping together," Bailey added. "Did you tell her that you wanted a relationship with her before she left?"

"No, because that wasn't our agreement." He looked past Bailey and stared at Luke. "And why are we rehashing this again? In public? In front of my sister?"

"Because we care about you, Noah." Sally spoke for the first time. "And we want you to be happy."

Noah wanted to protest that he was happy, but he wasn't that good a liar.

"When you had that chat with Jen after she said she was going back with Dave, what exactly did she say?" Luke asked.

"Do we have to do this now?" Noah complained.

"Yes. Think of it as an intervention," Bailey said encouragingly. "A lurve intervention."

"Fine." Noah crossed his arms. "I told her that I got it— that she wanted to try again with Dave, and that was okay with me."

Silence greeted his words.

"Hang on, you *told* her that?" Bailey asked. "Without actually *asking* her to explain first?"

"I wanted to get it out of the way. I needed her to know that I understood."

"How did she react?" Sally asked, her face alight with interest.

Noah paused to think. "She wasn't happy. She thanked

me for letting her be with Dave, which wasn't what I was doing at all."

"Except it was," Max interjected. "Go on."

"Then she said I should go away, think about what I'd said, and get back to her if I came to any new conclusions."

Bailey tutted. "Bro, you messed up really bad. She's basically telling you that you got it all wrong."

"I've thought about it a lot since, and I can't see how." He gazed around the circle of concerned faces and sighed. "I guess you're going to tell me."

Bailey raised her hand. "Number one, you didn't give her the opportunity to fully explain *why* she was going with Dave. You told her *your* take on it and acted like it was fact."

Everyone nodded.

"Two, you didn't tell her that your feelings for her had changed and that you wanted a proper relationship with her."

"How could I do that when she'd decided to leave?" Noah asked. "If she'd wanted more from me, doesn't she bear some responsibility for telling me, too?"

"Yeah, but she had more constraints," Luke said.

"You mean Sky? I love that kid. I'd be more than happy to take him on."

Bailey blew him a kiss across the table.

"That's not her only constraint," Luke said thoughtfully. "She's got to resign from a job she loves, find somewhere to live, and then there's all that business with Dave."

"Dave doesn't love her," Noah interrupted. "I'd bet a million dollars on that."

"Dave only loves himself, but you saw how he reacted when he found out you and Jen were close."

"He was pissed, and he got super possessive of Sky and Jen," Max said.

Bailey pointed at Noah. "Oh! And what about the legal thing you mentioned!"

"Yeah. When I talked to Jen last, she was really worried."

Luke nodded. "Dave threatened to take her back to court if she didn't go along with what he wanted."

"Why didn't you pass that little gem of knowledge along before she left?" Noah demanded.

"No wonder she didn't want you involved, Noah," Bailey chimed in. "She was probably terrified scumbag Dave would use her new relationship against her if he went back to the judge." She glanced around the table. "Courts can get funny about these things sometimes."

"Jen's family has already been screwed over and spat out by the court system before," Noah murmured. "And being Jen, she was probably trying to protect me."

Silence fell around the table as Noah frantically tried to rearrange what he'd discovered to fit with what he thought he'd known.

"I should've listened first," he said finally. "I made too many assumptions."

"That's because you're an ass," Max murmured.

"Hold up. I've got Dave on the phone returning my call. Talk about good timing," Luke said suddenly. "Don't do anything until I get back, okay?"

Sally handed around oatmeal cookies and more coffee while they waited for Luke to return. Noah's mind was reeling with possibilities. Could he salvage his relationship with Jen? Would she even be willing to hear him out?

Luke came back in with a huge grin on his face and sat down at the table.

"Okay, you're not going to believe this, but Dave's obviously bored with being a full-time dad, and we've made a plan . . ."

Jen unlocked the front door and stepped into the unusually quiet condo. It was already past ten at night and she was exhausted from both the traveling and the emotional aspect

of what she was about to do. The navy had been her home
and support since she was eighteen, and leaving everything
it represented and a job she adored was harder than she'd
imagined.

She set her kit bag at the bottom of the stairs. Dave might
have gone to bed, but it was most unlike him, and something
about the silence seemed wrong. She snapped on the kitchen
light and saw a note propped up against the pepper grinder
with her name on it.

She opened it up and read the scrawled lines.

*Hey Jen, decided to take Sky and a friend out to the
wilds of Northern California for the day and pick up
that rocking horse. Not sure when we'll be back!
Might stay overnight if Luke's okay about it. X*

"A friend?" Jen spoke into the silence. "God, not
Michelle . . . he wouldn't." She groaned. "Yes, he would."

Jen made herself some much-needed coffee and suddenly
didn't feel tired at all. She tapped her fingers on the countertop as she considered what Dave had done. He'd taken her
son and some unknown woman and headed up to the ranch,
where he'd recently pissed off his friends. There was no way
he'd be getting back tonight. It was a four-and-a-half-hour
journey on a good day. She knew that because on the days
when she missed Noah the most, she might have googled the
journey time.

As if he'd heard her thinking bad thoughts about him,
Jen's cell buzzed with a text from Dave.

Hey! Thinking of leaving Sky up here with the guys
for a few days while I show Michelle some of the
best hiking trails in the park.

Jen took a deep, steadying breath before she replied.

Don't you dare.

Why not? They won't mind.

Have you actually asked them this time????

Harsh, Jen. Remember I'm a new man.

Who's currently driving around California with another woman? Jen just about refrained from going all caps on him. Come home and we can sort this out together.

How about you come up here?

Jen considered her options. Did Dave think she'd be too chicken to go back to the ranch because of Noah? If she said no, he'd probably hope he could stay up there and avoid her for as long as possible.

Was she too chicken? She started typing again,

If I come, you must promise to stay put with Sky until I arrive.

It's a deal. See you tomorrow. X

Jen put her cell in her pocket, picked up her bag, and climbed the stairs. She had a strange feeling she was being manipulated into doing what Dave wanted, but she also needed to make sure Sky was safe and prove to herself that she had moved on from the Noah thing. She'd set her alarm for five in the morning and get moving. Her car wasn't great, but it would get her there by lunchtime.

The thought of seeing Noah and the others was both exciting and painful. They'd shared each other's lives for over a month, and they'd made her feel like family—something she'd never had outside her shipmates. Would it feel the same going back after six weeks of dealing with Dave and city life?

Perhaps it was time to be brave and find out.

* * *

"Jen will be at the top gate in ten minutes." Dave came into the kitchen carrying Sky on his hip. "She wants the gate code."

"It's one two three four," Sally said.

"Of course, it is," Max murmured. "I mean, who would ever crack that? Even Dave worked it out."

Sally gave him an affectionate pat on the arm as he went past her. "Luke said he picked something simple so that even people like you would remember it, Max."

"I just sent it to her." Dave turned to Noah. "Do you want to take the kid? I need to make sure Michelle's ready to hit the road."

"You're not going to leave before Jen gets here, are you?" Noah set Sky in his high chair at the table.

"I thought it might be easier. . . ."

"*Hell* no." Noah held Dave's gaze. "You owe her an explanation."

"I'm not sure why, when I'm doing all this just to get her up here for your benefit, Arkie."

"Dave, you brought another woman with you!"

Dave looked insulted. "No one said I couldn't make the journey more interesting. And Michelle offered!"

"You're not going anywhere," Max chimed in. "Try it, and I'll shoot out your tires."

"Fine. I'll talk to Jen before we go." Dave stomped out of the room, and Noah and Max looked at each other.

"He's so fricking oblivious." Max shook his head. "I really want to punch him."

"He's possibly one of the most self-centered people I've ever met," Sally chimed in. "The nerve of him."

Noah focused on getting Sky a snack rather than staring anxiously out the window for a sight of Jen's car. He'd been amazed at the changes in Sky even after six weeks. He was babbling more and was way steadier on his feet. He'd seemed happy in his father's company even though Dave had complained endlessly about how hard it was to be a parent.

Michelle, who was in her mid-twenties, was obviously enthralled with Dave and had been endlessly kind to Sky. She'd confided that Dave was so wise and such a great mentor that she didn't know what she'd do without him. Noah had thoughts on that, but he'd held his tongue and nodded politely along with everyone else. For their plan to work, they needed to keep Dave sweet long enough to get Jen on board. After that, what he did with Michelle was his own business.

Having blown it so badly last time, Noah couldn't think what he wanted to say to Jen. He kept hoping for divine inspiration, but so far had nothing. Bailey had told him to shut up and listen, and that seemed like the best advice he was going to get. Not that he'd have any trouble keeping quiet because he was basically terrified. If it came down to the wire, he'd beg, grovel, and plead if she'd give him the slightest chance to make things up to her.

"Where's Luke?" Sally asked.

Noah checked down the hallway. The farm office was empty and Luke's bedroom door was open.

"Probably in the barn." Noah noted there was no sign of Bailey either.

Max gulped down his coffee. "I'll get him. I might need his help to sack Dave if he makes a run for it."

"I heard that." Dave came back into the kitchen. "Michelle's just finishing our packing. Any sign of Jen yet?"

"She's just pulled up."

Noah said it like it was no big deal as the dogs started barking in tandem. As he strained to get a look at her through the glass, his heart was thumping so hard he had to remember to breathe. She was hugging Max and laughing, which made him want to rush out there and demand all her smiles for himself.

Jeez he was screwed. He was so in love with her.

Luke and Bailey joined Max, and they all moved toward the house. His sister was doing the majority of the talking as she obviously introduced herself.

"Here we go."

Noah thought he'd spoken aloud before he realized Dave had joined him at the window, his expression almost as apprehensive as Noah's. Dave had to sort out his shit with Jen first. After that, Noah would see how the land lay.

"She won't care about Michelle," Dave said. "She'll only care about what I did for Sky."

"You sure about that?"

Dave faced him. "We're coparenting our son, Arkie. There's nothing between us. She's spent the last six weeks looking like a woman who wanted to be somewhere else."

"Can't say I blame her."

Dave grinned. "You're funny." He braced himself and turned to the door as it opened. "Wish me luck."

In the crowd of introductions, hugs and pleasantries Jen noticed only the person who'd kept his distance after a brief *hi* and a pat on her shoulder. Sally was as delightful as Jen had imagined, and even Max was on his best behavior. The sense of coming home was both unexpected and emotional.

Sky pointed at her when she came in and smiled.

"Mama!"

Jen pressed her hand to her chest. "You finally said it!"

"Mama!" He said it again just to make sure she'd heard him.

"Maybe absence really does make the heart grow fonder," Jen murmured as she kissed Sky's head. He looked remarkably at home in his old high chair surrounded by dogs, cowboys, and various family members.

"It sure does," Noah said quietly before he moved away to give her some space to hug her son.

Dave cleared his throat. "We should talk."

"We should." Jen offered him a tight smile.

He gestured toward the farm office, and after making sure that Sally had her eye on Sky, Jen followed him inside.

Dave immediately held up his hands like he was warding her off. "Okay, I know you're not happy with me right now."

"Correct."

"But I think we both know things weren't working out between us. You're too . . . *much* for me, Jen." He sighed. "You expect things I don't have in me to give."

"Like loyalty, support, and honesty?"

He winced. "That's harsh. I guess I just want to live my life the way I want to live it."

Jen stared at him. "I guess you do."

"Look, I like my job, and I'm good at it. I'll go back to court and make sure to upgrade my financial contributions for Sky, but I can't be a full-time dad."

"Got it." Jen nodded.

"You could sound sadder about that." Dave actually pouted.

"Believe it or not, Dave, I want you to be happy. I also want to make sure Sky gets the financial support he needs, that I'm acknowledged as his primary caregiver, and that he'll get to see his father as often as possible."

"I could just say yes, I'll be there one hundred percent, but we both know I'm probably going to dick around and mess up sometimes."

"I'd rather you promised to do your best." Jen held his gaze. "I won't let you mess Sky around. If you say you'll be there for him, you've got to try and mean it."

"I understand." He considered her. "Just . . . don't set his expectations real high."

"I won't," Jen said. "But I won't ever stop you or Martha from seeing him."

"That's good because Mom would kill me." Dave started smiling again. He cupped her chin. "Thanks for being so understanding. I'm sorry things didn't work out between us."

"That's okay. You gave me Sky."

"Yeah." Dave nodded. "He's the best, isn't he?"

"Yes, he is." She finally smiled back at him. "I think we'll always agree on that."

He kissed her very gently on the cheek and headed for the door. "We'd better get going. Michelle and I have work tomorrow."

"I thought you were off hiking?"

"Nah, I just needed something controversial to get you rushing up here." He winked at her. "Seems like it worked."

"Don't ever try anything like that again, Dave Riley," she warned.

"I won't." He blew her a kiss and sauntered out into the hallway.

She remained where she was, trying to come to terms with the fact that Dave had no intentions of taking her back to court in a bad way and that she was safe, free, and clear of him. She took a deep, steadying breath. She'd still make sure she got everything in writing, because—Dave.

Now all she had to do was negotiate her way through the rest of her unexpected visit to the ranch. Was it time to be brave and put her wants and needs first for a change?

Her gaze roamed the farm office, a space Jen doubted Luke had altered since his father passed away. It spoke to her of home, family, and a permanent legacy she'd never had in her life. It was something she wanted for Sky, and she was willing to spend the rest of her life creating it for him.

"Hey." There was a gentle knock on the open door. Jen looked up to find Noah standing there. "Do you want to come and wave Dave off? Make sure he's gone?"

"Not really." She tried to smile. "I think we said everything that needed saying."

"Yeah?" He hesitated in a most un-Noah-like way. "That's good, right?"

"It's wonderful." She turned to look at him properly for the first time, drinking in the hard lines of his face and the cautious warmth in his brown eyes. "He's not going to take me to court."

"That was worrying you."

"It was totally consuming my thinking." She swallowed hard. "I couldn't deal with anything beyond that. I was afraid I'd lose Sky again."

"Again?"

"I wasn't here for months, Noah. What kind of mother does that?" She only realized she was on the verge of tears when her voice cracked.

His brow creased. "You were doing your job and serving your country. The only person at fault was Dave for not fulfilling his end of the bargain."

She tried to smile. "Thanks, but it doesn't matter anyway. I'm leaving the navy at the end of my contract."

He studied her carefully, opened his mouth as if to speak, and then closed it again.

"It's the only thing I can do." She gathered her courage. "I was thinking of finding a job up this way."

"Yeah?"

"I was hoping that . . . maybe after I get settled you might come and see us. Sky would love it."

"What about you?"

She locked gazes with him. "I'd like it, too." She gulped in some air. "Look, I'm trying to be brave and reach out for what I want like you suggested, and—"

He closed the distance between them and enclosed her in his arms, his mouth finding hers for a deep, mind-blowing kiss that gave her everything she wanted and so much more.

He backed her up against the door, his body aligned with hers, his breathing ragged.

"I love you, Jen."

"Oh." She gazed up into his harsh face. "Are you sure?"

"I've never been so sure or so terrified in my life." He kissed her again with a possessiveness that thrilled every inch of her. "I want us to be together."

"That's good. I've missed you so much." It was her turn to kiss him. "I'm sorry for all those mean things I said to you."

"I guess I deserved them."

"No! I just . . . panicked because I had to stop Dave from realizing how much I'd come to care for you."

"I worked that out—with a little help from my friends." He returned to kissing her.

Eventually he raised his head, his breathing as ragged as her own. "We can work out the logistics. We're both smart people. This is the important part."

"How we feel?" Jen asked.

"You were right about some of it." He sighed. "I keep lists and spreadsheets to make sense of the world—to stop it spiraling into chaos. I tried to put you in a box, but you refused to stay there and kept taking everything over. I didn't know how to handle it. I thought that once you'd left, I'd instigate plan two—operation get Jen back—because that was the only way I could rationalize how I was behaving."

"That's okay." She patted his bearded cheek. "I understand."

"You do, don't you?" He held her gaze. "I don't even have to explain because you're military, too."

"Combat does weird things to people's minds, No one is the same after dealing with that," Jen said carefully. "You create order out of your chaos rather than unleashing it on the world. That's admirable."

"Except when it comes to love. I nearly screwed that up."

"But you didn't." She lightly kissed his lips. "I'm here, aren't I?"

He wrapped his arms around her and buried his face in the hollow of her shoulder. "I feel like I've come home."

"You're not the only one," Jen murmured against his ear as a wave of thankfulness engulfed her.

Someone knocked on the door, making them both jump.

"Hey, just FYI that's my office. I really don't want to have to imagine you two naked in there every time I sit at my desk." Luke paused. "You're not *on* my desk, are you? I mean . . ."

Noah eased the door open and looked at Luke. "It's okay. We're done."

"Talking," Jen added, blushing as Noah took her hand. "Has Dave gone?"

"Yup. And good riddance."

As Noah appeared intent on taking her back to the family room, Jen went along with him. Everyone was sitting around the table, even Max, and they all looked up as she and Noah came in.

Bailey shrieked. "You did it, Bro! I'm so proud of you!"

"How does she know?" Jen murmured as she was hugged and petted by Noah's petite sister.

"Have you any idea how you look when you've been kissed?" Max, who'd unfortunately overheard her comment, shook his head.

Sally clapped her hands. "This is wonderful news. You're going to stay, yes?"

"If that's okay." Suddenly Jen was feeling shy.

"I'm really looking forward to hearing about your work overseas." Sally linked her arm through Jen's and drew her farther into the kitchen. "Can we chat while I prep dinner?"

"Yes, but only if you allow me to help." Jen cast one look back at Noah, who winked and gave her a thumbs up.

"That would be delightful." Sally raised her voice. "Noah,

dear, can you put Sky down for his nap? I've set the crib up in Jen's room."

"My pleasure," Noah called out. "Come on, little buddy."

Bailey and Max went out to the barn, arguing loudly about something, and Luke reclaimed his office, leaving the kitchen suddenly quiet.

"You look a bit shaken," Sally said gently.

"It's been a lot," Jen admitted. "I thought I'd lost him, and now . . ." She smiled into the older woman's eyes. "I feel like I've won the lottery."

"Noah's a good man," Sally said. "When he commits to something, he does it one hundred percent."

Jen nodded. "I'm just not used to getting what I want, or even daring to ask for it. I've always been the one making everyone else happy so they'd put up with me."

Sally's expression softened. "So I've heard." She enfolded Jen's hand in her own. "But please know this: After everything you've done for me and my family, you'll always have a home here, sweetheart. Always."

"Thank you. That means a lot."

Chapter Twenty-Three

Six hours after Jen's arrival, Noah was still walking around in what was the closest to a state of bliss he'd ever experienced. He sat and stared foolishly at her through dinner, ignoring both Luke and Max's jibes about his lovelorn state. He'd even lingered outside her room when she'd gone to get Sky up from his nap just so he could kiss her.

"Hey." Max snapped his fingers under Noah's nose. "Concentrate, lover boy. You're supposed to be loading the dishwasher with me."

"Sure, sorry." Noah rinsed off another dinner plate and handed it over.

"Jen's putting Sky to bed?"

"Yup." Noah started stacking the glasses.

"Okay, Bailey and I will take over the baby monitor so you're clear to head out to the snowmobile barn and make things ready for Jen."

"What?"

Max raised an eyebrow. "Take Jen to bed, doofus. Remember how to do that? Then come back when you're good and ready. We'll even manage the morning duties if you want to sleep in."

Noah tried to imagine a whole night sleeping with Jen.

"Is everyone okay with that?" He glanced toward the

family room, where Sally and the dogs were watching some nature show.

"It was Sally's idea." Max grinned at him. "Go on. I'll send Jen your way when she comes in."

"You sure about that?"

"Yeah." Max paused. "I think you're good together."

"Thanks." Noah wiped his hands on the dishtowel. "I appreciate this."

"Then get going."

Noah was out the door almost before Max finished speaking. The thaw had set in, making it far easier to make the trek up to the second barn. When he got inside, he paused and slowly smiled. Someone had obviously been in before him. The heating was on, the blinds had been closed, and a log fire burned in the fireplace.

There was a note in Sally's handwriting on the countertop, which had been set up with a tray containing two glasses, a vase of flowers, spoons, and fancy red napkins.

Ice cream in freezer, champagne in the refrigerator, feel free to ruin the roses, and scatter the petals where you will. X

Noah had barely finished his own preparations before the lower door banged, and he heard Jen calling his name.

"Come on up." Noah lit the candles and waited for her to ascend the stairs.

She took a slow turn around the room and grinned at him. "This is *nice*."

He shrugged. "I'd love to take the credit, but this was everyone else's idea."

"You're too honest." She took off her coat, and he hung it on top of his on the newel post.

"You of all people know that." He grimaced. "Sometimes too much."

She wore a cream sweater and soft grey yoga pants and she'd left her hair down on her shoulders. He could look at her face all day.

She frowned. "Have I got something stuck in my teeth?"

"Nope." He reached for her hand and took her over to the couch. "I'm just appreciating you."

"I like that." She smiled up at him, and something inside him just melted like the last of the thaw. "I feel very loved."

He kissed her gently, and she looped her arms around his neck and reciprocated in kind. She smelled of roses, coffee, and just the faintest hint of nurse, which was somehow the biggest turn-on of his life. Without breaking the kiss, she climbed into his lap. He settled his hand over her fine ass and let her move on him until his cock was hard enough to hammer nails.

"You ready to take some of those clothes off?" Noah asked hoarsely. "Because I want you naked and screaming my name right now."

"Oh, yes, please," Jen breathed. She straightened, pulled her sweater over her head, and attacked her bra.

Noah feasted his gaze on the sight of her naked breasts right where he wanted them. With a groan he licked her nipple and drew it into his mouth as she wriggled out of her pants and panties. He slid his hand around her ass cheeks and cupped her mound, rubbing his thumb against her clit as she moaned his name.

"Hurry up!"

She started unbuttoning his shirt. When she was three buttons down, he took over and used his only free hand to pull the shirt off while she unbuckled his belt. His cock was throbbing like a bad toothache, and he wanted inside her so bad he wasn't his normal measured self.

"Condom in my pocket," he murmured against her mouth as he tugged at her lower lip.

"Got it."

She shoved his jeans and boxers down past his hips releasing his hard shaft and covered him in one practiced motion. He didn't even need to beg her to mount him. She was on him so fast he almost lost control. He gripped her hips and held her pinned over him.

"I wanted this to be slow and meaningful, but I'm so turned on, it's going to be hard and fast."

"Fine by me," Jen gasped.

"Good." Before she could say anything, he flipped her onto her back and started thrusting like a madman, his whole being wanting to please her, make her come, make her scream his name, and then do it all over again.

She came fast, and he couldn't stop thrusting through the clenching of her internal muscles, which heightened his pleasure to such a frenzy that he had to bury his face in the pillow to avoid biting her throat. Her climax went on for so long that he was groaning her name while still banging her hard enough to make the couch shake.

Her nails raked over his back, and he bucked his hips and came with a roar that echoed off the beams and left him a shuddering, grateful wreck. Even as he forced himself to stay braced over her and not collapse, she gave him the hottest smile ever, squeezed him again, and came again in slow, luxurious waves that he got to watch pass over her face.

"More?" he asked and gently touched her clit.

"Maybe."

"You've been holding out on me."

She lifted her hips against the press of his thumb and climaxed again. "I always felt I was too greedy."

"Not for me," he assured her. "I'll take as much as you can give me."

She sighed and cupped his chin. "That's the nicest thing

you've ever said to me." She pushed gently at his chest. "Can we just cuddle for a while? I've missed that."

"Sure." He levered himself off her and disposed of the condom. "How about we make up the bed? We've got all night."

She sat up, her body rosy from his rough caresses, her nipples hard, and his cock stirred again.

"Maybe you'll get your socks off this time?" she asked.

He ran his hand over his already stiffening shaft, and her eyes went wide.

"Maybe." He glanced down at himself. "And maybe we'll have to make do with the couch again."

Jen opened her eyes into complete blackness and silence and for a moment couldn't remember where she was. A deep, resonant rumble under her cheek and Noah's familiar scent reminded her that they were naked together in bed at the ranch. They'd made love so many times that she'd fallen asleep in his arms as soft and pliant as taffy. She touched his chest just because she could, petting and owning each ridge of scarred muscle in a drowsy dream of lust and love she'd never experienced before.

Her hand moved lower, and he grumbled something under his breath, his fingers catching hold of hers.

"More?"

She smiled into the darkness, evaded his grip, and ran her finger down his half-erect shaft. He shifted against the sheets, offering her more access. She pressed her mouth against his warm skin and licked her way down, pushing the sheets aside as she moved between his legs. She pursed her lips and blew on his cock making him shiver and grow larger as she cupped his balls.

She lightly kissed the tip of his cock and then licked him with a final swirl of her tongue that had him raising his hips off the mattress. She liked the way he filled her mouth and the way he felt as she swallowed him deep.

"God, Jen . . ."

She stroked his balls as she sucked him slowly and thoroughly, just the way she wanted to. He didn't try and direct or control her, his hands remained fisted in the sheets while he cursed and groaned as she owned him inch by glorious inch. She took everything he had, keeping him there as his fingers threaded through her hair and held her like she was the most precious thing in his world.

After he came, he drew her up to lie beside him, his chest heaving, his voice hoarse.

"That was . . . amazing."

"You're welcome."

She was drifting back to sleep when he spoke again.

"Don't ever feel like you need to hide who you are or what you want from me, Jen."

She looked up at him. "I don't think I can. But it's still scary."

"Right back at you." He kissed the top of her head. "I'm worried I'll scare you away sometimes."

"Why?"

"Because I make assumptions, set up false scenarios, think everyone's brains work like mine."

"At least you know that about yourself." Jen drew small circles on his chest. "And I'm not afraid to call you out when I think you're wrong."

"True." He paused. "I guess that's one of the reasons we work well together." He squeezed her ass, his voice deepening. "And the sex of course."

"Mmm." Jen's eyes closed again. "Should we be getting back to the house?"

"Max said it's all under control if we want to come back for breakfast tomorrow."

"Really?" Jen sighed with pure bliss. "That would be wonderful." And she promptly fell asleep.

The next time she woke up it was to the smell of coffee and the sight of Noah clad only in his boxers approaching her with a mug. She'd never loved him quite so much.

"What time is it?"

"It's five thirty. Drink this." He handed over the coffee. "You've got time to take a shower, get dressed, and we'll still be back in time to wake Sky and have breakfast."

"Okay." She winced as she got out of bed and smiled at Noah. "I'm out of practice."

"We'll work on that."

She took a quick shower, finished her coffee, and dressed in the clothes she'd worn the night before, which wasn't great, but she wasn't in the mood to be picky. Noah was waiting for her in the kitchen, his expression calm, his gaze appreciative as he held out his hand.

"Are you ready to go?"

Jen glanced back at the couch, which Noah had reassembled. "What about the sheets?"

"Already in the washer. I'll pop back later and make sure they get dried."

"You're definitely a keeper," Jen said as she went down the stairs behind him, only to bounce off his back as he stopped dead and turned to face her.

"Am I?"

"Yes."

"Because I want to be in this for the long term, Jen. I want to stick around for you *and* for Sky," he said fiercely. "I didn't think I had it in me to be this guy, but somehow I am."

"I want that, too." She locked gazes with him. "And for the record, Noah, you've always been that person."

His smile was crooked. "Then maybe I just needed to find the right woman to let him fly free."

She went up on tiptoe and kissed him until his arms locked around her and he kissed her back.

He lifted his head and scowled down at her. "You realize Dave will never let us hear the end of this? That he brought us together and we both owe him?"

Jen rolled her eyes and opened the exterior door.

It only took a few minutes to walk down the slope to the ranch house. The sun was barely visible above the impenetrable line of dark green trees, and the barn and fields remained in shadow. Patches of snow remained on the yellowed hills, but the main pastures were clear, and the cattle grazed peacefully. Jen paused to listen to the stillness and heard instead the rustle of the breeze through the pines and the hum of the generators working to keep the ranch running. She reminded herself that even on a ship in the middle of a vast ocean you could still hear the engines that kept the boat in motion.

"What is it?" Noah asked.

"Just appreciating the view," Jen said with a sigh.

"You're one of the very few people who does. Even Bailey says the silence gets creepy at night."

"I like it." Jen continued down the slope and approached the house, where lights were already shining from the kitchen windows. "Someone's up."

"Probably Sally." Noah held the door open for her to go through into the mudroom and stopped short. "Hell, they're all up."

Jen almost balked at the table full of people enjoying eggs, bacon, pancakes, and maple syrup. Her stomach gurgled as she took off her coat.

"Used up a lot of calories last night, Jen?" Max asked as he pulled out a chair for her.

"Shut up, Max," Noah said as he joined her at the table

and stared suspiciously at all the smiling faces. "Why are you all up so early?"

Sally handed them each a warm plate and a mug of coffee. "Why don't you tuck in? We want to talk to you."

Jen was too hungry to argue, and even the thought of the conversation to follow couldn't stop her eating her fill. Noah ate well, too, ignoring Max and Luke's teasing and deflecting Bailey's attempts to get interesting details from Jen whenever he overheard her asking.

When they were all finished, Sally looked at Luke and nodded.

"You go ahead. It was mainly your idea."

"Okay, well, we were talking last night," Luke addressed Noah and Jen. "And we wanted to run this scenario by you. Dr. Carlo and Mom are looking to expand their practice, and someone like you, Jen, who's used to dealing with all kinds of scenarios would be a great asset to their team."

Jen blinked. "Are you offering me a job?"

"Yes." Sally sat forward, her hands folded on the table. "You'd start as the community midwife, but if you wanted to expand into general nursing and medicine, we'd be delighted. The pay isn't as good as you'll get in a major town or city, but there are several advantages."

Sally looked at Luke again.

"What Mom's trying to say is that if you chose to—you and Sky could live here on the ranch, which would save you housing costs." He grinned. "You'd also get to see a lot of this guy." He pointed at Noah. "And if you both decide to stick around, we're more than willing to build a house here for you. We've got one hundred and fifty acres to play with."

Under the table, Noah's fingers curled around Jen's.

"It's a lot to think about," Jen said slowly.

"But you will think about it?" Sally said earnestly. "You'd

be doing important work, you certainly wouldn't get bored, and you'd be greatly valued."

Jen glanced up at Noah, who was watching her carefully, his hand still gripping hers.

"What do you think?"

"I'd be cool with it." He hesitated. "But it's really up to you."

There was a noise from the baby monitor and Jen rose to her feet.

"Can I just get Sky?"

"Of course!" Sally smiled as she rose to her feet. "The little chap will want some breakfast. I'll get it started while you're getting him ready for the day."

"Thank you." Jen went to her bedroom, where Sky was standing up in his crib, beaming at her.

"Mama."

"Yes, sweetheart." She picked him up and hugged him tight. "Would you like to live here little one? With your Nono, Mama, Sally, and the cowboys?"

"Nono," Sky said.

Jen laughed. "My thoughts exactly." She kissed his rosy cheek. "I really love that guy, too."

In the kitchen, Luke cleared his throat. "Do you think one of us should go tell Jen we can hear her, or shall I just turn the baby monitor off?"

"Keep it on. Noah's actually blushing," Max said.

Sally walked over and turned it off. "None of our business, boys."

Noah nodded.

"She loves you, though." Max elbowed Noah in the ribs. "Just in case you didn't know that."

"Thanks for nothing," Noah growled. "And if anyone says anything to her when she comes out, I'll—"

"What?" Bailey asked. "Kiss her stupid in front of every-one?" She winked at Noah. "Although, from the state of the pair of you, I guess you've already done that."

"Bailey . . ."

Jen came in with Sky on her hip and stared at Noah. "What?"

"Nothing," he said hastily. "We were just talking about how much we'd all like you to stay here with us."

"I think I'd like that, too." Jen sat beside Sky, her expression serious.

"And if you need somewhere to live in San Diego while you finish out your contract, you guys can stay with me and the twins," Bailey offered. "We've got room and now we're family."

"That's so kind of you," Jen said.

"And there is one more thing," Noah said. "If you don't want to take the job here and prefer to stick with the navy, I'll come live in San Diego and take care of Sky full time while you're away on duty."

"Really?" she whispered. "You'd do that for me?"

"I love you." Noah shrugged. "I want you to be happy. If the job makes you happy then go ahead and do it."

Luke came to stand behind Noah. "It wouldn't just be Noah pitching in if you stayed here either." He glanced over at Max, who was nodding. "We'd all be here to help out. I mean, we're basically honorary uncles already, and Mom loves being a grandma."

Jen shook her head and Noah tensed.

"This is . . . so much more than I've ever been given in my life that I guess I'm having a hard time believing it's real."

Noah wrapped his arm around her shoulders, and she leaned into him.

"It's real, Jen. This is the best bunch of people on the planet, and you're part of our family. We all want you here."

"Then I think my answer will probably be yes." She held up a finger. "There are lots of details to be worked out, but—"

Noah kissed her, and everyone cheered, including Sky.

"I'm good at details." He held her gaze. "Just remember that we love each other, we're in this together, and we're a family now."

Max groaned. "I feel like I've stumbled into an alternate universe. Who'd ever have thought Arkie would take on a kid and a feisty woman?"

"Me," Bailey said, her eyes shining. "He's always been the best man I've ever known."

Noah felt an unaccustomed tickling in his throat as Jen and Bailey looked at him fondly. He frowned.

"Now let's not get too excited."

Jen rolled her eyes. "It's okay, you're still a badass marine." She blew him a kiss.

Max raised his mug. "I hate to say it, but here's to Dave. If he hadn't screwed up, we'd never have gotten to see Arkie brought to his knees."

"To Dave!" everyone shouted.

Noah looked at Jen, who was laughing along with everyone else. There were paths to be negotiated, and probably a few pitfalls along the way, but with Jen beside him, for the first time in a long while, the world seemed less of a hostile place, and for that he was truly thankful. Love had found him despite himself, and yeah, maybe he did owe Dave a drink. Not that he'd ever tell him . . .

Visit our website at
KensingtonBooks.com
to sign up for our newsletters, read
more from your favorite authors, see
books by series, view reading group
guides, and more!

Become a Part of Our
Between the Chapters Book Club
Community and Join the Conversation

Betweenthechapters.net

Submit your book review for a chance to win exclusive
Between the Chapters swag you can't get anywhere else!
https://www.kensingtonbooks.com/pages/review/